THE FINANCIAL LIVES
OF THE POETS

THE
FINANCIAL
LIVES OF
THE POETS

A Novel

JESS WALTER

HARPER

An Imprint of HarperCollins Publishers

HarperCollins books may be purchased for educational, business, or sales promotional use. For information, please write: Special Markets Department, HarperCollins Publishers, 10 East 53rd Street, New York, NY 10022.

FIRST EDITION

Library of Congress Cataloging-in-Publication Data has been applied for.

ISBN: 978-0-06-191604-5

09 10 11 12 13 OV/RRD 10 9 8 7 6 5 4 3 2 1

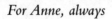

For Anne, always

Poets have to dream, and dreaming in America is no cinch.

—SAUL BELLOW

THE FINANCIAL LIVES
OF THE POETS

Another 7/11

—H ERE THEY ARE AGAIN—the bent boys, baked
and buzzed boys, wasted, red-eyed, dry-mouth
high boys, coursing narrow bright aisles
hunting food as fried as they are, twitchy
hands wadding bills they spill
on the counter, so pleased and so
proud, as if they're the very
inventors of stoned—

And behind the counter, the ever-patient Rahjiv makes half-
lidded eye contact with me as he rings up another patchouli-foul
giggler—Reese's Pieces, Pic-6 Lotto, Red Bull and a cheddar-
jack tacquito—Rahjiv probably thinking: *These kids, eh Matt*—or
maybe not, because Rahjiv doesn't know my name and I don't
wear a nametag. I'm just the middle-aged guy who leaves my gun-
metal sedan running when I come in after midnight. When I can't
sleep. And I've forgotten to get milk at a regular store. Milk for the
kids' cereal. In the morning. Before school.

The milk is like nine dollars a gallon.

For years, recent immigrants like Rahjiv have been a political Rorschach: see turban, think terrorist and you're a Red 'Merican. Assume Indian neurosurgeon fluent in five languages, stuck serving morons at midnight for minimum wage, and you're Blue, like me. Of course I have no more proof that Rahjiv was a doctor in Delhi than some Texas trucker does that he's a bomber. Rahjiv may have jockeyed a 7/11 in India too for all we know—so impeccable is he with change, effortlessly plastic-bagging Hostess Sno Balls and Little Debbies, Power Bars and Mountain Dews—"No wait . . . dude. Chocolate milk! And pork rinds"—as yet another stoner reassesses the aisles—"And ooh, ooh! Cool Ranch Doritos!"

Whenever I come in here, I invariably think of my own boys, at home asleep in their beds, still a few years from such trouble (or do they already dream of midnight at the Slurpee machine?).

Two tattooed white kids in silk sweat suits step to the line behind me and I tense a little, double-pat my wallet. The fat one juggles a half-rack of malt-liquor forties while his partner rolls away to yell in his cell, "Chulo! Don' do shit 'til we get there, yo." The door closes behind the cell-phoned gangbanger and I'm finally at the front of this line with my milk—"Hey Rahjiv"—when something goes terribly wrong at the soda fountain and the clerk and I turn together, drawn by a hydroponic squeal from deep inside the cave of a blue hoody. A pierced, lank-haired skater, board strapped to his back, has spilled his 72-ounce Sprite and now believes it is . . . *the funniest . . . fucking . . . thing . . . in the world*, and Rahjiv nods wearily at me again, no doubt wishing he were back cutting craniums at Mumbai General. He casually swings my jug past the scanner.

Then he hands me my milk. For the boys. For their cereal. In the morning.

It's like nine dollars a gallon.

I also think of my mother when I come in here. She was dying several years back and became obsessed with the terrorist attacks in New York. I hated that she should be so wracked with random anxieties as she wasted away, thumb jacking the morphine pump like it could save her life—it couldn't—her fear of dying manifested as a fear of things she had no reason to fear anymore: random crime, global warming . . . and most of all, terrorists on airplanes. "Matt?" she asked right before she died, "Do you think there will be another 7/11?" I thought about correcting her, but I just said, "No, Mom, there won't be any more 7/11s."

"Nice slippers, yo," says the cell-phone banger when I come outside with my milk. He's twenty or so, in a sagging shark-colored tracksuit, black hair combed straight over his ears, elaborate tattoo rising out of his shirt at the base of his neck. And right out in the open, in front of this convenience store, he conveniently offers me a hit on a glass blunt, a little marijuana pipe shaped like a cigarette. I wave it off, but sort of wish I hadn't—it's been at least fifteen years, but I didn't just spring from some relaxed-waisted suburbia with a Stoli martini in hand; I had my moments. In college they used to call me *Weedeater* because I devoured those Acapulco Gold joints, incense burning, black light on the walls, Pink Floyd thrumming down the dorm floor—

Oh, and they're not technically "slippers," but a casual loafer I got at the Nordstrom Rack with a gift certificate when I returned a cardigan that made me look like my grandfather. Of course I don't tell the stoned kid that, I just smile and say, "No thanks," but then I pause to get a closer look, instead of continuing on to my car. Maybe I'm just curious about this clever pipe or maybe it's the smell of the weed or maybe it's just this swiveling looseness I'm feeling, but I'm still in mid-pause when the fatter white gangster joins us, flat-brimmed ball cap worn sidesaddle, and now there are three of us standing in a little semicircle, as if waiting for a tee time.

"Hey," says the one with the neck tattoo and the blunt, "dude here can give us a ride to the party."

And I'm about to say I can't give them a ride because I've got to get home (and they look mildly dangerous) when fat-in-the-hat says, "Thanks, man," like he's surprised I'd be so cool and suddenly I want to be that cool. And then the fat kid looks down at my hands, and laughs.

"Damn, man. Why you buy your milk here? Shit's like nine dollars a gallon."

The clouds are low, like a drop ceiling suffused with light from the city. They slide silently overhead. And two dope-smoking bangers in tracksuits climb into my car.

I read once that we can only fear what we're already afraid of; that our deepest fears are the memory of some earlier, unbearable fear. If that's true, then maybe it's a good thing my mother never lived to see another 7/11.

"This a nice ride."

"Thanks."

"Seats heated?"

"Mmm."

"Feels funny. Like I pissed my pants."

"You pro'ly did piss your pants, yo."

"I'll turn it down."

"What kind-a-car is this?"

"Nissan. Maxima."

"How much 'at set you back?"

"Oh. Not much."

But this isn't true. With the winter floor mats, taxes and redundant two-year service contract, the car set me back $31,256. And because of several other recent *setbacks*—missed payments, ensuing penalties, house refi's, debt consolidations, various family crises and my untimely job loss—after two years of payments I still somehow owe $31,000. On a car worth eighteen. This is my life now: set as far back as it will go.

"My brother boosted a Maxima once," says the kid from the backseat. "Or an Altima. I can't keep 'em straight."

Car thieves. Nice.

The criminals' names are Skeet and Jamie. "Jamie?" I ask the kid in front.

"Yeah right, no shit, huh?" says Skeet from the backseat. "Dude's got like a chick's name, don't he?"

"Eat me, Skeet," Jamie says, and he offers me the blunt again and I surprise myself by taking it this time; I just want the smallest taste of that sweet smoke, or maybe I want to make sure they haven't done anything new to the pot. . . .

Oh, but they *have*!

I suppress a cough. Nose runs. Eyes burn. Someone is composting leaves in my throat. Scraping my lungs with a shovel. Wow.

"Good, huh?" asks Jamie.

I hack: "Not bad."

"Shit's designer. Like three hunnerd an ounce," Skeet says.

The next roll of coughs I can't suppress. "Really?"

"Definitely," Jamie explains, voice lilting with excitement. "In this lab in British Columbia? This Nobel Prize dude? He Frankensteined that shit? It's knock-off, but shit's still pretty good. They can do whatever they want to it, you know? Make it do a thousand different things to your mind, yo."

And I think that must be true, because a couple of old dorm-floor hits later my brain springs a leak and my life seems to trickle out, as I tell Jamie and Skeet my whole story: how I left a good job as a business reporter two years ago to start an unlikely poetry-and-investment website, how we got buried in the housing collapse just as my senile father moved in, how I scrambled back to my old newspaper job, only to get laid off eight weeks ago. How I got

fourteen weeks of severance from the paper, and have six weeks
left to find a job, because fourteen minus eight is six. How last
week it was seven, next week it will be five, but right now,

> at this moment,
> with Skeet in the backseat
> and Jamie in front,
> right now, as of this . . . very
> moment—and I hold the smoke
> in my chest as if I can make
> this moment forever—Hooooo—

"It's six. Six weeks."

And that's not even my most pressing deadline; I have all of
seven days to liquidate my retirement and pay off a $30,000 bal-
loon payment to the mortgage company, or risk losing our house.
And it is this second deadline, I tell the boys, that has given my job
search such throat-constricting immediacy, as I worry over thin-
ning want ads, shakily fill out applications and hope my references
still have the positions I've listed on my résumé, and how—this
part has just occurred to me—I've gone and *added another stress* to
a very shitty situation, because "Even if I do somehow get a job
interview now, they'll probably make me take a—"

"—drug test!" Skeet yells from the backseat, and he laughs and
I laugh and he laughs and I stop laughing and he keeps laughing.

"Don't freak, Slippers," Jamie says, "there's a million ways to
beat a piss test."

"Pecans," says Skeet from the backseat.

"Pecans?" Jamie turns back.

"Didn't I read about some kind-a pecan diet in O?"

"How the fuck I know what you read? An' what the fuck
Oprah be writin' about how to pass a drug test?"

"Dude, Oprah don't write *O*. She just own that shit."

"And what the fuck you be doin' readin' *it*?"

"My moms reads that shit, yo. . . . An' I don't know, maybe it was in *People*."

"So what the fuck the pecans do?"

"The fuck I'm supposed to know what the pecans do! Clean up your piss or somefin'."

"You crazy, motherfucker."

"You crazy."

"You crazy."

"You crazy."

"You so crazy you took the short bus to school."

"You *know* that shit was behavioral, yo."

And I must be high because this conversation makes sense.

Jamie waves Skeet off and faces forward again. "Don't listen to that shit, Slippers. Here's all you gotta do for that piss test. Get some of them pills. You know, online?"

Not you too, Jamie. Don't fall for the online lie—that everything we need is available at the click of a keystroke: all that shimmering data, the dating habits of the famous, videos of fat people falling down, porn . . . investment poetry . . . job listings, foreclosure information, poverty advice . . . and what about the thing my wife has begun seeking online?

But before I get too deep into a new round of self-pity, Jamie offers a lilting anecdote: "You could do what my cousin Marshall did? Fucker wore a catheter? Connected to a baggy? With some other dude's piss in it? And now he screens luggage at the airport? And he's up for a supervisor job with the NTSA? And a security clearance? I shit you not, Dude's got someone who warns him about random tests, and he keeps that catheter full of someone else's whiz right there in his locker? And when he hears about tests, dude loads that shit up."

In the rearview, I see Skeet drink directly from my milk carton.

Hey. That was like nine dollars a gallon.

Very good pot. Far better than the dusty brown ragweed we smoked in college. And I think of my mother again, and the trouble we had at Christmas break my freshman year when she was doing laundry and found a single joint amid the pennies and pocket lint of my 501's—she hated the sound of change rattling in her dryer— and I tried to convince her it was a rolled up note from a friend and she asked if I thought she was stupid and I said *No*, even though I was eighteen so of course my mother was stupid, and my parents were still together then but she *never told my father* about the joint, and I feel awful about her being so decent when I was such a shit; I feel awful for everything I did and everything I didn't do, and I miss her terribly, although it's probably good she's not here be- cause I couldn't bear for her to hear about Jamie's cousin Marshall screening bags . . . pissing someone else's piss as he watches for shoe bombs and keeps us safe from the dudes planning another 7/11.

No, it's exceptional pot—

And the party . . . is not a party the way I remember par- ties but eight young guys, short and fat and tall and lean, black, brown, white, rejected Abercrombie models standing in a flower bed outside an apartment building across from a closed pizza place, smoking and laughing and drinking malt-liquor forties, talking in likes and shits and dudes, and I fit in fine, although I can't re- member when I gave Skeet my slippers—but he's wearing them, dude drinking from my milk jug—and I'm in my socks, sucking that blunt like a scuba diver on an air hose as I track conversations that mean nothing to me: music I've never heard, and "skank- ass trippy chicks" I don't know, someone's "bus'-up ride"—and I gather from these conversations that my new friends are between nineteen and twenty-two, have a few community college credits, some minimum-wagey part-timey jobs, a possession charge or five, and I think about the semicircle that I used to make with the old neck-tied newspaper hacks in the newsroom around the 5 p.m. TV news, arms crossed, talking in our own code about our wives and our cars, about flacks and blogs and the Dow, and I think maybe the world is made up of little circles like this one and that one, that maybe there's no fundamental difference between the circles except the codes for the shared bits of data, that somewhere a pack of plotting terrorists is standing in their own little circle, bouncing on cold feet and ululating not about the great American devil but about Ahmed's skank-ass trippy girlfriend and Mahmoud's bus' ride, and that's when I picture *my boys* again, one day standing in their own circle, generational losers smoking ever-improving weed and talking about their loser dad who went in the tank after getting run in the Great Recession or whatever they'll call it in the history books, or the *history MP3 files* and Christ, I'm only forty-six . . . I don't want to entertain such *grandpa-thought,* but I feel so old, so unemployed, outdated, dead technology, impotent scrap-heap, unraveling, unraveling, unrav—

"Wait," one of the felons interrupts my time-dilated self-pity; it's tattoo-necked Jamie, the reliable one, quiet leader, and he leans in close: "Dude! Aren't you . . . like. *Starving?*"

And the thing is, bouncing on soaked socked feet outside this apartment building, blowing on cold hands that seem to belong to someone else, thinking of my sons at home in bed and the many ways I can still let them down, it's true—

Yes! I am so! Starving!
But maybe we're all starving
hungry for the warm lights
and tight aisles of nacho-corn-
sour-cream-onion-and-chive-

barbecue-goodness—and again
I drive my boys, Skeet and Jamie

—And I'm hypnotized by the set of cat-eyed taillights I'm or-
dered to follow as we arrive—because where else can you find the
hungry, a community of the hungry—you tail the dude in the
tricked-out Festiva—*damn he drive well*—and that smell? *Dude!* says
Jamie, and Skeet laughs proudly and Jamie says, *Lay off the milk,
Skeet!* and I crack with laughter as Jamie explains, *Dude's lactose-
infuckin'tolerant yo*—to the flat green and orange stripes—the sheer
hot white light goodness of . . .

. . . another 7/11. And here I am, just like my mother feared,
stoned off my nut, unemployed, a week from losing my house
and maybe my wife and kids, and I file in with my new friends,
as per—(1) banger in sweats (2) dude in baggie jeans (3) kid in
hoodie (4) another banger in sweats (and my slippers) and finally
(5) middle-aged unemployed man in Chinos, pea coat, golf shirt
and wet socks—*and yes, Mom, in a perfect world,* we could find an
open grocery, but there are simply going to be times when you
must go out in the world, into the dark uneasy dangerous places
and so I go. . . .

Straight to the freezer case and a siren of a meat-and-bean
burrito which I tear into, unwrap and microwave—bouncing in
squishy socks, watching that thing turn under the light like baby
Jesus in an incubator—and that's when Skeet freaks, he completely
freaks! loses it! "Turn it off, man! That shit's poison, man! They're
nukin' us with that shit, turning us into radiated zombies!" Jamie
trying to calm the poor kid through gritted teeth, "Chill, man,"
but Skeet won't chill, he just screams and points at the humming
microwave oven as the clerk, this store's Rahjiv yells: "Get that
trippin' guy outta here before I call the cops!" And everyone's yell-

ing, "Chill, man, chill!" and "What else he on?" and "He always
be trippin, yo!" and "Don't call the cops, dude's on probation!"

And that's when I remember: *I am an adult* and I can do . . .
something . . . I can fix this, protect my boys, make the world
okay, and so I grab Skeet by his round shoulders and feel his racing
heart, catch his sketchy eyes and say—

"Skeet. Look at me. It's not nuclear radiation. It's just waves.
Like sound waves," my voice getting softer, slower: "Tiny . . .
waves." A deep breath. "Like good vibrations, right? That's why
they call them micro . . . waves. See?" And he's still breathing
heavily when I nod and the microwave beeps, and Skeet looks
over, still panting. And it's quiet in the store.

After a second, Skeet nods back. Smiles. It's gonna be. Okay.

And I pat Skeet's shoulder, grab my steaming burrito and get
in line to pay—take my place with the starving and the sorry, the
paranoid, yawning with fear, the hungry lonely lost children let
down by their unemployed fathers, men zapped by history's mi-
crowave, a generation of hapless, luckless, feckless fathers with no
idea how to fix anything, no clue what to do except go home to
face the incubated babies staring at their dry bowls of Crispix and
confess—

—*Sorry. But Skeet drank all the milk . . . right before he freaked*—

Oh, I am such a shit father, shit husband, shit son, shit human
being . . . and I've lost my shit job, am losing my shit house, am at
the bottom of my shit-self when I glance over at the endless wet
roll of the Slurpee machine and it's instantly hypnotic—

Banana-blackraspberry-cherryCoke-piñacolada! So peaceful.
Around and around it swirls and I could watch the wet blend of fla-
vors forever—when Jamie sidles up and whispers, "I'm gonna mix
'em all, man," like a soldier volunteering for a suicide mission.

"Go with God," I whisper, and Jamie does, straight to a piñacolada icy blur, and then down the line, cherry Coke, black raspberry, and he smiles back, and I'm insanely proud as I step forward to pay for my burrito, eyes falling on the clerk's wristwatch when . . .

for just a second . . . I can't tell . . . if I've forgotten . . . what the numbers mean, or maybe . . . I'm just imagining . . . what it would be like . . . to forget what they mean . . .

I spend days staring at this guy's watch before the second hand finally moves—and the position of the hands against the little numbers correlates to a memory of how this particular mechanism works (a memory from kindergarten: Miss Bean in go-go boots standing above me moving the hands of a sun-faced clock)—and I connect the relation of these symbols to a system of tracking the movement of the earth around the sun as across a forest of synapses there sparks a pattern of theoretical constructs (time, space, go-go boots) flaring into an evolutionary fire that represents a near miracle of abstract comprehension, an Einsteinian leap of cognition: *It is four-thirty in the morning.* That means I can still make it home to watch my boys' last hour of sleep.

And in my mind, the Nissan Maxima of my responsibilities follows the Ford Festiva of my unraveling into *this* convenience store of realization:

Hey!

This is where they sell more milk!

But that shit's like nine dollars a gallon.

Outside the store, Skeet and Jamie go off with the dude in the Festiva and I wave goodbye with my new white jug and I am in love with the predawn cool black, in love with my boys, in love with two percent.

The drive home is glorious—streetlight rollers like tide at dawn.

I blow laughter through my nose. Key in quietly. Like I'm

sixteen again. My old senile father is asleep on the hide-a-bed in the living room, TV still on ESPN. This is what we were watching together when I left to get milk . . . almost four hours ago. Dad doesn't stir. I try to take the remote control from him but he's holding it against his cheek like a security blanket, so I turn off the set manually, old school. Every day now they show the top ten sports plays of the day—and I think: what if life was like this, and at bedtime we got to see our own daily highlights (No. 4: Skeet freaks over the microwave).

Lug my jug to the kitchen, milk in the door of the fridge—the food inside is also glorious: cheese stick, martini olives—*chomp, chomp*—I eat shark-like, without conscience, hover upstairs to find Lisa in bed, tousled short hair clinging to the pillow. My wife, she is cute—everyone says so, but lately that word has carried a kind of accusing overtone, as if there might be something unsettling about a grown woman who retains her cuteness well into her forties; and maybe that's our problem, maybe Lisa is *too* cute, curled up in her cute little ball, cute back to the profoundly un-cute space where I'm not sleeping. Her cute cell phone on her nightstand, where she no doubt set it after TM-ing her old flame . . . and I toy with waking her, begging for a little marital goodness—*smack, smack*—maybe we can fix this thing the way we fixed problems when we were twenty-seven, but we're in a smack-smack dry spell, and according to an online chat of hers that I reconned earlier, she's not a big Matt fan these days. Anyway, this might not be the best time to win my cute wife back, given my B.C. bud-and-burrito breath, and the fact that I haven't told her that we could lose the house as early as next week. (I imagine breaking it to her as we fire a couple off—*Yes, yes, yes! Uh-uh! That-feels-so-good-we're-about-to-be-evicted!*)

So I step back into the hall; the boys' rooms are across from one another, and I stand between them, fists on my hips. Sentry.

Superhero. All I want is to keep them safe, healthy, fed. But with no job? No prospects? No money? No house? What did the man say—*There is always hope, but not for us.* Mouth dry. Head weighs eighty pounds.

I look around at *my house*—for a while anyway—before it begins its journey back to Providential Equity, or whatever company buys the company that bought the company that bought the bundle of red bills in which ours is bundled. Or is that more melodrama, mere self-pity? (They don't just *take* your house. They want you to pay. You're just the sort of homeowner they want. They'll do whatever they can to keep you here.) No, all I have to do is liquidate, get some money together, show good faith, get someone from the mortgage lender on the phone and convince them we need a little more time . . . that's all . . . a month . . . what's one month . . . a single month for a journalist in his mid-forties . . . to find a job . . . during a recession . . . with newspapers failing faster than investment banks.

I slump against the wall, played out. Who am I kidding? I can't save anyone. Maybe Skeet's right. Maybe they *are* irradiating us; maybe we're dead already. Mom knew it, that there would always be another 7/11. And suddenly I understand her fear of terrorism wasn't fear *for herself*. She wasn't flying on any more airplanes. She was afraid for me, afraid for her kids and her grandkids, for all the hungry, lost boys. Afraid for the world she knew she was leaving. As she lay there dying, she must have realized there was nothing she could do anymore to protect the people she loved. Just as there's nothing I can do for my boys anymore, my boys who will one day freak out alone in the tight warm aisles of a world beyond their understanding. I may as well be dead for all the help I can be to them. (My boys stir, agreeing that it's their scary world now, their hard, hard world: *go on, old man; rest now; sleep.*) And in my fraying head there plays a news medley of war and instability, financial collapse and bad schools; forbearance, foreclosure, eviction; cynicism, climate crisis, 7/11—and the melody switches to my personal theme song (*Concerto of Failure and Regret in E minor*) as the life bleeds out from my feet and puddles in the hallway. . . .

And this is when the unlikeliest peace comes, and I smile. Because as fucked as the world is, as grim as the future surely seems to be, as grim as it revealed itself to be for my mother as she lay dying of the tumor that kills us all, there is a truth I cannot deny, a thing no creditor can take; even as my doomed boys stir in the cold unknowing of predawn sleep, even as the very life leaches out of me, soaks into the berber, into the cracks of my arid grave, I must grudgingly admit—

—that was one great goddamn burrito.

CHAPTER 2

Giving to Charity

"H EY, THE GUY'S COMING to blow the sprinklers,"
Lisa says as she blows through the kitchen,
in a billowing skirt, and I can barely keep
my head up—something I forgot to do?

Ah, I remember now: sleep. I forgot to sleep, after I got home
high from 7/11, spending instead the hour before dawn worry-
ing and flipping between CNN and Cartoon Network—endless
politics and the *Go Go Gophers*, international financial crises and
Klondike Kat.

And apparently I'm still stoned—and a huge proponent of to-
day's weed—big fan. In fact, I wish I could invest in the dude
who Frankensteined it up there in B.C. There used to be a cranky
old government reporter at my paper named Abe Cowley, who
always ranted that "kids now are fucked," because they'd never be
able to afford real estate or find jobs—I couldn't always follow his
rant—but if it ever comes up again I'll say, *Yeah, Abe, you're right,*

kids today have no future, but Christ, have you tried their pot? At the table Teddy reaches past me for the milk. I think of the hours and brain cells that went into getting that simple white jug and I feel strangely proud. Lisa blows through the kitchen again—we pass like storm fronts now—this time she has her jacket on and she tells me, "Before you take the kids to school, don't forget to turn off the water and roll up the hoses." When I don't say anything, she asks, "Matt?"

Beneath the table, I click my heels together. *"Jawohl, herr commandant."*

Note: for future marriage-enriching banter, avoid Nazi humor.

Smart, round Teddy slides the milk over to wispy little brother Franklin, who teeters it before finally pouring milk on the counter. He diverts the wayward stream toward the bowl, but it hits his up-turned spoon and splashes even more on the counter. Today's milk spill looks like the state of Florida. I grab a dishtowel and sop.

"Hell, I can blow out the sprinklers," my daft father says. He's having one of his sharper moments—eyes clear as he stares out the window, gray hair bursting cactus-like off his head. He watches the horizon for something. Grips his spoon over his coffee like a battle knife. Two white pills sit in front of him, right where I left them, Aricept, the medication he takes for his cobwebby memory.

"No you can't, Dad." I push Dad's pills closer, wipe milk off Franklin's elbow.

Dad pats the pocket where he used to keep his cigarettes. Then he tosses the pills in one side of his mouth and spews anger from the other: "Would you goddamn let me do one thing around here, Matthew!"

"I don't think you put the swear word in the right place, Grandpa," Teddy says. When Dad first came here, my boys would look shocked whenever Dad went Old-Faithful-profane, and I began to wonder if Lisa and I shouldn't swear more so Franklin and Teddy weren't so put off by curse words. But they've gotten used to Grandpa's eruptions; they don't even look up from their cereal unless it's to correct his grammar.

I try to be patient: "Remember Dad? You can't blow out the sprinklers because you don't have an air compressor anymore?"

"Where the hell's my compressor." His ears are bright red and he won't meet my eyes. I think he sometimes knows that he's forgetting, even if he's not sure what he can't remember.

"Look, we'll talk about this later."

Sometimes this answer is enough; other times Dad's creeping dementia makes him angry and frustrated, like now, and he argues with me. "No. Tell me now. Where the hell's my air compressor. Did you sell it?"

"No, Dad. You gave it to Charity. Remember?"

This is what I say when Dad persists. It is partly true. My father did give everything he owned to a stripper stage-named Charity—a young silicone-peaked girl he met when he went with some old Army buddies to a reunion in Reno that ended at six in the morning with lap dances at a strip club. Dad's and Charity's relationship was one of those classic May-December romances, a by-the-numbers affair, those numbers being (1) grind, (2) drunken proposal, (3) taking stripper home, (4) identity theft and (5) disappearance of stripper. After Dad drove her all the way back to his remote house in Oregon, she lived with him for exactly ten days, just enough time to clean out his bank accounts and ruin his credit, and to have her boyfriend drive up from Reno to load most of Dad's belongings—including his beloved air compressor—into a U-Haul and drive away, Charity waving bye-bye from the truck window.

Dad was so embarrassed he didn't tell me or my sisters for months, during which time Charity and her boyfriend lived high on Dad's cratering credit; his power was shut off, his gas cut, phone disconnected, and I arrived at his little fifteen-acre ranch to find him eating canned corn he cooked in his fireplace. It was too late to untangle him, especially since Dad couldn't remember the details of his undoing (although I notice he hasn't forgotten my childhood failings, i.e., the great Little League dropped pop-up of 1977). Now, when I explain—over and over—how a stripper ripped him off, Dad's biggest disappointment isn't that he gave everything away, but that he didn't get Charity's last name so we might track her down. When I point out that Charity is a phony first name, and that getting a phony *last name* probably wouldn't help us find her, Dad says I give up too easily.

"And you're going to see Richard today?" Lisa asks on her next lap through the kitchen. Richard is our financial planner, which is a bit like being Lido Deck Officer on the *Lusitania*.

"Yeah," I say. "Just to move some stuff around. Get some advice."

Lisa doesn't do financial crises very well—when she was twelve, her father died and she and her mom struggled—so I've been sparing her some of the specific details. Obviously, she knows I'm out of work and that we're in debt (she helped get us there) but she doesn't know, for example, that today Richard is cashing out what's left of my retirement so I can make a deferred balloon payment to the mortgage company next week. "After the meeting with Richard," I tell her, "I'll go see that employment counselor. Then I've scheduled a bank robbery. Then I'm selling my organs to buy food. It's a glorious day in Matt-topia."

Lisa has learned to ignore self-pity disguised as humor—my métier. "Don't forget to pick the kids up and take Franklin to speech therapy and Teddy to Scouts. And can you get over to Costco to pick up our pictures? I have a session after work." Lisa goes to a therapist every other week for the compulsive shopping binge she went on last winter, or more precisely, for the depressive episode that sparked her shopping binge, the same depressive streak that is now causing her to act in other mysterious, online ways—a social surfing habit that she doesn't know *I know* is getting more social all the time. She puts a hand on my shoulder, and for just a moment my wife is in my port and I put my hand on the lovely notch of her waist and look into those green eyes, but she sniffs the air around me, pushes away from the dock and makes a face. "God, what did you eat, Matt?"

"I had a burrito when I went to get milk last night." In the language of a fraying marriage, the truth often comes with ellipses. I had a burrito . . . *after I got stoned with some criminals* . . . when I went to get milk last night.

"Meat or fecal?"

"What's fecal?" asks Franklin as he washes his bowl in the sink.

"It means poop," says Teddy, who is ten and, left alone, would insert the word poop into every sentence he uttered.

Franklin is a tender, breakable eight. He giggles, as he always does when Teddy says the word poop. Frankie is the world's greatest audience for poop humor. "Dad ate a poop burrito?"

"I had to try the recipe before I make it for dinner tonight," I say. Franklin gives me the requisite *Eeww*, and I beknight him with my coffee spoon. "Now go get dressed for school, my young apprentice."

"I had a cigar made of donkey shit in Mexico once," my father says to Franklin as he squeezes past the counter. "It wasn't bad. Hard to keep lit. I bought it at a little whorehou—"

And as much as I'm glad to see Dad reminiscing, I step in. "That's enough, Dad."

"Eeww, Grandpa," Franklin says. "You smoked cigars? That's bad for you." Among the world's evils—fascism, ethnic cleansing, environmental degradation—smoking deserves the most severe curricular attention in my kids' school. At least my new friends Skeet and Jamie have escaped this indoctrination.

I glance out the window to see Lisa's ten-year-old Subaru backing out of the driveway. I wave, trying to recall whether she said goodbye. Or said anything. She's already on her phone. She's always on her phone now, or the computer. It's her new life. I make my way upstairs, glance at the computer, but I don't feel like doing recon on Lisa's online life right now, so I do a few push-ups, fewer sit-ups, take a shower—fourth in line, I get lukewarm—dress in the same weedy clothes I was wearing last night. Downstairs, Dad is planted in front of the television, where he spends his days, switching from old movies to news and back. He pets his universal remote control like a tiny cat.

Ten minutes later, I'm driving the kids to their little parochial school. When Lisa and I violated the first rule of real estate by buying a big house in a questionable neighborhood, we landed near a low-income public school—and after Lisa investigated ("I heard a first grader call her teacher Ass-face") we decided to shop around for the best private school we could afford. This turned out to be a little Catholic shop a few miles away—odd since neither Lisa nor I is Catholic. This whole private school thing would baffle my Dad: not that we're sending our kids to a religious school whose religion we don't practice, but that I drive the kids to school every morning when a perfectly good squash-colored school bus rolls past our house. It would seem insane to him that I willingly pay tuition *beyond* my taxes. In fact, Dad would be outraged by the whole idea of being a consumer of schools. My parents never *shopped* for schools. It would have been like shopping for water, like shopping for air. It wasn't that Mom and Dad chose to be public-school people; it just would never have occurred to them there was a choice. If a school bus pulled up, whatever children were in the house were expected to file outside and get on the bus. It didn't matter if the bus was going to the compound of a racist, survivalist, apocalyptic cult—bus pulls up; kids get on. Of course, the schools I attended were god-awful; that bus took me to a junior high that was more bong and nunchuk factory than school. So maybe education shopping isn't such a bad idea.

"I love you guys," I say as we pull up to the old brick school building; uniformed urchins seep from assorted foreign sedans and big Catholic-family Suburbans and Expeditions. "Have a great day learning about the evils of smoking."

"Whose hat?" Franklin holds up the flat-brimmed, black and silver Raiders cap.

"Skeet's," I say.

"Oh," Franklin says, as if this makes sense.

Teddy grabs the hat and somehow knows exactly how to wear it, cocked a bit sideways and off-center. It's amazing how this kind of knowledge filters like an aquifer beneath the adult surfaces of the world, how everyone under thirty speaks the same subtle cultural language. Our parents' parents blamed records, our parents blamed MTV, and we blame MySpace or some other Internet villain, but I suspect it's the microwaves I was telling Skeet about; maybe they're not benign . . . maybe they beam style advice to the young, and on some unseen command the children of the world will one day band together and slit their parents' collective—

"Take the hat off, Teddy."

"*Jawohl, herr commandant.*" He drops the hat in the backseat and the boys jump out, start walking toward the school in their wrinkly blue chinos and white polos, and I think these uniforms wouldn't be so bad if they didn't make the kids all look like bank tellers on casual Friday or the employees of a discount airline or— like me . . .

Truly amazing, this pot. I have gone through at least five strata of high since those first hits on Jamie's blunt: the calm and the paranoia and the weepy displeasure, then the euphoria and rolling epiphanies, and now I seem to have a hyper-fluent sense of the world, as if I've traded in my old vacuum tube eyes for a pair of high-def LCDs. It's no wonder jazz musicians are so certain they write better stoned.

In fact, maybe there's something there for me, too. Linking free-verse poetry and financial advice was obviously a bad idea, and thinking my two passions would translate to the larger world was out-of-control hubris, even in the epoch of hubris we are passing out of . . . but this new idea forming in my mind makes some real sense—

I will be the baked financial journalist, *Moneydude*, Stoned Stock Analyst. I'll start a blog, get high every morning and give stock tips with the clarity I've achieved from deep-frying my skull in B.C. bud: Tip 1. Time to take a flyer on Frito-Lay stock. Why? Because, man . . . that queso cheese dip? *Damn!* . . . Tip 2. Zig-Zag Papers are poised to make a second-quarter rally because . . . yo, it's all summer and shit. Tip 3. The P-to-E ratio on A-Metro Trans-Solutions makes it a can't-miss stock given the Democratic Congress's likely emphasis on subsidizing mass transit projects. (And, dude, their logo totally looks like *a vag!*)

I drive through a forest of leftover political signs, red and blue and black and white and good and evil; the experts say we are polarized again, but I think we've become *bi-polarized*, and I leave the parking lot, pull out into the world, merging into something larger than myself, perhaps bleeding into the flow of history as we're on the verge of . . .

What? What was that? I lost it. Shit. A merge on the verge of the surge of . . . Tyger! Tyger! burning bright . . .

Damn. What was I thinking about?

Sprinklers? Internet? Forbearance? Unraveling? Slurpees?

No, it is very good pot.

CHAPTER 3

Social Networking

M Y WIFE TYPES HER life, key-by-key
site-by-site, primarily at night,
on the home PC where I try to find
work while she's drowsing, instead
find the history of her browsing,
surfing her lost past for evidence
that she wasn't always this sad—

Still, I'd convinced myself, at least until last night, that Lisa's
new online hobby, social networking, was a healthier compulsion
than the brief, eBay shopping spree she went on last year (our
garage lined with unsold remnants, nine boxes of commemorative
plates, plush toys and china figurines). At one time, Lisa man-
aged this online life at work, but the optometrist's office where she
rots as a receptionist for thirty hours a week without benefits put
an end to personal computer use, so every night now Lisa spends
two hours on our home computer, managing her Facebook page

and her Linked-In page and her MySpace page, responding to ass-sniffing inquiries from old friends on Classmates.com and Google-imaging people she used to know. I don't say a word about any of it—this was our couples-counselor's advice—but I worry that what she's really looking for is not the people she once knew, but the *her* she once was, some happier version of herself living a better life than the one she has with me.

Of course, it's unwise to diagnose the mental condition of one's spouse. But if I had to trace Lisa's current malaise (and if I didn't trace it to the moment she accepted my marriage proposal) I would say that it began when her confidence was battered by leaving her career to birth those two boys eleven years ago. Before that, Lisa was a world-beating, self-assured businesswoman, in charge of marketing a doctors' group that specialized in sports medicine, and she ventured out every day in curvy business suits that made me want to coax her into elevators for inappropriate workplace contact. But then I spermed her up and she left that good job, and since I was earning decent money and making indecent profits on some canny investments, we felt safe and maybe even wise—perhaps even morally good—having Lisa quit her job while she nursed, nested and nurtured those thankless little shit-heels. Then, a decade on, with the boys safely ensconced in papist school, we figured she'd just go get another job like her old one, but she ventured back into the job world two years ago with none of the hot confidence she'd had before we procreated. I try to put myself in her position—one day you come home from work a vital twenty-nine-year-old *babe*, whom the fellas at the office actively lust after (a real pro, too, trained in the latest technology, terminology and theory) and next day you go out looking for work a nearly forty-year-old *Mom* who colors the gray and doesn't even know PowerPoint, a short-tempered *lady* who didn't get any sleep last night because one of the kids pooped his bed (how do you *poop a bed*, anyway?). Six months of résumés, referrals and rejections took their toll and Lisa accepted the first job she was offered—receptionist for a dull optometrist who calls the women in his office *gals*, and whose idea of a Christmas bonus is twenty-five bucks at a craft store.

I hated seeing the woman I loved lose her confidence that way. And yet, in the deepest reaches of my psyche, I wonder if there wasn't a part of me that was glad she didn't go back to the gym-toned guys at the sports medicine clinic. Our marriage was typical, I think; we deluded ourselves that it was made of rock-solid stuff, but there were trace elements of regret, seams of I-told-you-so, cracks of martyrdom. In the last few months—with things around here deteriorating—I've even asked myself if I didn't take some pleasure *keeping my wife* at home, that maybe I subconsciously preferred a depleted Lisa because I was threatened by the sexy, confident one, the one I couldn't control, the one I could lose. If so, then I am an even smaller man than the out-of-work, out-of-gas loser who greets me in the mirror every day, and maybe I deserve my unraveling fate, pushed away from this beautiful beaten wife, who goes out every night on the Internet in search of her better self—pre-child, pre-forty, pre-me.

More self-pity. It's ugly. Counterproductive. I constantly warn my sons about the dangers of self-pity when they're moping about being the only kids in the world without a Nintendo Wii. And honestly, with Lisa and me, it hasn't been that bad. Beneath our current troubles, I think we still like each other, and as flatly unromantic as that might sound, it's amazing how many of our couple friends genuinely *don't*. Lisa and I still root for each other, still make each other laugh, still have fairly successful sex at least once a week, sometimes more—at least we did until about a month ago, when this dry spell started. We have similar goals and interests. Share the same politics. And (I realize I'm making the case to myself) we don't even argue much. Certainly we *did* argue some last winter and spring, when our finances fell apart, but even then Lisa and I didn't argue so much as *not talk*—our little ballet of sighs, pursed lips and hushed voices as I worried over mortgage statements and retirement bulletins and over the increasingly terse letters from various lenders and financial institutions—grim reams of paper that have led me today to the office of Richard Blackmore, our financial coroner . . . I mean, planner.

When the hole started opening two years ago, Lisa and I congratulated ourselves because at least we weren't in one of those La Brea Tar Pit adjustable-rate home loans. We had a normal thirty-year, with a normal fixed rate, and even though we'd unwisely cashed in equity for a couple of costly remodels, we were still okay. We had some normal debt: normal credit cards, normal furniture layaways, normal car payments, some uncovered medical bills, Teddy's normal braces and Franklin's normal speech therapy (*Oh, for God's sake, just say your 'R's*). But then my perfectly normal dream of starting my own business, the afore-derided *poetfolio.com*, turned out to take longer and be more costly than we thought, and we found ourselves taking another line of credit on the house, going deeper in debt. Then came Lisa's abnormal online shopping binge, and our credit cards rolled over on us a couple of times and the car payments lapsed and the ground began slipping away and the only thing that seemed rock steady was the house, so we took another chunk out of it, just to catch up, we said, to temporarily cover living expenses, and we refinanced at the peak value; like a snake eating its tail we borrowed against our house to pay the house payment of a house leveraged at forty percent more than the house was worth. When the dip came I scrambled back to the newspaper, but with the hole growing deeper and monthly interest charges eating us alive, we fell further behind, missed a few house payments and our helpful mortgage lender offered us an "agreement of forbearance," six months leeway (with interest!) to get on top of our payments, and we jumped at that lifeline, but then I lost my job and maybe we were distracted by that and by my father's collapse (we dragged him into the hole with us) because while we fretted and waffled and stalled, the stock market went out for milk, got stoned and lost forty percent of its value, depleting my 401(k), which, due to my stubborn love for financial and media stocks, had already begun to look more like a 4(k). That's about the time I stopped showing Lisa the grim letters about the house, with their phony warm salutations ("Dear Homeowner . . .").

This is how a person wakes up one morning to find that he's six days from losing his house.

The advice you get when your mortgage is in danger is to "contact the lender." The last time I contacted my lender, some twenty-five-year-old kid answered the phone and talked me into forbearance, this six-month amnesty of procrastination. I should have known it was a bad move when I contacted my lender the next time and found out the kid had been laid off, that our mortgage had been bundled and sold with a stack of similarly red paper to a second company, and that the second company had been absorbed by a third company. Now I have no idea how to "contact my lender." I seem to spend hours in automated phone dungeons ("For English, press one") desperately looking for a single human voice to gently tell me I'm dead.

Clock ticks. Planet turns. Six revolutions from now whatever bank owns my mortgage will start foreclosure proceedings unless I can either beg more time or come up with the balloon forbearance payment of $31,200. Meanwhile, I try to figure out how to tell Lisa about this looming deadline—keeping in mind that (a) she adores this house, (b) she was raised to connect financial security to love and (c) I'm quite possibly losing her anyway. So I go it alone.

In the office of Richard Blackmore, Idiot Financial Planner, on the third floor of a squat downtown building, the reception area's littered with *Forbes* and *BusinessWeek* and *Investors Daily*: crisis porn, full of emphatic dirty-talk about "Hidden Opportunities in the Wreckage," climaxing charts, "How to Make Money in a Crash," photos of wet-browed, bug-eyed investment experts looking for full relief in this overheated climate.

The meeting is as predictable as coffin shopping. Richard keeps his diplomas on the wall, and I wonder why journalists and poets don't do that. He tells me that losing the house might be inevitable, but that it's only the beginning of my trouble. "Look," he says, and he plays his adding machine like Jerry Lee Lewis, shows me various groupings of red numbers, offers painfully obvious advice. I could go into deeper detail, but frankly, I'm not that interested in the further specifics. Except these two points: (1) my money guy Richard is going without a tie now, like a politician who wants to appeal to the suffering common man (or perhaps every morning his firm takes the ties and shoelaces away from the brokers and financial planners to keep them from offing themselves); (2) Richard's basic advice is to liquidate, sell, sell, sell, dump, sell, scale down, sell some more, live "like a fry-cook in the '70s," try to get a job, any job "very fucking fast," beg my lender for more time, and with a great deal of luck we might avoid losing the house *and* going bankrupt.

This is something like taking your car to a mechanic, only to hear this: *I hope you have good walking shoes.*

"And by 'scale down,' you mean . . ."

"Scale. Down."

"Right. And by 'down' you mean . . ."

"Down," Richard says. His mouth is car-ported by a black mustache, an effective tool for delivering bad news: "Down down down. I'm talking public school down, used-car, canned-food down, lower-middle class down, Matt. Not 2004 upper-middle class down—not eight-person Jacuzzi and lawn guy down—but

1977 generic-food buy-your-clothes-at-K-Mart down. I'm talking dump your car payment, have a garage sale, clip coupons, Christmas shop at Goodwill. I mean—look at these numbers." He spins a red page. "You see anything I don't?"

I see London. I see France. Flood tide below me! I see you face to face! Heat check: still high. "Richard, if we cash out everything, is there any tax benefit to—"

"Tax benefit?" Richard's mustache spits laughter. "Jesus, Matt. I don't think you understand." And he leans forward, his bleary eyes darting around my face. "Once this starts, you can't stop it. I've seen this before. You're parked on a hill without a parking brake and your car is rolling toward you and the only move is to get out of the way . . . and you want to talk about tax benefits?"

I should point out that my money guy Richard is not the best money guy in the world. (My first clue in this direction came in the late 1990s, when I was doing pretty well on my own, blindly investing at the height of the tech boom and I let Richard talk me into what he called "a safer bet"—*Mexican shipping bonds*. So while I had doubled my own easy bets on Microsoft and Cisco, I lost thirty cents on the dollar on Richard's great tip—that anchor of the business world: Transmaritime-Pacifico.) But if Richard is not the best number guy, he's a brilliant word guy—probably the reason I stay with him—and should anyone doubt it, the man shifts metaphors while I'm still marveling at the idea of our finances as a rolling car.

"Look," Richard says. "I'm gonna give you the straight diagnosis, Matt. You are severely hemorrhaging here—not just on the house, in every area possible. Credit-card debt, health care debt, the equity you took on your house, unpaid creditors from your little business venture, your stubborn insistence on riding those bank and media stocks into the ground. And I don't know who talked you into forbearance, but that's the worst thing you could have done. It's just a way for lenders to squeeze the lemon once more. Did anyone tell you that ninety percent of the people who make the big forbearance payment still end up losing their houses?"

I seem to have missed that part of the sales pitch.

"Listen," Richard says, "unless you're about to inherit some money, what we're talking about here is irreversible, fatal. You have fiscal Ebola, Matt. You are bleeding out through your nose and your mouth and your eye sockets, from your financial asshole."

See! Fiscal Ebola? My financial asshole is bleeding? This was exactly why I started *poetfolio.com*; there are money poets everywhere.

Richard slides a small check across the table to me. "Here's another way to look at this. The last thing you can afford right now . . ." And he pushes the folders from my file over to me. ". . . is a financial planner."

This is why I'm here, of course. To cash out. I am pretending to need advice, but what I really need is whatever cushion I have left. So . . . I hold my breath and pick up the check. It's in the high . . . four figures. Nine thousand four hundred and twelve dollars. I laugh. "That's it?"

"I wanted to diversify you, Matt. You insisted on media and financials."

This is true. In my past life as a business reporter I'd decided *I* was the expert and I clung to a tip from a banking guy who, I can only hope now, is lying dead on a sidewalk somewhere. But I can't entirely blame *him* either, because I rode those stocks up for years, and when the financials first cracked, I stubbornly refused to sell. Then I got distracted by my own job loss and by Dad's senility meltdown. And every time Richard begged me to let him unload those bad stocks, I reminded him of his last advice, *And buy what? Mexican Shipping Bonds?*

So . . . as I say, here we are—

"After penalties," Richard's mustache continues, "taxes, commissions . . ."

"Wait." I look down at the check again as Richard stands. "You took a commission? Do travel agents take commissions on flights that go down?"

Richard ignores *my* choice metaphor. He apologizes, then walks me to the lobby and asks me how everything else is going—which is a bit like asking the Prime Minister of Poland how *everything else is going* in the fall of 1939—you know . . . other than the Nazi invasion. I tell Richard that, all in all, I'm not in a bad mood—probably because I got high at a 7/11 last night.

"You got high at a 7/11?"

"Well, we actually got high in my car, and at this apartment building. But I had an amazing burrito at the 7/11 afterward. You can't believe the pot they have now, Richard."

"Yeah, I know," he says. And then, he leans in and sort of wistfully, adds: "It's supposed to be a myth, the increased potency."

"It's no myth."

"No." He smiles. "No myth."

And then something hits me. "Wait. You smoke pot, Richard?"

"Now and then," he admits. "When I can get it. Doesn't everyone?"

"I didn't." And I tell him how it had been at least fifteen years, how I assumed that, after Lisa and I had two impressionable kids, two hypocrisy-sensing laser beams of sweetness, my weed-smoking days were long behind me.

Richard hums laughter. "Hey . . . I've got a question about that." Then he looks both ways and leans in close. "Can you get me some?"

Outside, after the meeting, it's cold—air crackling with the sudden turn to late fall. Leaves are giving up, like newspapers, becoming insolvent all over the streets. I walk to the car. It was disconcerting at first, to be out in the world in the daytime, when everyone else was working. This is the first fall since I was fifteen I haven't had a job of some kind. Sadly, I'm getting used to it. Right now the editors will be coming out of their budget meeting and the reporters will be trying to avoid their eyes, or pretending to be on the phone so they won't get assigned a weather story ("Colder temps move in") or a brief about last night's trailer fire ("Suspected arson at mobile home park") or a feature on the Eagle Scout who built a bike out of aluminum cans ("Recycled cycle leads to scholarship").

I call Lisa from the car as I drive to Costco.

"Well," she says, "How'd it go?"

"You know Richard," I say, "always the optimist. Thinks we should invest in cyanide."

Polite laugh.

"Would you have ever guessed Richard is a weed smoker?"

"How did that come up at a financial planning meeting?"

"I don't remember."

"So what's his advice?"

"Well, first, we can't panic . . . and second . . . if we were going to eat one of the children, which one would you pick?"

Lisa laughs a little more heartily; her voice always gets lower, throaty, when she thinks something is genuinely funny. It's very hot. "I suppose the older one," she says. "That little one looks gamy." And suddenly I'm filled with warmth and sadness and I am rushed with nostalgia—*for the marriage I'm still in*. I can't believe how much I want this woman and it kills me—*kills me*—knowing what I know.

This: Right before I went to 7/11 for milk last night, I considered telling her about the letter from the mortgage company. But when I went upstairs she was asleep. I signed onto her FaceBook page (it had taken me three days to figure out her password) and saw that she'd put up a better picture of herself with her cute new pixie haircut (a picture I took) and I also saw that she'd been carrying on a three-day "chat" with an online buddy named Chuck, which, not coincidentally, is the name of her old high school boyfriend, a guy I was never jealous of before, because, frankly, Chuck sounded like a bit of a chuck, and not like the sensitive, successful guy he turns out to be, at least in the online realm. The subject of this chat seemed to be the flat parallel trajectories of Chuck's and Lisa's mildly disappointing lives ("ever wake up and wonder what happened")—lives that must've seemed boundlessly perfect when they were eighteen, sneaking off to his parents' lake place to squirrel their boundlessly perfect young bodies into positions that I'd give anything to replicate. And it seems clear from their familiarity that this was not the first chat between Lisa and Chuck, not the first time the sad subject of their sad lives has come up. As the Face-Book conversation continued, Lisa and Chuck went back and forth about themselves ("trying to get back in shape" "Y? U look great") and their jobs ("not the best time to be looking for something" "but U R so talented") people from high school ("Dana looks like a manatee—ooh, that's mean" "U could never be mean") and while it was all vaguely above-board, it also felt . . . I don't know, intimate . . . and then Chuck wrote, "Temted to get all hot and steamy agin" as if the very words made him too worked-up to type straight and she ignored his misspellings and suggested two simple letters, "TM?" and either she was trademarking his stupid sexy-talk or, more likely, suggesting that he should take his nastiness to the text messaging world—*agin*—so she could see it right away— *agin!*—huddled over her cell phone, breathless, in our bed . . .

   . . . while I cluelessly watched sports highlights with my buggy old father—*agin*—who responded to every Colts highlight by re-

minding me how good Unitas was, every Eagles highlight by re-
marking what a slow stiff Jurgensen turned out to be—as if quar-
terbacks were declared extinct in 1968 . . .

. . . and I saw that I couldn't tell her about the house, at least not
yet, not after coming across the trail of this crushing deception,
because God knows I've flirted and daydreamed and committed a
thousand tiny betrayals—but . . . this tore me up . . . my broken
little black heart bleeding out through my mouth and my eye sock-
ets and my asshole and . . .

. . . I'm dying here. Of emotional Ebola. And I just wish the
little bugs would get it over with and gobble me all up, so that I
could stop suffering, because I know the world goes on without us;
my mother taught me that; it goes on and on, turning us over like
broken sod. And hell, maybe it's nothing, a little late-night nasty
smack-smack talk between old lovers—harmless! But *agin*? *Agin*?
And when I imagined my wife's narrow tapering back in our bed
last night, cute face bathed in the blue light of a nasty cell phone
message from the boy who used to sleep with her—Jesus, it hurt
more than I could bear . . . and that . . .

that . . .
that
. . . was when I went out for milk and ended
up baking my wounded skull.

Of course, this is just the kind of melodramatic, twisted logic I
will refuse to accept from my boys when they are teenagers. (You
went out and got high with delinquents because you were jealous
of your girlfriend? Do you know how stupid that sounds?) But last
night I did just that, went to the 7/11 and, sulking over my wife's
flirtation with her old boyfriend and the knowledge that I was losing
her house, I fried my nut with the delinquency dream team.

On the phone now with Lisa, I don't tell her that Richard says the house is almost certain to go to the bank. And I certainly don't mention her "chat" with Chuck. And I definitely don't confess my emotionally retarded response. Instead, as I pull into the Costco parking lot, into this temple of buy-bulk-big-box consumerism at the opening bell of a planetary recession, I take a moment to simply pass along to Lisa our pothead financial guy's more mundane recommendations, the long list of luxuries we can do without in the upcoming belt-tightening: "Richard says we should cancel cable and get rid of the Internet," I say, with no small amount of conniving joy. "We sure as hell can't afford these cell phones anymore."

"I don't know if I can live without a cell phone," Lisa says after a moment.

"Well," I say, and I laugh giddily, "I guess we're just gonna have to find out."

CHAPTER 4

A Brief Political Manifesto

I WAS DRIVING AROUND THE packed Costco parking lot
looking for a space and listening to some guy
on NPR talk about America's growing suburban poor
when I saw this woman with four kids—
little stepladders, two-four-six-eight—
waiting to climb in the car while Mom
loaded a cask of peanut butter and
pallets of swimsuits into the back
of this all-wheel drive vehicle
and the kids were so cute I waved
and that's when I saw the most amazing thing
as the woman bent over
to pick up a barrel
of grape juice:
her low-rise pants rose low and right there
in the small of her large back
stretched a single strained string,
a thin strap of fabric, yes,

the Devil's floss, I shit you not
a thong, I swear to God, a thong,
now me, I'm okay with the thong
politically and aesthetically, I'm fine
with it being up there or out there,
or wherever it happens to be.

My only question is:
when did Moms start wearing them?

I remember my mom's underwear
(Laundry was one of our chores:
we folded those things awkwardly,
like fitted sheets. We snapped them
like tablecloths. Thwap.
My sister stood on one end,
me on the other
and we walked toward each other
twice.

We folded those things
like big American flags,
hats off, respectful
careful not to let them
brush the ground.)

Now I know there are people out there
who constantly fret about
the Fabric of America:
gay couples getting married, violent videos, nasty TV,
that sort of thing.
But it seems to me

the Fabric of America
would be just fine
if there was a little bit more of it
in our mothers' underpants.

And that is the issue I will run on
when I eventually run:
Getting our moms out of thongs
and back into hammocks
with leg holes
the way God
intended.

CHAPTER 5

The Recession Hits
Stehne's Lumberland

Banded stacks of blond boards
sit out back of the lumber store
and if you squint they look
a little like leftover cakes.
God, the end of a party
is always so sad

"This economy must be killing you guys," I say at the lumber warehouse store where I'm pretending to shop for materials to make a tree fort for my boys. I hope I don't sound *too* hopeful about the economy killing this particular business.

"Things have certainly slowed," says Chuck as he flips through a catalogue for the kind of metal brace he is certain would be perfect for the imaginary tree fort I'm supposed to be building. "Luckily, the last few years were busy enough that a slowdown won't be the worst thing in the world."

It is cold inside this big warehouse store; the ceilings must be thirty feet high. Each narrow aisle is stacked nearly to the rafters with boards and posts and dowels and bags of concrete and plywood and doors and window sashes. The effect of all this scale is to shrink the people in here and I feel like a leprechaun, a tiny sprite come to this mystical woodland to shop among giants for a place to store my magic beans for the winter.

I have lived in this city most of my life and yet I'd never ventured into this lumber store until I found out—from Lisa's chat last night—that her ex-boyfriend Chuck worked here. Setting aside what my never-going-to-a-lumber-store says about my manly bona fides, the important thing is that I'm here now, confronting my enemy, or at least seeing the infamous Chuck for myself. I am totally undercover. Chuck has no idea who I am. He hasn't asked my name, and I don't know why he would, but if he does, I've decided to go with the nom de guerre Jamie Skeet.

And here is my lightning quick assessment of my enemy's strengths, relative to mine: (1) Chuck is taller. (2) Chuck is a few years younger and clearly in better shape. (3) Chuck really does have dreamy eyes. (I heard Lisa make this claim to a friend of ours once, when we were out with another couple, talking about why we fell for our first loves and Lisa said, "His eyes. Chuck had dreamy eyes." Sadly, it's true—a couple of dreamy blue orbs jut from that Cro-Magnon skull.) (4) Chuck looks good in his Carhartt work pants and does not seem to have the middle-aged disappearing-ass issue I've been battling the last few years (just being coldly objective about this). (5) Chuck is—I have to admit it—heartily handsome, those eyes astride carved cheeks over a square jaw. (6) Chuck is employed.

Another list—this one offered in my defense—of the reasons I may have underestimated my opponent for so many years, this strapping and friendly man's man who, I was well aware, had slept with my wife back in her nubile, flexible, childless years: (I) Whenever she mentioned this old boyfriend Chuck she would smile slightly, which I misinterpreted as an expression of disbelief that she'd ever dated such a monumental tool before finding true love with the man of her dreams. (II) Complacency led me to believe that Lisa and I had such a strong relationship that it didn't matter who she'd dated before; her ex-boyfriends could've been George Clooney, Kobe Bryant and Abraham Lincoln and I wouldn't have been smart enough to be intimidated. (III) I made the classic arrogant white-collar mistake of thinking that because I used my *brain* to support my family (back when I supported my family) I was superior to some dude who stacks lumber for a living. (IV) *Dude who stacks lumber for a living* is not the same as *dude who works for hugely profitable family business, which he stands to inherit.* (V) Whenever Lisa mentioned her ex-boyfriend Chuck Stehne I always spelled it in my mind Chuck *Stain* and, honestly, who could ever worry about a guy named Stain?

"Top ten rejected attractions at Disneyworld," I say. "Number ten: Lumberland."

Prince Chuck of Lumberland smiles politely and spins a photo of the steel double-reinforced brace, or whatever it is, so I can see it for myself. "This one."

"Nope, all wrong," I say. "That's not what I'm looking for. Not even close."

Chuck spins the catalogue so that he can see it again. "No, I really think this is what you're looking for. I built a fort for my kids and this worked great. See, it stabilizes the posts here and here and—"

"You have kids?"

"Three."

I glance at his ring-less left hand. "Married?"

"Divorced." But he looks a little confused by this line of questioning, as if he can't imagine what it has to do with fake tree fort construction.

I pretend to look back at the brace. "I don't know. That looks pretty dangerous. I have two boys that I love more than anything. Love my boys *and* my wife. Their *mother.*"

"Sure," Chuck says, looking at the catalogue. "Well, maybe a different style. We have some books." He walks toward an aisle, and after a moment, I follow. We walk past all sorts of weapons that could be used on Chuck's back, hammers and nail guns and pry bars—

Divorced. Shit. How do I fight divorced? Means he probably has his own house somewhere (probably not about to go into foreclosure); I was hoping the logistics of sneaking around might at least be difficult for them, but if he's got his own place . . . shit, shit, shit.

Lisa is not someone who would stray from a marriage lightly but I see why now, because I know exactly what she's attracted to—confidence, security, strength, stability—all of which Chuck has, none of which is exactly seeping from my pores these days.

He stops in the aisle of how-to books and clicks his tongue as he runs his hand across the spines of books that show how to do simple electrical work and how to repair a carburetor and how to fix a clogged sink and how to build a porch and how to stain your fence and, finally, how to build a tree fort. This long bookshelf seems taken directly from my insecurities—an entire library of things I cannot do. In the next aisle of this hell-library would be books about how to manage your billions and what to do with your foot-long penis.

"Here we go," he says, and pulls out the book and hands it to me.

"You can look through this and see if there's a style you like better."

I take the book and pretend to leaf through it. Each tree-house picture makes me feel more incompetent than the last.

"You might just buy the book, take it home and look through it to make sure you get the right one," he says. "There's no rush, I'm guessing."

I look up at him.

"I mean, you're not going to build a tree fort in the winter."

"In the winter? No." I laugh. Scoff. "Of course not." I purse my lips and look back down at the book, make my own clicking noises with my tongue. I wish I'd said I was building some-thing else, *anything else*—a catapult or gallows or balustrades—anything but a stupid tree fort. Four years ago, when we moved into the house we're about to lose, I promised the boys that I'd build them a tree fort. Four years later, there's no tree fort and that sad fact is probably not even in the top ten ways I've let the poor boys down.

"So, you built one of these for your kids?"

Chuck is looking through his own copy of *Building the Perfect Tree Fort*. He shows me a picture. "Kind of like this one." Then he closes the book and puts it back. He looks off a little wistfully. "It's at their mother's house."

"Ooh. Sorry," I say. "It's tough when a marriage breaks up. Let's hope there's a special place in hell for anyone who would break up a—"

But by putting the book back, Chuck has opened the door for a man's man in coveralls who was waiting for his help, and before I can finish my pointed little comment about cuckolders deserving Dante's seventh circle, this guy slides his lumber wish list in front of Chuck, like he's the goddamn Lumber Fairy, and I wonder why the jerk can't go get this stuff himself. He looks ca-

pable. He's in coveralls. Still, Chuck excuses himself to go help the
real customer.

> And I stand alone holding a book about
> how to build the tree fort
> I will never build
> in the freezing thirty-foot-high aisle
> of my many deficiencies
> while the man stealing my wife
> goes off to gather more wood.

//

CHAPTER 6

My Stupid Idea

M-Tronic Reports Strong Q3

Higher than expected orders and
a reversal of its earnings direction
have led to an upward adjustment of
M-Tronic's third quarter projection
and revived hopes for a sector move
despite several analysts' rejection.

I know it sounds stupid in hindsight, and perhaps in foresight too, but my idea was that someone needed to start a website that gave financial news and advice . . . in verse.

Actually, it's not *quite* as stupid as that. My idea was that the site would not just feature poetry, but a higher level of financial writing—think of it as money-lit. People spend so much time thinking about business and finance, about their mortgages, about investing, about their retirement and college funds; hell, after 7/11, it was all anyone talked about, as if we'd had a collective midlife crisis. But the writing about those things has always seemed so dry. My site was supposed to remedy that, by featuring all sorts of *literary* writing about the financial world—creative essays, profiles of brokers, short fiction about business, and what I called "investment memoirs"—first-person chronicles by investors and professionals (for instance, a commissioned broker piece: *My Season in Purgatory: How an Otherwise Savvy Trader Fell for the Convertible Bond Lie*). The hook, though, was poetry—not because I felt there was some great demand for a quatrain about consumer confidence, but because I thought people would simply be drawn to the anachronism of it— like the European TV channel where the news is read by topless anchors. Investment poetry would draw in the curious, get newspapers and TV stations to do bemused features about us, and this, then, would open the door for a literary discussion of the thing that most of us spent so many days thinking about: our money.

And so: *poetfolio.com*—conceived in overheated-but-honest passion, its home page still pinned to my laptop like the refrigerator-taped ultrasound of a stillborn baby. I can close my eyes and still see that beautiful beta page: a humor piece about the return of tech stocks written like a horror story (*Night of the Living Tech*); a frankly mediocre investment memoir from a woman who funded only socially progressive companies (*Redefining a GOOD Investment*), a handful of smart, short rhymed business shorts down the right side, and my favorite—a rollicking heroic poem about the first step in saving for your kids' college (*The Ballad of a 529 Plan*).

Even with that perfectly reasonable explanation, and perfectly realized home page, I still feel the need to defend my idea, by tracing the synaptic misfires that went into creating it. My thoughts went something like this: A. people don't read poetry much anymore. B. I *like* poetry, or at least I did in college. C. I'm not sure

I understand the poetry I read in journals now; it seems like another language, disconnected from my undergrad Keats, Stevens and Neruda. D. This new poetry seems rooted in abstract language and has little to do with the real world. E. I have spent most of my life covering the real world as a journalist, first for a small business publication and then for the local newspaper. F. In that time, I've noticed that business writing is the driest, boringest, least imaginative writing in the world. G. At one time, I wanted to be a poet. H. It's really too bad people don't read poetry; they should. I. Early middle age is such a creepy time, and I constantly find myself wishing I were more like the younger me. J. Perhaps fiscal poetry is the perfect union of my overworked, analytical, continuous-list-making left-brain and my seemingly ignored creative right.

Conclusion: I shall now quit my job and endanger my family's future to follow my youthful dream of writing stock news and tips in pedestrian, amateurish verse.

The thing that finally tipped me over the edge was when I read a story about the heiress to this big fortune leaving a huge pot of money for the advancement of poetry. I wrote a grant proposal and a business plan, and shocked myself by getting some actual funding (though far less than I ended up needing). Whenever I described the idea, people smiled and I suppose I mistook their bemusement for enthusiasm. I bought two new computers, hired a tech/ad specialist to help create the website and to sell advertising, rented a little office, and, hell, when you get a grant and people are smiling and the start-up costs are minimal, you kind of have to go through with it. I quit my job, built my site, quickly burned through the tiny grant, emptied our savings, went in debt, stalled, spent six months fretting, and then got ice-cold feet, realizing at the last minute, days before we were supposed to go live, that no way in hell was anyone ever going to use the Internet to read poems about—

"Dan Fouts," my father says as we watch football highlights on SportsCenter, as we always do after dinner. "He threw the prettiest ball. He had a beard you know."

"Yep," I say. My dad always brings up the old bearded quarterback, Dan Fouts.

"I don't know how he played in that beard." My father pinches his face when he watches TV, like a trial judge unhappy with the lawyers in his courtroom.

"Hmm."

"Had to be itchy."

"You think?"

"Sure. You know who else threw a nice ball?"

I can hear typing coming from upstairs, the rackety tap-tap of plastic keys, Lisa on the computer again, no doubt telling Chuck how she dreams of caressing his—

"Joe Willie Namath. Before his knees went to shit." Dad shakes his head. "He could sling it. Maynard and Sauer and Boozer and Snell. Great team. Last of the great ones."

The last great football team was in 1968 . . . I just say, "Yeah."

I hear footsteps on the stairs and look over my shoulder. Lisa has changed into yoga pants and is clutching the grim stack of monthly bills and bank statements from the top of my dresser.

So it's time for our monthly descent into the finances . . . *agin.* I stand and follow her to the kitchen, where we lay out the bills and bank statements, and I give her the basic outline of our trouble (while sparing her the grisliest details). I can see by her face that she suspects it's even worse than I'm letting on; in my defense, the only thing I hold back is the *immediacy* of some of our troubles. For instance, Lisa knows we're way behind on our mortgage payment; what I don't feel the need to show her is the letter in my messenger bag threatening eviction if we don't come up with the $31,200 forebearance payment *next week.*

I tell myself that I'm like the kindly oncologist who lays out the severe treatment the patient faces without depressing her with the long-odds prognosis. And even without the scariest details, Lisa agrees with most of the draconian steps Richard and I discussed: cashing in our retirement and my pension, seeking another grace period on the house (during which time I will find a job, I swear), selling my car to get out from under the payment, combining the rest of our debt into one loan, which we'll then chip away at, buying health insurance only for the kids, and cutting back on all extravagances (cell phones, restaurants, vacations, Christmas presents). But there's one obvious measure that she simply can't seem to get her mind around.

"Public school?" She frowns again at our bank statement. "Are we there already?"

"I know," I say. And I do know. We'd just moved into this neighborhood four years ago—finally getting the big old house we wanted—when I drove past the neighborhood elementary, smiling as I always do whenever I pass a school. I watched as four boys, eight, maybe nine years old, walked away from the recess pack toward the tree-lined fence; I thought, that school doesn't look as bad as the realtor made it sound (ninety-two percent free-and-reduced lunch, he'd said, the liberal in me bristling at the disturbing equation he was proposing: *poverty=bad school*). That was when one of the walking boys pivoted and took up a sentry post while the other two began beating on the fourth at the edge of the playground. It was like watching a prison documentary. I was stunned at first, and kept driving, but finally stopped my car and jumped out. I ran back along the fence line, yelling something like, "Hey, stop that!" and one of the nine-year-olds yelled, "Fuck off, faggot," and I was struck dumb. Thankfully, a playground aide heard the yelling and ran over and I hoped she was going to break up the fight, but the kid getting beaten (the kid I thought I'd saved) jumped up and told the playground aide that I was "a perv" who'd asked them to get in my car. It was ingenious, and I saw that I actually *had* saved the kid—not by yelling, but by giving him and his bullies a new, common enemy, so that he could be aligned with the thugs and show himself to not be a snitch, but a stand-up guy. I stood there as the playground aide gave me a sharp look and I thought: do I really want my kids to go here? Do I want to explain the politics of prison beatings and snitch avoidance *to my fucking six-year-old*? And I hurried off, Mr. Public School admitting to himself that I'd teach my kids at home before I'd send them to Alcatraz Elementary.

Parenthood makes such sweet hypocrites of us all.

"Public school," Lisa says again. She sighs and stares at that bank statement like it's in some code. "I just don't know if I can do that, Matt." —As if I'm suggesting we sell the children for medical experiments.

"We could try moving to a neighborhood with a better school," I say lamely.

Lisa points out the obvious, that it would be insane to sell now, when "we owe thirty percent more than we could get" in this market. (Try fifty, I think.)

There is a scholarship program at the school, Lisa says, but she doubts we'd have much of a shot because we aren't parish members . . . aren't, in fact, even Catholic.

"I'll join," I say.

"I don't think it's that easy," she says. "I think there are classes. Rituals."

"I'll take a blood oath. A spanking."

But no matter what I say, I can't seem to get her to look up at me. Those eyes move from bill to window to bank notice to bill, but won't rise to meet mine. "It's a religion, Matt, not a fraternity. You have to go to class, get baptized, that kind of thing."

"I'll get baptized," I say. "I'll get exorcised. Simonized."

She smiles. A little. But still doesn't look up.

"Euthanized?" Finally, I give up and my eyes follow hers to the bills and budget sheets between us, and I can't help but think of the boxes of her eBay shit in our garage, as Lisa, no doubt, thinks of the money I wasted on *poetfolio.com*.

Airline Deal Proposed

Buffeted by fuel costs soaring
and with labor costs surging
Delta and Northwest are exploring
the possibility of merging.

Or maybe she isn't thinking about my lame business at all, but fantasizing about Lumberland Chuck, about running off for some therapeutic skin-slapping teenage *humping* in the sturdy sex fort he's no doubt building in some big phallic tree on his property. (Chuck being the sort of guy who would own property.)

That Lisa would be lost in such a fantasy seems even more likely when the back doorbell rings and she overdoes the surprise in greeting her happily divorced friend Dani—"What are you doing here?"—bottle-blond Dani, packed into her teenage-daughter's jeans, with the forty-year-old single-gal wrist tattoo and gravity-be-damned implants that I get in trouble if I notice, Dani the friend Lisa always seeks out when she's unhappiest with me.

She has come bearing two skirts roughly the size of headbands that she "tragically can't fit into anymore," but which will be perfect for Lisa—"with your hot little bod"—and this feels like a slap at me, somehow, as if I don't deserve my wife's bod, as if Dani is pointing out how Lisa would kill (like herself) out on the open market—what a team they would be! And even the skirts feel like a lie to me; it's as if Lisa expected them, as if they were part of a cover story. Lisa says, "Want to come in for a glass of wine?" and of course Dani does.

"Hey Matt," she says, and I say, "Hi Dani," and that's all we get as the women encamp at the kitchen table over fishbowls of Merlot, chattering (for my benefit, I think) about their kids, and waiting for me to leave the room so they can get down to the real talk. I slowly finish loading the dishwasher and drying the pans, scooping up the bills and bank notices until I can think of no other reason to stay in here and am forced to leave.

Dad's watching TV, so I go upstairs to check on the kids, who are supposed to be getting ready for bed, but are engaged in futuristic cartoon battles on their Game Boys instead, Franklin pleading, "Can't I just play until I die?" I know that he means until his little Game Boy character dies, but it chokes me up anyway (I'm so *weepy* these days), and I watch my boy's digital avatar bounce around in what looks like a giant spit bubble until finally, it passes on. (No service; in lieu of flowers, go to bed.) In addition to his little speech problem, and his pooping problem, and his oversensitivity, Franklin is frailer than his big brother. Teddy would probably survive just fine at that tough public school. But lisping, tiny, day-dreamy, slow-to-read Franklin? He'll be some yard-thug's second-grade bitch.

"Can't I stay up?"

"Wish I could let you, but I can't."

"Why?"

"Federal sleeping statutes."

"Please."

"Out of my hands."

"Please?"

"You know if I could do anything at all, I would."

"But I don't want to go to bed."

This reminds me that it's been roughly forty hours since I've been in a bed. This is, of course, the great dream for a kid, staying up all night. Were I to tell Franklin that I didn't go to bed at all last night, his eyes would get huge. *Wait. You've seen the undiscovered territory, the world after bedtime?*

"Sorry, pal." I pull the covers up over his chest and ruffle his hair.

He grabs my arm. "Don't leave."

My Kid Is a Plagiarist

He's stolen all of my best-loved stuff:
the quivering jaw, endless drinks of water,
clutching for arms as Daddy tries
to retreat to the TV; but this isn't
new work, he has to know,
the boundless fear
of being left
alone in bed
in the dark
forever.

When I picture those bullies at Baghdad Elementary walking Franklin to the edge of the playground my mouth goes dry. I comfort and kiss him, then check in on the older one; but Teddy's post-kiss now. Too tough. Squirms when I try. Reading, he waves me off, "'Night Dad," without looking up. I find a cup on his dresser though; this will work.

At the top of the stairs, I slip off my shoes. Walk quietly downstairs, half a step, half a step, half a step onward. Edge into the kitchen with the cup . . . and that's when I hear it.

Leaning in toward one another at the table, Lisa and Dani

are clearly *not* talking about children anymore and I only hear a snippet, but it's more than enough to make me Chuck-spicious. They're whispering—but I hear the words *"so romantic"*— Dani covering her mouth, shaking her yellow head as Lisa tells her something vitally important . . . something that causes them to stop talking and straighten up when they see me, causes Dani to look at me like an accident victim, or so I imagine. I can't say how I know they're talking about Chuck; I just know. Because the other line I heard, just before I came in here, from my wife's frothy best friend was this: *Oh my God, are you gonna do it?*

My mouth goes dry. "Do what?"

"Nothing." No eye contact. "We're just talking about Karen's candle party."

"Oh." I put the cup in the sink and have no choice but to leave again. I sulk into the living room to watch TV with Dad, who watches the box nonstop now, and who is going to be crushed when I tell him we're canceling cable. It's quiet from the kitchen. They must be whispering.

And the night speeds up: the back door closes; Dani goes home; the boys fall asleep; Lisa drifts upstairs to retreat into her social-networking life; and here we all are, alone in our dying house—

"You know who else threw a nice ball?" Dad asks me. "Dan Fouts. But I don't know how he played with that beard. You ever have a beard?"

These are the loops you learn to live with when you live with someone suffering from dementia. Perhaps it's no different than the rest of our lives, the shit circling back around on us: bearded QBs and recessions and death and blue-eyed Chucks come to take your wife. And weed, which took a long twenty-year swing back into my life.

Dad wields his trusty remote, turning it—to another sports channel, as if on that one, it might be 1970. In the quiet I notice the tapping upstairs has stopped. I guess Lisa and Chuck are done blog-fucking, or whatever it's called, or else they've moved *agin* to the TM intimacy of their cell phones. It's surreal, imagining what's going on up there. I wonder if Chuck wrote anything about the sorry putz who came in to Lumberland today to build a tree fort for his kids. Dad and I watch the top ten plays of the day, and he tells me once more about Dan Fouts's beard.

"Itchy," I say.

"Yeah . . . that's what I think," he says, as if I've read his mind.

When I finally go upstairs, Lisa's in bed, just closing her phone. She's wearing her giant, unsexy, population-control pajamas, made of burlap, fiberglass insulation, razor wire.

"Sorry. Were you on the phone?"

"Just checking my messages." She picks up a magazine and starts reading. I stare at her dainty little red phone, which sits closed on the nightstand agin. I think about throwing it out the window. I think about going online to check tonight's browsing history, but hell, I know who she's chatting with, what she's browsing for. I think about telling her the truth about the house, but I'm worried it will be the final nudge for her . . . I think about climbing into bed and begging her to make love—smack-smack—zero-population-growth pajamas be damned. I think of asking her to quit this, whatever it is. It's all so . . . shitty. I know it's shitty. She knows it's shitty. We both know it's shitty, going broke, going down the drain. I don't want *this*. I don't want to spend every night tailing her online like some Internet P.I. I don't want to be sneaky and I don't *want* to catch her cheating or thinking of cheating or wishing she could cheat. And hell, if she does cheat, I'm not even sure I want to know about it. I'd rather be the blithe idiot: get up in the morning, go to a job, come home, help my kids with their homework and go to bed with my wife, clueless. Especially now—

with this noose tightening around my neck and the sense that it's all getting away from me . . . I only want comfort. Peace. I don't want to have to work on my marriage; I just want to have it.

But it's all . . . broke. We're broke, Lisa and me—something important cracked in us. And I have no idea how to fix it, any more than I know how to keep from losing our house, or for that matter, how to build a tree fort. All I know is that I have a check in my pocket for less than ten thousand dollars, a check that represents the last threads of the money we always assumed would serve as our safety net, and *that* might be the stupidest thing we did—not starting a poetry-business website or buying shit on eBay or taking the six-month stay of financial execution, not emailing old boyfriends or getting high at a convenience store—no, the truly stupid mistake was believing that when we fell, a net made of money could catch us.

And just like that, I know what to do. "I'm going to the store."

She doesn't even roll over to answer. "What for?"

"Milk."

I drive. Sigh. Park outside the 7/11. Stare at the sign: red stripe, green stripe, orange stripe. I watch people come and go. These are my people—hungry, cold, desperate. No one shops at a convenience store for convenience. They shop there out of desperation. I fiddle with the radio. Find a lunatic radio show where the loons are talking about the United Nations taking over our country— New World Order and Mao suits—and as I listen to the paranoia seep from the Bose speakers, I think we're all losing it, suffocating in our paranoia—and then I wonder if my fears about Lisa and Chuck are symptomatic of this paranoia pandemic and that's when I switch over to sport talk, where they're rating college quarterbacks, and now I'm onto a Dad-loop because I actually think of calling in to ask if there are any quarterbacks now who play with beards and maybe I'm going crazy.

It's especially crazy to assume that Skeet and Jamie will return to this 7/11, but I don't know where else to look for them. Finally, after an hour, I give up and drive over to the apartment building where we stood outside last night smoking weed. And I see the tricked Ford Festiva among the rust-buckets in the parking lot, but I don't know which apartment belongs to the dude who drives it. So I sit in my car agin, waiting, until finally, I see a loping young black kid in huge jeans and a dirty tank top walking toward the building. I don't recognize him from the other night, but I jump out of my car anyway.

"Hey. I'm trying to find Jamie and Skeet. Or the guy who drives that Festiva."

"I don't know what you're talkin' about," the kid says, too fast, and I can see that I've spooked him.

"I'm not a police officer or anything. I just . . . I want to ask them something."

The kid looks around, shifts in the glow of a streetlight, and then lowers his eyes. "You were here last night. Dude with the slippers."

But Skeet has my slippers now, and I'm wearing running shoes, so I say, "Yeah, that's me." I don't exactly remember this kid; they all kind of blurred together last night, because I'm so old or because I was so fried. "Look," I say, and I step in close. "I just want to buy some of the weed we smoked last night."

"And you're not a cop?"

Remembering my upcoming Catholic training, I cross myself. "I swear."

And maybe this kid was raised Catholic because this seems to convince him. He cocks his head and says, "How much you want?"

"Well," and I take the $9,400 check from my pocket, "how about this much?"

CHAPTER 7

The Last Days of the
Newspaper Business

I DREAMED I WAS ON my bike, delivering the last paper
to the final porch and I tossed that rag at least a mile—
last dream of a democratic press—and the end of papers
fell like a snowflake onto the faded wood planks
of my old man's porch, and he came out in slippers,
picked it up, slipped off the rubber band—and the thing
exploded with fresh despairs: new Vietnams and
Watergates, Mansons and Patty Hearsts, not to mention
Andy Capp and Hi and Lois, horoscopes, a Crossword puzzle,
box scores—even the obit of my poor mother. And
my old man told me not to cry, that even good things die,
son, and he folded that paper back up and tucked
the only good thing I ever did under his arm, easing back
into the warm house of my dead childhood to take
his morning shit.

CHAPTER 8

The Last Days of the Newspaper Business, Part II

M Y DREAMS TEND TO be either so obscure as to seem random, or so obviously connected to my subconscious that it's embarrassing—as if even my hidden depths lack depth. When I was negotiating my severance from the newspaper, I really did dream one night that I'd delivered a paper to my own father, and that it contained my mother's obituary. Of course, any good Freudian would accuse such a dreamer of ginning up his dream to please his therapist (this kind of behavior has a name like Stockholm Syndrome or Des Moines Disorder or something). But I swear: I really am that shallow.

Sometimes, in the same way one might try to piece together a fading dream in the morning, I'll try to re-create the stupid chain of events that caused me to quit a solid newspaper job two years ago. The industry decline had already begun, of course, but I didn't think for a moment that it would be fatal. I'd always assumed that, no matter what, I could just go back to the paper . . . that I could go home. It never occurred to me that a newspaper could *die*, any more than children think their parents will one day die. In fact, it was right around the time my mother passed away that I first began to feel the urge to leave my job. It felt like *I was dying*, like I was missing some opportunity to do something grand, something meaningful. Destiny. It felt like my creative soul was being suffocated by the cycle of writing for a newspaper, the slumping, slacking, always-behind feeling of being a news reporter. And then the stories themselves even seemed to shrink—pieces about this insurance company laying eighty people off . . . or that hospital joining a health consortium—as if there was a deflation of journalism's ambition alongside its news hole.

But I never disliked my job. Worse (and it's with great shame that I admit this), I took my job for granted. Worse yet, I never believed that my job was worthy of me. I thought of myself as more than a simple newspaper reporter, somehow better than the mean of my colleagues. I offer no excuses for this arrogance, and no rationale, either; I simply felt *bigger* than what I did for a living, like I was slumming, like I deserved more money, more respect and more esteem than any grubby newspaper could offer. I suppose it's one of the reasons I became a business reporter in the first place. I preferred wearing suits (most reporters tend to dress like substitute teachers) and I liked swimming amid the sorts of fearless executives who made multi-million-dollar decisions the way the rest of us decided on a restaurant for lunch. When it became clear that Lisa and I had higher material aspirations than we could satisfy on the sixty-or-so-grand I could make as a journalist, I considered public relations for a time, but I'd always seen that as a pasture for old glue horses. So I began augmenting my salary freelancing stories to various national business magazines, and more significantly, I applied what I learned as a reporter to my own investing. And, Mexican shipping bonds aside, I did pretty well for a while. In my best move, I managed a nice pivot from technology stocks to financials and media before tech blew up. In some years, I made nearly as much investing in the markets as I did writing about them. I even had a popular investing column for a couple of years, although, in the interest of full disclosure, this *was* during the late 1990s, when you could've trained a puppy on the newspaper stock section and made twenty percent a year investing where his turds fell.

It was also during this late '90s entrepreneurial euphoria that my tumor of discontentment first began to replicate cells, as I sat chained to my desk and watched various friends and colleagues slip into phone booths and emerge as dot.com superheroes. It's the devil's taunt—watching people stupider than oneself making fortunes. Even when that bubble burst, I still told myself that my lack of ambition and imagination had cost me a chance at . . . I don't know . . . wealth? Happiness? Some fulfillment of earlier promise?

Over the years, this tumor grew and metastasized until, by 2006, with my mother gone and my dad smoking his life away on a ranch in Oregon somewhere, with my own mortality throbbing, with the Dow climbing to its peak, with our house assessed at fifty percent more than we owed on it and my financials-heavy retirement account looking like an act of genius, with my marriage seemingly steady, the thing broke within me . . . and . . .

. . . I jumped. And landed. On *poetfolio.com*. It wasn't that I believed I had some great talent as a poet. I knew my poetry was pedestrian and sentimental when I tried, silly and sophomoric when I didn't. In fact, on top of the FAQ page of my prototype website was this little self-directed zinger by Alexander Pope:

Sir, I admit your general rule,
That every poet is a fool,

But you yourself may serve to show it,
That every fool is not a poet.

But I jumped anyway. I walked into my evil editor's office
(imagining the zingers I would deliver) and said simply that I was
giving my two-week notice. Every working person fantasizes this
moment, but it's ultimately unsatisfying. I packed my desk into
two boxes, took some files and . . . I jumped.

Splat.

Parked in front of the newspaper now, I wonder what would
have happened had I not quit two years ago. I likely wouldn't have
been laid off, for one thing. My newspaper had a vague seniority-
by-department layoff rule (which the evil editor took joy in
manipulating and subverting, by transferring his enemies to de-
partments he would then gut)—*last one in, first one out*—so while
I had a total of eighteen years at the place, when the last round of
layoffs came, they only counted the four months since I'd come
back. But I'm not sure staying would have been much better; those
four months were an anxiety-dream version of my old job: there
was real fear in the air, a sense that this was more than some kind
of business trend, that it was the end. Four years earlier we had
complained about too many ads in the paper (less room for our
brilliance) and competed for designer beats (*cultural trends reporter*);
now we sighed with relief when the slender paper had any ads at all
and eagerly accepted pay cuts and broad, hyphenated jobs created
by the loss of our colleagues (*courts-cops-schools* . . .).

No, it was clear. The newspaper was sick. Dying. And when
the next round of inevitable layoffs came, there I was, at the top of
the to-go list, the company not at all unhappy to lose my top-scale
salary and four weeks of vacation, my three-plus benefits pack-
age. My demise represented a nice chunk of savings. And when

they cut me a little fourteen-week pity severance check, the sweet Human Resources minx Amber Philips pointed out with no sense of irony that I was "lucky" to get so much severance because they could have only counted my service from the four months after I returned.

"Lucky," I said.

Now, as I take the elevator up to the fifth floor and that Gitmo of offices, Human Resources, I pray to God or the Pope, or whichever saint is in charge of humiliation avoidance that the elevator doors will NOT open to the third floor, that old cauldron of a newsroom, but of course the Pope—knowing that I haven't taken the required classes yet—causes the doors to open *exactly* on the third floor. And, not satisfied with this, the Pope causes to step on my elevator the last person on earth I would want to see, the Idi Amin of journalism, the Pol Pot of my newspaper, he whose name cannot be typed without befouling a keyboard, the very editor who accepted my resignation two years ago and then took me back, only to force me out four months later, the evil M—. With him is one of the young women he likes to hire, unfailingly busty reporters he is tireless in his willingness to . . . uh, mentor.

"Oh," says M— as he steps onto the elevator. His back stiffens. He looks like he's seen a ghost, the ghost of someone he whacked. "Matt. Hello. How are you?"

"Excellent," I answer. "Much happier, thanks. Taller."

We ride in silence. M— is an awkward clunk of a man who constantly strokes his pencil-thin chinstrap beard, which due to his substantial girth, is more like a *double-chin* strap. I suppose it's unfair, blaming this bloated despot for ruining my newspaper, since every paper is similarly suffering, the big-picture decline of my newspaper no different than the decline of newspapers in most towns. Specifically, the timeline looks like this:

1950s: TV arrives and it turns out that most people prefer having their news delivered by a guy on TV with molded plastic hair, smoking a cigarette.

1960s: Evolution and improved diet cause the first father in history to give up reading the paper on the toilet . . . much like the first fish that walked on land.

1970s: Literacy and newspapers reach their peak just as, ironically, actual reading begins to decline. (Side note: the guy reading the TV news quits smoking on air.)

1980s: Cable TV arrives and steals ad dollars from newspapers; soon entire channels are devoted to 24 hours-a-day news with three main components: (1) stories about celebrities, (2) police chases filmed from helicopters and (3) angry political hacks yelling at one another.

1990s: The Internet arrives, stealing even more advertising, and compelling the last reader under forty to cancel his daily newspaper subscription so he can devote more time to masturbating to online porn.

2000s: eBay and craigslist combine to kill off classified advertising and car and house listings, which turn out to have been the financial backbone of newspapers. The recession crushes display advertisers, coolly finishing the job.

Present: After a long period of newspaper panic, publishers do increasingly stupid things to drive away what readers they once had, speeding up their impending death, which is now estimated to be somewhere around 2015.

Of course, the specific details vary. At my mid-sized newspaper, the soul-disabled publisher scoured the various newspaper chains until he found the perfect budget-hacking delusional jargon-monkey, a man driven out of every crappy newspaper he ever ruined, a man who—in my humble opinion—is at the very least a narcissist, and at worst, a complete sociopath (thus, his in-house nickname, Idi Amin). Like any tyrant worth his sadism, M—'s first move was to force out any managers who might disagree with him, and his second move—right out of the Khmer Rouge playbook—was to target and demote any intelligent people left who might question his propaganda, until before long, he had systematically dumbed down management to a flock of morons whose only qualification was loyalty. Oddly, M— seemed to have no real interest in the city his newspaper was supposed to cover; his only passion was the business itself, a thing he called *newspapering*, and he constantly made us all uncomfortable by professing a creepy, nostalgic love for this made-up word, a love he seemed to mainly show by wearing a '40s-movie fedora and getting weepy whenever he reflected back on the fourteen months he spent as a libelous reporter waterboarding the English language. "The man loves journalism the way pedophiles love children," we used to say.

Meanwhile, M— continued to promote his sycophants and to build himself the Taj Mahal of offices, even as he oversaw round after round of layoffs. Like some medieval doctor, this self-aggrandizing bully claimed he was saving the paper every time he bled it, and throughout the long decline, continued to waste a reporter's full salary each year flying to journalism conferences where he could bloviate alongside the other Saddams about the future of newspapers (whose very death they were ensuring). We dreaded whenever M— went to one of these conferences because he invariably came home with a whole new batch of *bad ideas*, and like a delusional general moving his shrinking forces across fronts that only he could see, he would announce one day the future of newspapers was an entirely online edition. (Advertisers read this proclamation, shrugged and cancelled their ads in the print edition, leading to yet another round of layoffs.) Then, without ever acknowledging a misstep, M— would proclaim the future of newspapers was putting print reporters on television! (Anyone who has ever *seen* a newspaper reporter knows how this turned out . . . more layoffs.) Then the future was putting the newspaper on radio! ("Radio? My God, we're going backwards in time," my colleagues said. "What's next? Cave-painting?") In the waves of layoffs that accompanied these paroxysmal death-throes, this bearded shit-in-a-suit whacked the newspaper's most profitable sections and bureaus and its best writers and shooters, all to protect his ring of beholden pets, a phalanx of talent-challenged ass-sniffers and the cadre of bulbous interns that he hired from his Midwest alma mater and its pretentiously named H— School of Journalism (there are two things that should never be named: j-schools and penises), an equally overrated institution that he hoped to eventually return to in some kind of endowed bean bag chair.

But I suppose death comes for tyrants too. Because recently, I've heard from my former colleagues that M— is being forced out himself, that the publisher is finally tired of his blustery bristling incompetence, and has given him two months to find another job. Like any delusional dictator looking for asylum, M— is planning to make it look as if he's fed up with years of laying people off and has decided to fall on his own sword (a weapon profoundly dulled from the heads he's chopped with it). Then he can go out and seek ingratiating, flattering profiles of himself (One Editor Takes a Stand) in industry publications that should know better. Ah, well. Cheaper than sending out résumés, I suppose.

And what of the ship that this Queeg of journalism has run

aground? My old paper, which I still irrationally love, is half the number of pages it was just a few years ago and one rail narrower. The once plucky staff—my old colleagues and friends—now resembles the nervous crew in one of the *Alien* movies, their numbers shrinking as they look over their shoulders and wait for one of those mean little pink-slips to burst out of their chests.

So there's that.

On the elevator, M— stares straight ahead. Like any bully, I know that he is driven by his own insecurities, and for a minute I have some sympathy for this awkward, friendless stump, who somehow believes that chinstraps aren't just for boy bands, and who is, after all, on his way to being out of work himself. But none of that excuses his behavior; only bullies respond to being bullied by being bullies, and all I have to do is recall the way he walked so many good people to the edge of the playground and my sympathy dies.

Ding. My floor.

"Have fun mentoring," I say.

M— just snuffles.

The elevator doors close. Why are those snappy things I imagine myself saying so unsatisfying when I actually say them? Then, into HR where I wait in the waiting room, waiting.

"Matt. How are you?" asks Amber Philips. Amber was the head of the HR department for the newspaper when I worked here. Now, four rounds of layoffs later, Amber pretty much *is* the HR department. That has to suck, too, the head of HR laying off almost everyone in HR. We shake hands. Though no great beauty, Amber has that slightly-slutty business look just this side of inappropriate, her suits 0-2 fastballs—little high, little tight—her shoes a bit drastic for an office setting. (If Amber ever has to lay herself off, she could always commit suicide by jumping off those pumps.) And she's a genuinely nice person.

Perhaps the most pathetic thing about long-married guys like me is the delusional list that each of us keeps in our heads, a list of women we think are secretly attracted to us. Amber was always at the top of my delusional list. Even now, in my beaten-down state, I can't help but have a kind of muscle-memory that she's crushing on me a little (*ooh, out-of-shape middle-aged unemployed guy, yum*)—an assumption for which there is absolutely no evidence.

"What can I do for you today, Matt?"

I explain that Lisa and I have an investment opportunity for which we might need some immediate cash; and I need some information on my tiny newspaper pension, and what kinds of options I might have for tapping it early.

She looks mildly horrified. "How early?"

"Um. Now?"

"Wow. Is it that bad out there, Matt?"

"In the words of Robert E. Lee, 'you have no idea, Pumpkin.'"

"Remind me." She smiles as she looks up my file on her computer. "Who did Robert E. Lee call Pumpkin?"

"He called all his soldiers either Pumpkin or Sweetie. I know he called Nathan Bedford Forrest Doll-face. At Appomattox he called Grant—General Snuggles."

Her smile goes away as her cursor arrives at my dainty little pension, which I'd always counted on to pay for a tee time or two when I turned sixty-five. "I'm glad you still have your sense of humor, Matt."

"Actually, I don't," I say. "I'm just really stoned."

This is true.

Of course, I wasn't able to buy nine thousand dollars' worth of pot last night, but the kid did call my old felon friend Jamie, who drove over to the apartment building and said it would take a few days to get such "significant weight," a term that should've scared me off, but instead made me feel sort of exhilarated. As an act of good faith, I gave Jamie back Skeet's Starter hat and told him to ask Skeet for my slippers. He said he would. We smoked a little in the apartment of the kid I'd flagged down in the parking lot, whose name turned out to be Larry, and whose apartment was—there is no other word for it—fetid. There were beer cans and pizza crusts all over the place and when I sat on a pizza heel, Larry shrugged and said, "I don't like the crusts," which didn't explain why he needed to throw them all over his apartment. But I was a guest, so I just smiled and told Jamie and Larry that I really did want nine thousand dollars' worth of pot because I needed some immediate cash and I thought some of my fellow old pothead middle-classers would buy it up. Jamie said that for that much money he could probably get me a couple of pounds. Meantime, he gave me a little taste at a bargain price, an ounce for the three hundred I was able to squeeze from a cash machine.

We smoked a little last night, and I tucked the rest of my rolled Ziploc into a top dresser drawer and tried to go to bed, but I still couldn't sleep—Was that a smile on Lisa's dozing face?—so I got up and watched the sunrise, fed the kids and drove them to school, came home, showered, got Dad settled in front of the round-the-clock-politics-and-economic-crisis-dither-fest on CNN, and immediately took my wares to my baked broker, Richard. I sold Richard half of my deep green stash—what Jamie called four-eighths (and not a half, which is apparently different, or else Jamie is just bad at math)—feeling not even a hint of guilt for charging him three hundred, all I had invested to that point, even though it was an inflated price (and more evidence that Richard is not the financial genius I once thought he was). I also made Richard pay me twenty bucks for the pipe Jamie gave me for free. And I made him light up and give me a hit right there in his office. We blew smoke and stared at one another.

"What?" Richard asked.

"I don't know," I said. "I just wouldn't have figured you as a pothead—although that might explain your tip on Mexican shipping bonds a few years ago."

"In this economy?" He shrugged. "I'd get stoned every day if I could." Then he smiled wistfully. "I only smoke a couple times a year now. Partly because it's so hard to find. And Liv hates when I do it." Liv is Richard's wife. He hummed some distant memory. "After college, I lived with this painter, Anya. She was wild, nothing like Liv. She liked to wake and bake—a quick bowl in the morning—and then have sex. Something like that sticks with you." Richard considered the little pipe, and then took another hit, his mustache keeping a lid on his mouth as he fought coughing. He said, through gritted teeth: "God, I miss her." Then he lost the smoke in a combo sneeze-cough-seizure-laugh. His eyes went wide and he said, "Wow." The last thing he said when I left was, "I'll take as much of this as you can get."

And now, sitting in the HR office of my old newspaper, Amber leans in, legs crossed, makeup perfect, and smiles rather wickedly. "Are you really high, Matt?"

"Oh yeah." I was so sure that I was done being a pot smoker. I was a two-drink, twice-a-week guy. Sober. Straight. Clean. Like a lot of parents, I anticipated the questions my kids would ask when the time came, and had prepared a speech to deliver when I sensed they were at the age temptation might arrive. *No, son,* my speech went, *I did not smoke marijuana. I am proud to say that drugs have never touched this body.* Here was my rationale, worthy of a politician eyeing a presidential run: if, as scientists say, every seven years the human body remakes itself with all new cells, then after fifteen years, I was *two full people* removed from that loser who smoked weed in college. And the truth was: I didn't miss getting high. Not at all. I could honestly tell my kids that it was bad stuff. It made you stupid. Lethargic. And it was illegal!

I felt good about spouting this company line, partly because I assumed I actually had *company* in my line, that the rest of the adult world around me had also stopped getting high.

But now I'm beginning to feel like the only jerk not invited to a great party, because it appears that while I was repeating my Nancy Reagan mantra, every other responsible adult was smoking bud like reggae musicians. Amber confides that she was a twice-a-weeker until her regular dealer moved six months ago, and her boyfriend, a drywaller whose drywall work has dried up, has been in a funk for months, has even considered moving somewhere where it's easier to get a medicinal prescription. After some light negotiations, I give Amber a better deal than I gave Richard, because Amber is better-looking, and because she didn't take a commission off my severance check, which Richard would probably have done. Amber buys the rest of my weed for two hundred, straight profit for me since Richard took care of my nut this morning.

I've only been in the business a few hours and I'm up 66 percent! Amber writes me a check. On the subject line she writes: "lawn care." We giggle.

As for my pension, it's not good news. With penalties, it would only be about twenty-six hundred dollars. Still, I tell her, get the paperwork started. (If I can make sixty-six percent on that twenty-six hundred . . .)

"Wait," says my friend Ike over lunch an hour later. "You're like . . . a pot dealer now?"

Ike and I have skipped our usual how's-your-family and how-is-Idi-Amin-ruining-the-newspaper-now small talk and gone straight to my new career choice.

"Yeah, I guess I am," I say. This is the crux of it, I know. This is what we're really talking about here. I am apparently buying marijuana and selling it. For profit. This is, I believe, the definition of a drug dealer. "But it's only temporary."

"Wow." Ike was the music writer at the newspaper for years, and oddly enough, given that position, among the squarest people I know. Married. Three kids. Asthmatic and frail. He was probably the only other adult not getting high the last fifteen years. He's recently been transferred and is covering politics and city government now. On a shrinking staff, a music writer is an extravagance they can't afford. I feel bad for Ike, who spent years developing that weird, specific music-writer vocabulary (the *thunky wallop* of the bass . . . the *womb-like, plangent* guitar) only to find it doesn't quite translate to covering politics (the state Senator's speech "lumbered along like a fussy cover musician scatting a complex hook").

"What about your kids?" Ike asks.

"I'd rather not sell to them if I can help it, although I probably can't afford to rule out their friends."

"You know what I mean."

I do know what Ike means. And it is something I've tried not to think about—what would happen if my kids found out, if Lisa found out.

Ike is a pale, skinny enrolled member of one of the California casino Indian bands—I can never remember which one—bifocaled and smart, he's the best kind of newspaper guy in that he is a chronic underachiever, doomed to spend his life working for people half as intelligent as him. He's my favorite writer at the newspaper, laid back and modest, one of those natural stylists whose effortless flow seems typed within the genetic code of his sentences, so that when you finish an Isaac Watts story you are unaware of its inherent art. Ike's talent and intelligence are not without their blind spots, however; he was the one person genuinely excited about *poetfolio. com*, and in fact was even going to contribute a monthly column on real estate using a pen name: Frost Peltier. Ike and I started at the newspaper at the same time, eighteen years ago. He's figured he was "safely above the water line" of layoffs, but he keeps watching others he assumed were safe, like me, "get sucked under, thrashing as they drown." I have to say that, like my financial planner, sometimes Ike's way with words is, at times, too evocative.

"I can't believe it," he says again. "You are seriously thinking of dealing weed."

"I'm not thinking of dealing weed. I'm up two hundred and I just put in a buy order for almost ten thousand dollars."

"Is it really called that . . . a buy order?"

"How do I know what it's called," I say. "I just started. Look. This is a bad idea. I know that. But I'm only gonna do it until I get back on top of my mortgage, or until I get a real job, whichever comes first. But if today's any indication, it might just work—"

Ike agrees: "Every other person I know smokes weed."

"It's like prohibition," I say. "In hard times, people crave the old stuff. Pot is nostalgia for a lot of people our age. Selling weed is like opening a speakeasy in 1933."

"I think prohibition ended in '33," Ike says.

"Either way, I'm only going to do this for a few months, just long enough to make some house payments and keep my kids in Catholic school. Then I'll quit."

"Wait." Ike lowers his head. "You're selling pot to pay for Catholic school? Drugs for private school? That's so Iran-Contra."

Ike and I are in a favorite old haunt, a lunch place and donut shop on the edge of downtown called The Picnic Basket—the walls painted like a park, picnic benches for tables. The place has great chicken, sandwiches and pies, and transcendent maple bars. It's owned by an old New York transplant named Marty, who runs it with his wife and adult son and the boy's hot girlfriends. Marty loves talking politics, and he always corners Ike and me, leans in and asks us, *Fellas, what's really going on,* so certain is he that we have inside information that the general public doesn't know. It's probably the other reason we come here—aside from the great food—there aren't many places where the chef makes a big deal out of newspaper reporters. Even now, Marty delivers a half-chicken-in-a-basket to the table next to ours, and gives us a knowing wink.

And that's when my cell rings. I pull out my phone . . . look at the number. It's Jamie. I look up at Ike, who holds a forkful of potato salad in midair. I mouth: *It's them.*

I look around, then open my phone and clear my throat. "Hey?" I say, which is what I assume drug dealers say into phones.

"My guy needs to meet you first," Jamie says. I can hear the announcer for the Madden Football video game in the background. Okay. It's on, then. They want to meet me.

"Sure. Sure. Um." I am aware that we are to be very careful about what we say on cell phones and I speak slowly. "I would like that. To meet your friend."

"You okay, Slippers?"

"Yes," I say. "Don't worry. I'll come alone."

"What?" Jamie says. "What the fuck you talkin' about. Who else would you bring?"

"Oh . . . no one. I don't know. I just . . . thought I should say I'll come alone."

"Look, don't freak out on me, man. These guys can be a little paranoid."

"Sure. Sorry. So . . . should we meet at the 7/11 . . . what, at midnight again?"

"Do you think we could meet a little earlier? I have a midterm tomorrow." I shift the cell phone at my ear. (Stoned stock analyst side-note: Nokia's 6700 is perfect for setting up buys.) We agree to meet at 10 p.m. I click off the call. Ike has had his potato-salad-laden fork at his mouth throughout the call. His eyes are wide.

"That . . ." I put my phone away. ". . . was my contact. The deal goes down tonight."

"Holy shit!"

"I know!" I say.

"Holy shit," Ike says again, and leans forward, over his rice. "I can't believe it. You're a drug dealer!"

A woman at the next table looks over.

"I know," I say more quietly.

"Holy shit," Ike says again.

"I know!"

We eat our chicken quietly. Wait. I—am a drug dealer? "Holy shit," I say.

"I know," Ike says. Then he leans in, cocks his head. Something else has occurred to him. "Hey," he says, "this is . . . I don't know, I was thinking about what you said about nostalgia . . . this is probably crazy, but . . ." He looks all around The Picnic Basket—people licking fingers and rolling eyes—and then back at me. "Do you think you can get cocaine, too?"

CHAPTER 9

Twenty-Four-Hour News, a Haiku

Iᴛ's ꜱᴏ ᴅɪꜱᴛʀᴀᴄᴛɪɴɢ
how sexy the women are
on the TV news

Here's what Dad and I do during the day while the kids are at school and Lisa is at work (at least I pray to the patron saint of pathetic husbands that she is at work): we sit with cups of coffee and flip from channel to channel watching overheated experts argue about the crises in housing and banking and credit. We can't turn away; it is financial porno.

But this isn't our only reason for watching. Because even if the world financial crisis is somehow solved, we will still tune in to ogle the twenty-four-hour news babes. When one comes on in her smart suit, we say to each other, "Wow," (me) or "I wouldn't mind ten minutes alone with that" (Dad) or "I think she's changed her hair," (me) or "Love to get on that" (Dad again).

There is even one of these women—Tamara—for whom I routinely declare that I would violate my marriage vows. I first got lumberland for Tamara's lovely talking head long before I found out that Lisa was on the verge of carrying on a virtual affair—or a real one, jury's still out, there—with her old squeeze, Chuck.

My thing for Tamara is in no way a betrayal, like Lisa's Chuck-obsession is. For one, Lisa knows all about my Tamara-lust and knows I couldn't act on it. Tamara is, in the particular parlance of our marriage, my *mulligan* (what others might call a freebie), that one guilt-free unattainable, purely theoretical woman with whom I could cheat without penalty. Sometimes Lisa and I go with the obvious: say, a little swing with Angelina and Brad; other times, more obscure: say, Lisa Bonet and Jason Patric; or erudite: Jhumpa Lahiri and Paul Krugman; for a while, when things were best between Lisa and me, we had time-travel thought-experiment cheats: 1967 Ann-Margret and 1972 Robert Plant. This is how solid we were, our marital bonds so strong we *joked* about infidelity! Only recently did my mulligan become this whip-sharp MSNBC anchor, whose lovely eyes and soft mouth make the ongoing crisis in the world credit markets and the loss of trillions of dollars sound, to my ears, like spank-me dirty talk.

"One time," my father growls to the TV screen. "One time in my life, I'd like to flop on something that tight."

Should anyone doubt that our miserable time here on Earth is just a sad existential joke, here is the cruelest thing I can imagine describing: my father (who is obsessed with sex, like a lot of dementia sufferers)—at seventy-one years of age, frail, balding, with a paunch that looks like it should wear its own pair of jockey shorts—recently had ten days of crazy sex with a twenty-two-year-old stripper with long smooth legs and two big round silicone funbags, and *the poor son-of-a-bitch doesn't remember a thing about it.*

This is the first metaphysical question I have planned for the church hierarchy once my Catholic training is complete: *Okay, your holiness. Seriously . . . what the hell?*

My dad pats the pocket where he used to hold his cigarettes, back when he was allowed to smoke. Then he looks over and I think maybe I see some of the old sharpness in those eyes, maybe one of those brief flashes of clarity he gets, like the one yesterday when he remembered buying a donkey shit cigar in a Mexican brothel (sadly, I can't predict which lights will come on in there). "Hey, kiddo, I ever tell you about the woman who worked at Lannigans?"

Usually when my father says *Did I ever tell you about*, he tells me something he just told me, but I don't recall hearing about a woman who worked at Lannigans. I do recall Lannigans, because it was the bar I occasionally had to stick my head inside to see if Dad would be joining us for dinner, or for the weekend, or for Thanksgiving, or for my high school graduation.

The doctor has prescribed a handful of activities to help with Dad's dementia, alongside his medication: I. that he do crossword puzzles, play games, and do little jobs around the house (given certain tasks and chores, Dad can concentrate and this sharpens his overall acuity); II. that he look through photo albums; and III. that I indulge him whenever he wants to tell this kind of story, so that he might better reconnect with his past.

But as quickly as it arrived, the old clarity is gone. "Tell you what?"

"You were going to tell me about the woman from Lannigans."

"Lannigans? We should go there." He pats his shirt again.

"It closed years ago, Dad."

He turns back to the TV. I know it's frustrating for him, too, feeling like he can't keep it all straight. This is not a man who likes thinking of himself as incapacitated. After the Army, he married my mom, and eventually got a good job at Sears, working his way up to manager of the automotive department. Every day, he put on a tie and went to work, and once there, he put on coveralls and grabbed a clipboard. It was important that his necktie peer out of his shop clothes like that but I don't think it was something he consciously thought about; it was more like an innate Darwinian drive, a man in a tie and coveralls being the missing link in the evolution of my family's male drive from *lower-middle-class, rural blue collar* (Dad's dad worked on cattle ranches and in lumber mills) to *upper-middle-class urban white collar.* (I've never worn a pair of coveralls; my private-school kids have never seen them.) But while every father hopes his sons will use their brains to make more money and have a better life than he did, something was lost when Dad crawled out of the primordial labor swamp and put on that tie. Dad's dad, my Grandpa Stan, could fix anything—tractors, cars, washing machines. (Give the man a socket set and a Phillips head screwdriver and he'd get this economy going again.) My dad is half-as-handy as his father was and I . . . well . . . I can change light bulbs. Sometimes. I always planned to have Dad show me some . . . stuff. I imagined his later years as a master class on plumbing and sheet-rocking and auto repair, Dad and I retreating to the front porch for a beer after . . . I don't know . . . patching the holes in my driveway. Instead, we watch TV and Dad talks about quarterbacks from the 1970s, pats himself for the cigarettes he no longer smokes and tells me which female news anchors he'd like to nail.

He can still be his old self for a minute, commenting on politics or sports and then, bang: he skids on the ice and his mind spins sideways. And I think he knows he's spinning because he makes a little groaning sound and nods at the TV, and says, of the woman on-screen: "God, I wouldn't mind planting my carrot in that garden."

Eventually, he falls asleep and I edge out of the room. The rest of the afternoon and evening, I'm more nervous than I've been since the layoffs. This is probably understandable since I have in my coat pocket an envelope with $9,000 in it—a two-inch stack of hundreds—for the drug deal that I am planning to make later. When I cashed the check earlier today, I inexplicably put $400 in our checking account. I'm not sure what you'd call that—taking your last $9,400 and putting $400 of it in the bank while you buy pot with the rest. A $400 hedge? Yes, your honor, I did go into the drug business in a last-ditch effort to save my house, but I managed to sock away four hundred bucks in case something went wrong. (And honestly, what could go wrong with this brilliant plan?)

Since I've got some time, I spend an hour on my little side project: "contacting my lender" about the $31,000 payment we owe next week. This is not easy. The new company, Providential Equity—which bought the old company that purchased the bad mortgages in which mine was bundled—insists that "all inquiries come via email." I've sent four emails, but all I get back are "automatically generated" responses that begin: "Do not reply to this message." These auto-responses insist that my "correspondence is greatly appreciated," and that my "file is being reviewed" and that "a loan specialist will contact you soon." I did track down a 1-800 phone number on the website for the company that ate the company that bought the bundle of mortgages of which mine is one—but it led to a Cretan labyrinth of telephonic dead ends: "Welcome to the Providential Equity Help Line. For English, please press one . . . if you know the extension, please press . . . for customer service questions not regarding current mortgages please press . . . if this is about an adjustable-rate mortgage, please press . . . if this is about a fixed-rate mortgage, please visit our website at . . . the number you've reached is currently unassigned. . . ."

Last week, I tracked down the Providential Equity home office, in Benicia, California, but the main number simply returns you to this chase-your-own-tail voicemail system. Today I'm trying an old reporter trick, starting with the prefix, 392, and then tapping in random digits, praying that a phone will ring in a cubicle where an actual human being works, but this particular company seems entirely computerized now, perhaps taken over by the mainframe that wiped out humanity in the Terminator movies. I'm just about to give up, after forty minutes on the phone, when a carbon-based being suddenly answers, "Client services, this is Gilbert."

"G—..." For just a second I can't speak. "Gilbert?" I feel like weeping. "Gilbert! Thank God. I need to talk to you. Don't hang up!"

"Certainly, sir. What can I do for you?"

I patiently explain: (1) I had a mortgage. (2) Lost my job. (3) Fell behind. (4) The mortgage got sold along with a bundle of others. (5) The company that bought these mortgages was bought by Gilbert's company. (6) Before the sale, I foolishly got a forbearance agreement. (7) And now I have a "Dear Homeowner" letter in front of me that says I'm going to lose my house in less than a week unless I make the necessary reinstatement payment. (8) But I've got some things brewing and if I could just have another month or two, I could catch up. . . .

Gilbert says, "Sure, sure," and "Oh my," when I mention forbearance, and "I'm sorry," that I lost my job, and, "Of course," I need a little more time, and "We want you to stay in your home as much as you do, Mr. Prior." Gilbert is brilliant, loveable. He takes down my name, email, phone number, looks up my account, says it's going to be okay. I can hear his organic, nonautomated fingers typing. I tell him I'm going to write a letter about what a star he's been. Gilbert laughs gently and tells me that's not necessary. Gilbert isn't surprised that I've had trouble getting anyone on the phone; he confesses that "things are a little crazy right now" at Providential Equity. But he knows exactly who can help me. There is a program for homeowners like me and I should be eligible for "extended mortgage modification"—and I'm near tears when Gilbert mentions another person's name and title and extension and says that I should use Gilbert's name, and while I look for a pen to write down this new human being's name—Joyce or Joe or Joan, I didn't quite catch it, Anderson, Addison or Amberton, I'm not sure, either the senior client service manager or the special claims administrator, at some number like 478-2344 or 874-2433 or 487-3342—Gilbert transfers me to—

"Welcome to the Providential Equity Help Line. For English, please press one—"

The phone flies. Cracks against the wall. Not only don't I recall Joyce Joe Joan Anderson Addison Amberton's extension, I can't remember the number I dialed to reach Gilbert. I try a few combinations but they ring into the void and I imagine Gilbert alone in his little cubicle, pants at his ankles, surrounded by ringing phones as he goes back to surfing for fetish porn, or managing his fantasy football team.

I'm beaten for the day. I'll try again tomorrow. I stuff the Dear Homeowner letter back in my messenger bag. Slump back next to Dad. He pats his smoke pocket. Time bleeds. Wife comes home with kids. We eat pork chops. Dad picks at his. Lisa and I look away from each other.

At dinner, Franklin and Teddy are full of heartwarming stories about school, as if they've somehow intuited that their parents may not be able to afford tuition anymore, each story a testimony to what a beacon of academic achievement their little parochial school is, what a warm nest of intelligence and security, what a refuge against the cold, hard world, what a failsafe ticket into a blissful Ivy League future.

"The Math-Quest team is raising money to go to nationals again this spring," Teddy informs me. Of course, when Teddy's Math-Quest team goes to nationals, he will be over at Alcatraz Elementary, learning to make a plastic spork into a shiv.

Lisa finally meets my eye, her fork in mid-air. She doesn't grimace or shake her head, she does something far worse: she smiles sympathetically, her eyes drooping at the corners, as if to say, *Don't worry, Matt. We'll figure this out. It's okay.*

And her reaction pisses me off because it would be so much easier to lose my wife if she were an asshole, but she has consistently refused to cooperate in this way. Even when I was single and my buddies were required by law to hate my girlfriend, she was unfailingly easy to be around and they grudgingly paid her the highest buddy-compliment: "Nah, man, Lisa's cool. . . ." I was twenty-four when we met, my first year at the newspaper. And she *was* cool, twenty-one, a marketing intern at a hospital I covered. I first saw her at a press conference for the hospital's new outreach program for addicted teens. I only went because I was working on an enterprise story about the hospital's pending labor trouble and when the spokesman whined that "you never do anything positive about us," I wanted to point to the two paragraphs about that outreach program buried deep in the business section. I walked into the conference room and immediately saw this girl—bemused eyes, broad lips, toned legs in a just-above-the-knee skirt, and, like a beacon: a pair of expensive-looking, out-of-place, fur-lined boots. It was one of those inane "press conferences" where there's only one actual member of the press—me. I sat in one of the fifteen chairs they'd put out "for the media" as the hospital spokesman stood at a podium and read me—word for word—the same stupid press release I held in my hand. Then he asked "Anyone have questions," and being the only anyone, I asked, "How many teens will this serve?" and the stumped spokesman directed me to fur boots—"Lisa McDermott is facilitating this program, she has those specifics"—and I know it sounds corny, but in my mind I thought, *Lisa Prior*, as she strode over with a brochure for the program, which had some ridiculous, concocted acronym—N.O.D.O.P.E. or G.O.C.L.E.A.N., and I said, "Nice name," and fur boots said, "Yeah I know, right?" and—her back to the spokesman—she made a little fist and gave the universal sign for jacking off.

And that was it for me: love.

There were early signs of trouble, of course. Lisa was one of those people you don't ever feel like you've reached the center of; not that she withheld herself, there was just always another, deeper layer that I didn't have access to, boxes inside boxes. . . . And there was the money thing, always the money thing. Like most guys, relationships progressed physically for me (I kissed her . . . we made out . . . we had sex). Like a lot of women, Lisa's progressions were more financial, security-based steps (he bought dinner . . . he took me to Napa for the weekend . . . he wants me to move in). But at least Lisa was always up-front about it; her father had died when she was twelve and she and her mother were dirt-poor for a few years. "I have to warn you, I can sometimes mistake being spoiled for being loved," she told me on our fourth date, and then she smiled perfectly as she took a bite of her $65 entrée, winked knowingly and said, through a mouthful of seared-scallops-in-truffle-butter: "But I'm working on that."

No, even Lisa's quirky nature was alluring to me, partly because she was so open and cool about it. Even when she was suffering in the unfriendly job market, she was cool. Even during her online shopping binge—cool. She felt awful, apologized until I couldn't take it anymore, volunteered to see a counselor. Hell, even now, when she's possibly thinking of straying, I can't seem to *blame her*. I'm terrified that she'll find out I might be losing her dream house and leave me, but I can't seem to blame her for that.

Maybe it's because I feel so incapable of doing anything about it right now. Or because I knew the rules going in.

And—as long as I'm assessing my wife's strengths, a painful thing to do right now—the woman's not hard to look at. Hell, if I were being honest, I'd have to admit she's still attractive and smart enough to be on cable news . . . I mean, she'd need some makeup for primetime, or CNBC during the heavy market hours, but she's more than cute enough to take an overnight shift or as morning referee between blathering political pundits. In fact, maybe when she's living with Chuck in the cabin he builds from tree bark and his own nut hair, when she is *agin* distant, a pair of fur boots against a wall . . . totally unattainable . . . I'll choose her as my mulligan.

"I'm going upstairs," Lisa says when we finish the dinner dishes. Then she looks back at me. "Everything okay?"

"Everything . . . is great."

I help Teddy with his math homework. Listen to Lisa tap away up there on the computer. At bedtime, I read a story to Franklin about a snake that doesn't want to grow old and shed his green skin. Christ, I despise children's books. They used to be mysterious and disconcerting, filled with odd Seussian creatures and Wild Things meant to scare the kids to sleep; now they're aimed at scaring the parents, or worse, *fixing us*, thinly veiled attempts to get us to shape up, subliminal messages from Oprah's insidious army of self-help authors trying to get us to be more responsible and loving. I get it, okay? I'm the snake who won't grow up. I kiss Franklin, pry my arm away from his worried grip and escape downstairs.

"Let's not watch TV tonight," I tell Dad.

So we play an insane game of Scrabble instead, but my father only seems to know dirty words or made-up words that sound dirty.

"Cumshok? What is it—some kind of late-life nocturnal emission?"

"It's a fish." He pats his pocket for a cigarette, like an amputee looking for a limb.

I slowly reach for the dictionary. His eyes follow my hand, and then rise to meet my eyes. "A fish?" I ask.

"Go ahead. Look it up. It's a fishing lure." He stares at my hand on the dictionary.

"A fishing *lure*?"

"Yes. It looks like a bell."

He knows I don't know shit about fishing lures. Oh what do I care? I'm glad he's sharp enough to mess with me. Make-believe words are an improvement. Fine. Cumshok. I remove my hand from the dictionary. Write down the eighty-one points and lose to a senile old man by sixty.

We go back to watching TV. He looks over and sees the Scrabble game still on the table. "We should play that sometime," he says.

Upstairs, the typing has stopped.

Dad sighs. "You know what I really miss?"

I know this loop; there are six main things that my father misses and they come up a lot now, as if, right before he says, *You know what I miss,* Dad spins a tiny wheel in his head. And I make a game of trying to guess which of the six things he will land on. The six things my father misses are: (1) chipped beef (2) Angie Dickinson (3) Dandy Don singing at the end of *Monday Night Football* (4) the old pull tabs on beer cans (5) *The Rockford Files* and (6) Joe Frazier. It is a good sign, the doctors say, anytime Dad references the past, and so I always ask what he misses, even though it's mildly disappointing that he never seems to miss my mom, or even my three sisters—scattered across the country by the limited employment opportunities of themselves and their husbands—or his job at Sears, or I don't know, his bowling ball. Instead, it's always one of these six inane things, and usually it's chipped beef. I even made chipped beef for him one night, but he ate it without saying a word, while the boys made faces and Lisa pretended to get a phone call. Two hours later, Dad said, "You know what I miss? Chipped beef." But I suppose the doctors are right: it is a good sign that he's remembering at all, connecting images or things to his past, building himself out of the things he no longer has. And so I don't take it personally, I just lodge my mental guess . . . I go with the odds: "Chipped beef?"

"*Rockford Files*," Dad says.

It is garbage night in America, the night I glide room-to-room emptying plastic garbage cans and get the full measure of what's really going on in my family's life. No surprises in the kitchen can—except more banana peels than I remember us having. This is the problem with our cultural paranoia: something as harmless as extra banana peels can send the addled mind a-reeling (. . . *playing off the sweet memory of their pet name for his lumber, Chuck sends Lisa a bouquet of bananas to her office* . . .). The bathroom bucket has nail clippings, toilet paper tubes, disposable razors and the forensic clues to that still mysterious world of feminine-parts care; it's depressing to think of these cycles of male and female hygiene, to imagine landfills full of the shit it takes every day just to keep us all fresh, un-rank, wiped and de-whiskered. In Teddy's room, the basketball hoop garbage can reveals what I have suspected: dude's hitting his Halloween candy a little harder than he's supposed to. It's a killing field of Reese's, Sweetarts and Musketeers. Franklin's garbage can is like the kid himself, heartbreaking—a half-eaten sneaked sucker thrown away in guilt, a pair of crapped underpants he hoped to hide, a scary picture of a monster he's torn from a book.

It's 9:30—thirty minutes until my meeting with Pablo Escobar. Both boys are asleep, sprawled across their beds like window jumpers splayed on a sidewalk. I pull the covers over them. Teddy's hair is in full revolt on his pillow. I smooth it down.

In our bedroom the garbage can is empty, and while I'm not above assigning meaning to this fact, in my overheated season of allegorical discontent I can't quite decide whether an empty can symbolizes a bankrupt marriage or the withheld nature of our relationship, i.e., that we're not even sharing our garbage with one another.

Lisa is in bed already, her reading glasses low on her nose as she flips through a magazine. Apparently, there will be no phone texting tonight. Maybe Chuck has his kids. Or maybe there was a band-saw accident at work and he lost his fingers and can never type again.

"I was thinking . . . if it's okay," Lisa says, without looking up from her magazine, "I might go see a concert with Dani on Saturday."

I stand there holding my bag of shit. "With Dani?" And I remember Dani last night: *So romantic* and *Are you going to do it?*

"Yeah." No eye contact. "She asked if I wanted to."

"What concert?" I ask, as if she'd start down this road without a cover story.

She mentions the name of a band I don't know: "Blue-Eyed Jesus? Supposed to be good. Kind of alt-country . . . Wilco-ish."

"Oh sure," I say, pinned. "Blue-Eyed Jesus. Yeah, they're good. No, you should do that. It sounds fun." And then, devilishly: "I know how much you love Wilco."

Lisa hates Wilco.

"No, I just thought a concert sounded fun. And since Dani has an extra ticket, it wouldn't cost us anything."

"No, you should go. I'd go if I had the opportunity."

"Oh. Did you . . . did you want to go?" She glances up at me. My God, we change. Arms go flabby, guts grow, hair gets gray; everything changed on those two people whose eyes met at that press conference; everything, that is, but their eyes. Hers look away.

And I pretend to consider it. "Maybe."

"I would have asked you," she says, "but I know how much you hate concerts."

I do hate concerts. I have hated them ever since we went to an outdoor festival once and were nearly trampled to death. I hate paying three times the cost of a CD just to stand in an unruly crowd and think one of two things: (A) this song sounds just like it does on the CD or (B) this song sounds nothing like it does on the CD.

Lisa closes her magazine. "You want me to look for a sitter, then?"

Here we are. Our poker hands on the table. Antes in. Time to either bet my bluff or get out of the way. Or . . . wait . . . "Can I think about it?" I lug my bag of trash downstairs, happy with myself for my open-ended play. This is what we call a check in poker—the third way.

I stack the recyclables on top of our wheeled garbage container and push the whole thing through our leafy backyard toward the alley. The truly undesirable part of our undesirable neighborhood begins at the alley behind our big house; our alley is the DMZ of gentrification. Everything in front of the alley, like our house, has come around, owners tidying up lawns, painting, planting and putting on new roofs, parking new cars in driveways. Behind the alley is an unsettling world of chipped-paint, junk-cars and sofas-on-porches, and it's not uncommon to see police lights strobe the clapboard rentals or to hear loud reports of drunk love—*Get your fat ass inside for dinner, Damien!*—that make Lisa and me feel pathetically superior about our more-sober parenting style. (And yet, I'll bet most of those screamers have jobs.)

I push the garbage into the alley and turn back toward my home—

My home . . .

God, this view is breathtaking. This is the view that sold us on the place. The homes on the front of our block sit on wide lots and I still lose my breath at this angle of my house, from deep in the backyard: a long, gently sloped hill leading to big majestic maple trees on either side of our angular, two-story, 1917 Tudor, a street-light on the corner, and the mist of late October rain bands the street with fog so that our big brick house glows in soft light like a movie set of Old London. From back here, the money and stress, the lifetime of work it will take to pay for this place (I remember calculating the total we'd pay over thirty years and feeling sick) almost seems worth it. Up close, the clinker brick and uneven roof make our house look like it was drawn by the unsteady hand of a child, but from back here, if you squint, there is the faint line of a country manor. This is the house we fell in love with, Lisa and I—the house that has become, in every way, the third party in our marriage, the very sort of big drafty place we always saw each other in when we imagined our married adult lives.

I wonder if a house has ever represented as much as it does now, for people like Lisa and me. It has been the full measure and symbol of our wealth and security over the last few years; every cent we threw into it and every cent we took out, seemed so smart, like such a good bet. Every time we got ahead, we borrowed against the thing to remodel, and every time we remodeled the thing we congratulated ourselves on our wisdom, and every time we saw a house go up for sale on our block (*They're asking three-eighty-five and it's half the size!*) we became like derivative-crazed brokers; we stopped thinking of the value of our home as a place of shelter and occupancy and family—or even as the aesthetic triumph witnessed from our alley—but as a kind of faith equation, theoretical construct, mechanism of wealth-generation, salvation function on a calculator, its value no longer *what it's worth* but some compounded value that might exist given the continued upward tick of the market, because this was the only direction housing markets could ever go: up. All the geniuses said so. If housing had survived the dump of the technology bubble and the brief realization after 7/11 that we weren't alone in the scary, scary world, then what could possibly stop its march? In eighty years, the geniuses told us, actual housing values had only fallen once. *One time in eighty years?* I can still close my over-leveraged eyes and hear two decades of such party talk: real estate is the only safe bet; real estate can only go up; they aren't making any more real estate.

Yesterday, Dad and I watched a news story about half-empty subdivisions in Nevada and California, dead sprig saplings slumped in the rolled seams of sun-fried sod, backyard pools green with neglect, swarming with clouds of malarial mosquitoes visible over cedar fences. *Idiots*, my father said, and while I wasn't sure whether he meant the buyers or builders or the bugs, borrowers or banks, Congress or me, or people in general, how could I disagree? Idiots.

I'd love to go back to a 2004 cocktail party and beat those sure-sounding real estate idiot optimists to death with a For Sale sign. I'd take a good whack at myself, too, because while I suspect that housing prices will eventually bounce back (five years? ten?) I'm also sure of this: I'll never fall in love again. I've lost my innocence. And my disappointment is not that my own home has lost half its value. What disappoints me is me—that I fell for their propaganda when *I knew better*, that I actually allowed myself to believe that a person could own a piece of the world when the truth is that anything you try to own ends up owning you.

We're all just renting.

And this is how the poets failed us.

The poets were supposed to remind us of this, to regulate the existential and temporal markets (*Let be be finale of seem./The only emperor is the emperor of ice-cream.*) and to balance real estate with ethereal states (*One need not be a chamber to be haunted,/One need not be a house*). Hell, we don't need bailouts, rescue packages and public works. We need more poets.

Yes. Standing behind my own home like this, I imagine letting go of this dream of solvency . . . let it go . . . float away into the sky . . . let someone else live in the big house; I'll live above the garage, finally get some sleep, spend the rest of my life as a simple servant (*Matt? He's our poet-driver*), let the boys forget that I was once their father, now just the kindly old poet-driver who brings the car 'round front. Rest of the time I'll disappear in my little writer's garret, grow a goatee, write bad verse and smoke good weed until I can't recall those people who loved me, or how much I owe on their big house ($485,592). Write during the day, and at night hang out with Skeet and Jamie, read them my poems while we fry our skulls and haunt Rahjiv's convenience store aisles for Fritos. And this is such a pleasing thought—Fritos!—that of course my mind can't hold it and it goes the last place I'd like it to go: Lumber-Chuck moving in, taking over the parenting, the payments, the pampering and pleasing of Lisa.

And that's what finally snaps me out of my self-pitying funk. Not the thought of Chuck inside my house, but the thought of Chuck rooting around inside *my wife* snaps me out of this delusional hole, and I run across the backyard, ready to reclaim my house, my wife, my life. I'm suddenly aware again that the air is sharp and cold; winter's here. A gun has gone off in my head and I know what to say: this is insanity, Lisa, this place we are going! We have to stop: dope dealer? Mistress of the Prince of Lumberland? No, no, no! Is this really who we are?

Who cares if we lose the fucking house next week? This house isn't us. We are us. *One need not be a house* . . . So what . . . we default? Declare bankruptcy? Big deal. It doesn't matter where we go, what we do. Hell, I'll wash dishes, tend bar. You can clean houses.

We can take the kids out of school, walk away from this big house, drift. Go from town to town, see the world, work menial jobs. Live. *Let be be finale of seem!*

Through the kitchen, I take the stairs two at a time, fired up to reclaim my life: *Damn it, Lisa. Why are we doing this? Come back—*

But she looks up at me from bed and there's something in her eyes that stops me cold. She closes her phone. She's seen my earlier check and . . . she raises the value of the pot: "I called Dani. She doesn't know if she can get another ticket for the concert."

My knees lock. "Oh."

"She's pretty sure she can't."

"Ah."

"You could probably still go. You just might not be able to sit with us." And Lisa shrugs, pretends to go back to her magazine, phony nonchalance. She's steady, unmoving, but beneath the covers I can see that she's wiggling her toes nervously. God. She really wants this. That's what hurts. What's the last thing I remember her wanting this badly? Oh yeah. The house.

How do you know when you've gone too far? When you can't go back? I think of my home from the alley again. Sometimes you can't get back in. You just have to live outside for a while. "You know what? You guys go ahead. I'll stay home, save us the cost of a babysitter."

"Are . . . Are you sure?"

"Go. Have fun."

I grab my jacket and wallet, trying to keep my hands from shaking.

"Where are you going?" she asks.

I don't even turn back. "We need milk."

CHAPTER 10

Dave the Drug Dealer Wants to Look Up My Ass

I DON'T KNOW WHAT I expected—no
maybe I do, Al Pacino from *Scarface*—
but this drug dealer is more like Al Pacino
at the beginning of *The Godfather*
reasonably bemused, untouched by his
criminal world, sitting with Diane Keaton
whispering about Luca Brazzi, not yet asleep
with the fishes, or like Al Pacino
from *Glengarry Glen Ross*, although actually,
now that I think about it, he's not
like Al Pacino at all but more like
Kevin Spacey from that film, and who's
ever been afraid of Kevin Spacey?

"Okay, then," says the drug dealer, whose name is Dave. He's
probably thirty, with short hair and deep acne scars. He wears a
sports coat over a button shirt, and I think, *Hell, since I took a buyout*

and stopped showering, I look more like a drug dealer than you. Then Dave stands and I get queasy, thinking: why is Dave the Drug Dealer standing? And it's clear I should stand, too, when Dave gives a little roll with his hand and says, "Should we get to it?"

Preceding *getting to it*, I have so far on this night: (1) left home pretending to get milk *again*, leaving Lisa alone again so she could presumably scurry to the computer and email the Prince of Lumberland—*He fell for the concert story. See you Saturday night and we will have sex* (2) hurried to the 7/11 near my house, arriving promptly at 10 p.m. to find Jamie already there, bouncing in the cold drizzle, blowing on his hands, wearing not his silky sweat suit but a pair of dark jeans, a sweatshirt and a watchman's cap that make him seem just a bit dangerous (3) driven in my car with Jamie to an even older, sadder neighborhood, where the blocks of huge 1890s Victorians have been split into unfortunate apartments—this particular house an old four-story beauty whose original grand floor plan is long gone, replaced by cubby apartments with mismatched numbers and letters hung on the doors, so that we somehow walk past Apartment 5 to get to Apartment G (4) met the owner of this cozy book-and-candle Apt. G, a tall, leggy, striking girl named Bea or maybe just the letter B or maybe the insect Bee, not sure, her long blond hair pulled in a ponytail, her no-doubt banging body effortlessly buried beneath a pile of tights and sweaters and scarves— she is a walking coat rack—and as we shook hands, Bea fixed me with the most alarming blue-eyed stare of my life, the kind of stare in which you think some potent subliminal message is being passed along (*Run away with me* or maybe just *Run away*), before Bea said she'd get out of our hair so we could "get to it" (5) waited about five minutes until Dave the nonthreatening Drug Dealer swept into Bea's place, shook the rain off his overcoat, and I thought, *what kind of drug dealer wears an overcoat*, as I also noted that Dave has a key to Bea's apartment, a fact that broke my pathetic little heart, since I had decided to fall in love with Bea, and as Dave set his briefcase next to the couch, we engaged in a little political small-talk (like everyone I know, we seem to agree on everything) before Dave stood and said, as reported earlier: "Okay then. Should we get to it?"

And here we are, about to get to it.

The best part of Apartment G is Bea's wall-length hot-English-major bookcase, filled with the comfortable spines of all of the books we were supposed to read in college but which we only got a few chapters into, and enough contemporary fiction to make it clear that reading is not just an assignment for lovely Bea. Alarmingly, though, on top of the bookcase there is also a family portrait of Bea with two just-as-striking blond-and-blue-eyed sisters and a pair of handsome proud Nordic parents, whose stares make me aware of the vast age difference between Bea and me, and I am profoundly ashamed to be here buying drugs in this girl's apartment. What I'd really like to do, I think, is lie down on this couch and take a nap.

Jamie elbows me. I stand.

"Okay," Dave says. "Take off your clothes."

"My . . ."

"I need to make sure you're not wearing a wire or anything." And then he pulls out a small flashlight. "And I need to look up your ass."

I turn to Jamie on the couch. He is surprisingly unsurprised, impressively unimpressed.

"What . . . would possibly be up my ass?"

Dave says, "It's just a precaution I take."

"I'm no expert," I look over at Jamie, "but if I was wearing a wire up my ass, how would the police even be able to hear it? Wouldn't it be muffled?"

Dave stares at me. I look over at Jamie again but he has picked up a copy of *The Sun* magazine and is flipping through it.

"I don't understand," I say.

"This is what I do," Dave explains. "It's the same search you'd get in prison. I do it to make sure people aren't stealing from me. I might do it any time. You never know."

"But . . . I haven't even bought anything from you yet."

Dave is starting to get a little more threatening. "And you aren't going to buy anything until you take off your clothes and I get a look up that ass."

I look over at Jamie again but he won't meet my eyes. There's a twitch in his neck tattoo.

So I take off my shirt and, for some reason, fold it before setting it on the arm of the couch. I try to remember the last time anyone has looked up my ass, which would be, oh, let's see: never. I begin to unbutton my pants.

And that's when Dave spits laughter. "I'm just fuckin' with you," he says.

My hands are still on the buttons of my pants.

"Man," a disappointed Jamie says, "I can't believe you were actually gonna let him look up your ass. What's the matter with you? You some kind of ass exhibitionist?"

My shirt is off and my pants are two buttons down and I am dumbfounded. "You mean you don't need . . . I don't have to get undressed?"

"It just proves my point," Dave says. "You can get people to do anything."

I put my shirt back on, button my pants and we all sit again.

Then Dave picks up his briefcase and opens it on his lap. "Jamie says you need some pain relief."

"Um, yeah." I reach for my coat, which has the money in it. "Nine thousand dol—"

"Bup, bup!" Dave interrupts me. "I didn't ask how much." He

holds up his hand to stop me. "Wait. . . . You brought the money *with you?*"

"Well . . . yeah."

"First—I don't handle money. And second—" He looks over at Jamie, shakes his head, and then back at me. "You brought nine grand to a meeting with someone you don't know?"

"What if we were planning to rob you, Slippers?" Jamie asks.

I scratch my head, embarrassed that I hadn't thought of that.

"What if we rolled you? You gonna go to the cops and say you got robbed in a drug deal?" Dave asks. He taps my skull. "You gotta think, man, if you're gonna work with me."

"I . . . I'm sorry," I say. I glance over at Jamie, who has the look I sometimes see on Teddy's face when I take him to school, or roller skating, or anywhere: *please don't embarrass me anymore, Dad.* "Look, I don't usually do this."

"That explains why you seem to think you can just go out and buy two pounds."

"Look," I say, "I really am sorry. I'm just trying to make a little money, and I have some friends who I think would buy some—"

"Bup, bup!" Dave says again, and he puts his hands over his ears. "Don't ever tell me how much you want or what you're doing with it. All I wanna know is what condition you got."

"Uh." I nod. "Okay."

Jamie leans over and says quietly, "Glaucoma."

Dave waits.

"I've got . . ." I look over at Jamie " . . . glaucoma?"

Dave smiles, opens his briefcase. Takes out a tabbed folder marked CONTRACTS. He opens this CONTRACTS folder and sets two short stacks of pages on the coffee table.

Then he holds out a pen and spins the first contract so I can read it.

"This," Dave says, "is a simple agreement between Party A, which is me, and Party B, which is you, obviously . . . stipulating that you are not a law enforcement officer, that you're not in any way or manner working with state or federal law enforcement in any investigatory or information-gathering capacity, either as an undercover agent or as a paid or unpaid informant, and that you will not knowingly provide any law enforcement agency with any material information regarding this transaction."

Before I can read the language in the first part of the contract, Dave is already on to the second: "This stipulates that you and I have not discussed any intended usage for what will heretofore be known as *the medicinal product*, that I will introduce you to a grower but if you are planning to use *the medicinal product* for usage other than medicinal, I have not been made aware of this fact, and thirdly, I have made no promises or guarantees that in any way indemnify you, should you, upon your own actions, outside the basic language of this contract, end up as the subject of any outside investigation for any prosecutable criminal offense. To wit—"

And he flips to the second, longer set of contracts. "This is a series of riders in which you agree that you will not engage in selling *the medicinal product* within 400 yards of a school, that you will not sell *the medicinal product* to minors, nor use weapons in any way connected with *the medicinal product*, that you will not use the Postal Service to mail it, nor cross any state borders with it, nor in any other way, knowingly or unknowingly, commit any material infraction in connection with *the medicinal product* which would represent a real and severe breech of this contract in any substantive manner and which might violate any and all state or local statutes, as well as the federal Controlled Substances Act, 21 U.S.C., and all its subsections herewith, nor commit any willful act that can be defined as an extenuating circumstance superseding the standard guidelines as defined by the federal mandatory sentencing laws, which, for the purposes of this contract, shall include any laws now on the books, or any laws passed in the future, in perpetuity, etcetera, in all states and territories, etcetera, etcetera. . . ."

"You're a lawyer?" I ask.

"There appears to be some question with the bar about that," Dave says. And then he hands me a final, single contract. "This last one simply indemnifies me, and releases me from all liability, all claims both criminal and civil, should you, knowingly or un-knowingly, alter *the medicinal product* in any real and/or material way by cutting it, or crossbreeding it, or enhancing it through the addition of any artificial stimulants or other substances covered by the Controlled Substances Act or by federal sentencing guidelines or by FDA regulations, those substances including but not limited to, cocaine in all its forms, PCP, heroin, methamphetamine, insec-ticides, fertilizers, artificial sweeteners, etcetera, etcetera."

I am staring at this pile of contracts when Jamie holds up the magazine he was reading to reveal an arty black-and-white photo of a nude woman standing in the shade of a doorway. "I like this kind of tits," Jamie says.

"Pointy," Dave says.

"Artificial sweeteners?" I ask.

Dave shrugs. "Some people like it sweeter. Most people use honey, but some assholes go cheap and douse it in old liquid sweet-eners."

Jamie leans in. "That shit causes cancer, yo."

I look at Dave, who is still holding the pen out to me, and I picture the real estate agent that Lisa and I used to buy our home, a tool named Thomas Otway, his tanned face set in a constant half-smile. Thomas had a funny Australian accent that always seemed phony.

"This is all pretty much boilerplate," Dave says, another thing our real estate agent used to say, except with his Aussie-r-dropping-vowel-twisting accent—bolah-plite.

I take the pen and begin signing. "Here," Dave says, removing flagging tape from each section, "and here, here, and here . . . and one more . . . here." Dave puts the signed contracts back in the CONTRACTS folder and then he takes from his briefcase another folder: MENUS.

He opens the MENUS file, takes out one of the sheets and hands it to me. The menu lists what are apparently various kinds (breeds? brands? makes? models?) of marijuana down the left column: AK-47, Arrow Lakes PB, Haze, Purple, Trainwreck, Snow Cap, OG Kush, Canadian Black, Cambodian Red, Schwag, F-1, ChemDog, Sour Diesel, White Russian, Jumping Jack and Northern Lights. The prices are listed in two columns on the right—the price ranges from $35 to $80 for an eighth and from $250 to $575 for an ounce.

I stare at this sheet, not entirely comprehending it. Jamie points out one of the cheaper middle brands—Arrow Lakes PB—and nods. This must be the B.C.-Bud-Nobel-Frankensteined shit that I've been smoking the last few days.

Dave goes on: "The blends are italicized, and anything with an asterisk is a name brand. I work mainly with a local grower, so what I tend to feature are locally produced versions of these brands—think of them as knock-offs, but every bit as good, sort of like generic prescription drugs. Not everything is going to be available, obviously, and these prices are subject to availability and other market forces."

"And you can get me—" I recall I'm not supposed to mention amounts "—enough?"

"First, I'm not *getting you* anything. I don't handle that part of it, because of my allergies—I'm allergic to spending the rest of my life in prison. I introduce you to the grower, help you broker a fair price, that kind of thing, all for an hourly fee, but I don't want to know how much you're buying or what you're doing with it. I assume you have a prescription. After that, you're responsible for paying for it, and for transporting anything you buy. I don't ever see dope or dough. I'm simply a lawyer who gets paid for whatever billable hours I spend on various negotiations, contracts and introductions—none of which involves the actual transaction of drugs or money. I am not the person providing you with the product. We're clear on that?" Dave taps the stack of contracts I've signed.

"Uh. Yes?"

"Good." Dave begins packing up his briefcase. "Then take this menu home and read through it and I'll call you tomorrow."

When his briefcase is packed, Dave looks me in the eye, smiles and winks, and once again, I think of Thomas, the agent who represented Lisa and me when we bought our house.

Our house . . . for another, what . . . five days and nine hours? Lisa's inside it right now, bent over the computer keyboard while our boys are nestled in their beds—no idea of the insanity going on around them, foreclosure, affair, dope deal, all that unraveling—and it's almost as if I can hear our old real estate agent's phony accent: *I'm so bloody 'appy for you, this is the house-a-ya drimes*, slick son-of-a-bitch pushing papers like they were made of fine glass, *Lisa, Matt, this is the pa'ht I love*, papers that chained us to a death ship for thirty years, for the rest of our lives, or until next week, *I have a feeling you're going to be so 'appy heah*, and it dawns on me that Drug Dealer Dave's sales strategy might be a good one for realtors, too, beginning the home-buying process by pretending to want to search your asshole.

Because, honestly, after that everything goes pretty smoothly.

CHAPTER II

Turns Out There Are Only Four Eskimo Words for Snow, However—

Ace auntie atshit bammy banana bash
bart bazooka black-mote block (and) blue-bayou
bobo bone boom brick budda (botanical name:
Cannabis sativa) charge cherat chips chira
chronic daga dope funk ganja giggle grass
grefa hemp jack jane jay jolly juju
(and the deliriously sweet-sounding) kiff.
A loaf a log a lid (which is what we called
an ounce when I was a kid; what they now
call a can) loco lucas ma mak mary-jane
marijuana—(which is Mexican
for something no one can ever agree upon
and then comes the sweet string of—)
meggie moocah muggles numba noma paca
pat pin pot pretendo rat red reefer rye
sen sez spliff snopp stink straw
stack thai thumb wollie what yeh

yen-pop yesca zambi (then back a bit to
end on my own personal favorite)—weed.

"Why are you Googling pot slang?" Lisa asks. I didn't hear her
come in the room and now she's looking over my shoulder. She is
dressed in a tight-fitting black shirt and skirt; she looks great. She's
been dressing up more for work the last few weeks. It reminds me
of when we were first married, how it used to break my heart a
little every morning when she'd make herself so beautiful to go
market the sports medicine clinic and I'd think: wait a minute: I'm
the guy who married you. Why don't *they* get the sleepy woman
in the zero-population-growth pajamas and *I* get the business babe
in the hot suit?

"I think we need to be ready, that's all," I say, thinking quickly
to explain the list of stoner synonyms on the screen. "Those boys
are going to be teenagers soon and when they start sneaking around
I don't want to miss any of the code words."

"They're ten and eight, Matt."

"You want to have your head in the sand, go ahead. I'm gonna
be ready."

Lisa shrugs off the latest sign of what she surely must see as my
fatal case of mid-life imbalance. "Curt is supposed to get back to
me today about going full time and getting on the benefits pack-
age," she says. When she's nervous, like now, Lisa bites her bottom
lip. It goes white under her teeth. "I'm not optimistic, Matt."

"I know you're not."

"So what should I say if he says no?"

"I wouldn't say anything. I've told you before I think you
should look for another job, but you probably shouldn't quit this
one until you have another one."

"Yeah," she says, and she looks past me, out the window. She
clears her throat and says, "So what do you have today?"

I list off the day's chronological indignities: (1) Dad's doctor's appointment, in which he will be given a routine dementia exam—SATs of senility—to determine the rate of his decline and the effectiveness of the meds he's on (2) a meeting about the one job prospect I've been tending, with a wealthy developer I used to cover who claims to want to start an online newspaper with me as editor (3) a twice-postponed afternoon appointment at the Unemployment Office with my job counselor, Noreen.

What I don't mention is that I'm also: (4) going on day three without sleep (5) desperately trying to "contact my lender" to fend off foreclosure for another month and (6) waiting for Dave my drug-dealing lawyer to call so I can order nine Gs of primo skank—at least two logs of meggie, or two bricks of block (or is it two blocks of brick?). Eight loafs of juju. Thirty-two cans of chronic. Two-hundred fifty-six eighths of zambi. Eight hundred spliffs of bammy. (Stoned stock analyst side-note: Texas Instruments makes a fine calculator for figuring this out.)

"I'm sorry to ask again, but do you think you could pick up the boys? And feed them dinner? I might be kind of late."

"Sure." I notice that she hasn't offered an excuse and I don't ask for one. I just turn back to the computer screen and Lisa exits this little room we call "the office," to go finish getting our future potheads ready for school.

What I was actually doing when she came in was trying to figure out the words on Dave's marijuana menu, but it is like trying to learn Spanish, this pot-language; there are apparently national and regional dialects (how would you ever know where to smoke wollie, or yeh?), native slangs giving way to brands and hybrids, formal and informal constructions, questions of singular and plural (can you have two sez?), an ever-shifting slang meant precisely to exclude creepy old dudes like me. In fact I'm beginning to suspect that every noun is slang for pot, and every verb also means to get high. Raise a flag? Pound a nail? Shoot some hoops? Park the car? Feed the cat? Well . . . that might just be feeding the cat.

Voices trickle up the stairs: "Bye, Dad." "Bye, Dad." "Bye, Matt." The house is wrung of its young people and it's just my dry old man and me, both of us staring into flat, diode screens.

I call down the stairs. "You okay down there, Dad?"

"When does *Rockford Files* come on?" he yells back up.

"Nineteen-seventy-five."

I finish my dope research and check Lisa's Facebook page, but she's gone underground. No more public flirtation. Usually when I do recon, I come across a dozen harmless chats back and forth between Lisa and her old college friends—they send each other good karma and E-hugs and online invitations and it's no different than grade school, folded notes going back and forth. Usually, in a single night, Lisa receives, and responds to, dozens of these passed notes. Last night there were twenty entreaties to her from various "friends" and she didn't respond to a single one. It's all Chuck all the time now, and either she's learned to keep their conversations private or they've moved to a safer platform.

I remember, at a party in college some girls asked me what represented first, second and third base at my high school. These girls were loudly and drunkenly agreeing that first base was kissing and a home run was sex, but second and third were open for debate—everything from booby-outside-the-shirt to heavy petting to making out to blowjobs. I said that at my school, first base was group sex, second base bestiality, third base necrophilia and a home run an elaborate weeklong orgy that ended with a snuff film. The joke, as I recall, fell somewhat flat, ending the usually solid party topic of sex bases. Lisa did always say that my sense of humor was an acquired taste. Like beef heart.

Anyway, I think there must be a sort of electronic version of those bases now—first base being a simple wall-posting on Facebook or MySpace, second being a private email, third a text message to one's phone leading to . . . I don't know . . . phone sex or masturbating in front of a computer camera. That's a pleasant thought for one's wife and the prince of lumber.

I push away from the computer, spend ten minutes in mortgage-company automated-phone hell (*por español, dos*) but my heart's just not in it. I need to sell some jack. I do push-ups. Sit-ups. Shower. Take a dress shirt from the ignored side of my closet, whisper to the despondent ties: stay alert boys, any day now, any day! Downstairs, Dad has given up ever finding Jim Rockford on TV and is watching news swing back and forth from a plane crash to the recession and back again, until they begin to seem like the same thing. "Look at that," Dad says of a certain twenty-four-hour news babe. "I'd like to bend her over her anchor desk."

As my father fantasizes rough sex with this pert professional on her crisp news set, I run a comb through his wispy gray hair. He pats his chest for a cigarette.

Dad follows me to the car, where he rides like a vet-bound dog, facing sideways, the world streaming past like the façade of an old arcade game. There is a for-sale sign in the back passenger seat window of my car. Such new details are always alarming to Dad—they must signify something—so every once in a while he looks back at the sign. "You selling this car?"

"Yeah."

"What kind of car is this?"

"Maxima."

He sighs. "Do you know what I miss?"

"Dan Fouts?"

"Chipped beef."

"I know you do, Dad." The sky is clear again today, world

sharply drawn, trees clear of leaves, their anguished branches rising like clutched fingers. It's quiet in the car. He first had it in the Army; shit-on-a-shingle, they called it. My mom used to make it for him, too. She preferred the description "chipped beef"—which, now that I think about it, is what he says he misses, not shit-on-a-shingle. Huh. So, he misses Mom's chipped beef. Maybe he misses Mom.

"Dad, what do you say we have that for lunch today?"

"Have what?"

"Chipped beef."

"I miss that."

"Yeah. Me, too."

He looks back. "You selling this car?"

"Yeah."

"What—"

"Maxima."

He is not happy in the doctor's office waiting room. For the dementia patient, all of life is a waiting room in which you can't remember what you're waiting for and your turn never comes. In this *actual* waiting room are the kinds of people my father would never choose to spend his morning with—whiners, sniffers, the weak, complainers. I think about asking a nurse for something to help me sleep; I got an hour or two last night but I suppose you can't really complain about not sleeping if you're not actually going to bed.

The nurse calls Dad's name and he looks at me. I nod and we start to the back of the clinic. She takes his blood pressure and weighs him. He's lost six pounds in six months. She glances over at me. I know. I know. I'm not feeding him enough chipped beef.

We sit in the doctor's office. Dad shifts, crinkles the paper-covered table. He stares at a crosscut drawing of the female reproductive parts, trying to figure out what he's looking at: some kind of plant? map of the Gaza Strip? carburetor? Finally, I think his mind gets around what it is, and he winces and looks away.

Dad's doctor always seems grumpy about our appearance, even though she schedules these routine appointments. I always feel guilty that we've taken time away from her important life-saving for a routine maintenance check on Dad's failing mind. She spends a few minutes on his health; she's glad he's quit smoking, even though I fear he's just forgotten it.

"Okay, Jerry," she says. "I'm going to ask you a few questions. What year is this?"

My father looks at me, pissed that I've done this to him. Last time he guessed 1997.

"Nineteen . . ." He rubs his dry lips. "No." And he smiles, because he's not falling for the trap this time. "One thousand eight."

"One thousand eight?"

"Yes," he says.

"And the month?"

"November."

"So it's November of one thousand eight?"

"If you say so." He smiles at me. One thousand eight? Maybe it's not terrorists we have to fear, the dudes planning another 7/11. Maybe we should be more worried about the Norman invasion. Or the plague.

"Where did you work, Jerry?"

"I worked at the . . . place." He looks at me. "Sears," he says, relieved.

"And what did you do?"

He pats himself for a missing smoke. Then he looks at me again. After managing the automotive department at Sears, Dad worked briefly in the Sears insurance offices but I think he missed his coveralls. He says, "What did I do? Hell, I did my job, that's what."

"I'll bet you did. And what did you have for breakfast today, Jerry?"

He looks from the doctor to me. Blank. I can't help him. He is pissed. If this test is the SATs of senility, Dad is headed straight for the Yale of assisted living places. "I have to go to the bathroom," he tells the doctor.

While he's gone the doctor looks at his chart. "He's lost six pounds."

"He's eating," I say.

"Does he have any favorite foods you can make?"

"Shit-on-a-shingle?"

Maybe Lisa is right and I do have an inappropriate sense of comic timing; or maybe some people just don't laugh when they should, this doctor, for instance, who looks down at the chart.

"He comes in and out, has good days and bad days," I say, which is pretty much the outlook the doctor predicted six months ago.

"More bad days, though? More days like today."

"Not really," I lie. "Half and half."

"Have you talked with your father any more about assisted living?"

"A little," I say. "He's had some financial trouble . . . we're sorting out his insurance now. But honestly . . . I think he'd rather eat a gun than go live in one of those death warehouses."

I'm not sure why I'm doing this—shit-on-a-shingle and eat a gun and death warehouses . . . as if the rough drug dealer is already emerging. Maybe I'll whack this doctor.

Dad comes back in the room. "Two thousand eight," he tells the doctor. "I think I said it wrong before." I recall the calendar at the nurse's station. Dad glances over at me, and smiles, and I don't think I've ever loved the old guy more than I do right now.

He drifts in and out like this during the remainder of the test, knows some things I wouldn't guess he'd know but can't come up with others that seem basic to me, like two of my three sisters' names. Simple math crushes him, and when he's asked to repeat a list—wallet, telephone, car keys—thirty seconds later, he's angry about the trick question. "What list?"

"I said to repeat those three things," the doctor said. "Remember?"

"Well, they must have been stupid things," Dad says. Right again.

I drive Dad home and put the TV on financial news, slip into a sports coat and drive back downtown for my meeting with Earl Ruscom. I park ten blocks away to avoid paying for a meter. I'll buy nine thousand dollars worth of pot, but I won't pay fifty cents to park.

Outside the restaurant, I call Dave the Drug Dealer to put in my order. He asks if I've read the menu. I say I have and that I'm interested in Arrow Lakes PB. I'm careful not to say how much.

"Good choice," Dave says. "Very good for glaucoma. Let me get back to you."

He hangs up and I go inside.

I first met Earl Ruscom in 1997, at a public hearing I covered as a reporter. Earl was there to get the county to waive environmental cleanup for a cluster of houses he wanted to put on the site of an old railroad depot. Somehow, Earl got it in his mind that I was *on his side* in this dispute, because while my stories described him accurately as a voracious fat-ass developer trying to get around reasonable environmental laws, in the profile I called him "bombastic" and Earl took this as a compliment. "Just glad to have you on my side, Matt," he used to say, even though I explained that reporters weren't allowed to take sides, and, were I allowed to take sides, it wouldn't be with a guy who wanted to build cheap houses on a polluted hillside soggy with oil leeching from old buried tanks. "Yeah," he said, "but you're fair. I can smell the fair on you."

In the late 1990s Earl first approached me with the idea of starting his own newspaper. Earl's newspaper would be "business friendly," he said, and would contain none of the "liberal bias" and "anti-growth bullshit" that he believed were choking off development and keeping capitalists like himself from making money and filtering it back into the economy through the companies that made yachts, Jacuzzis and Scotch. I always liked Earl though, and we played golf together a few times. But I always thought he was talking out his ass about owning his own publication. Then he began drawing up a business plan, and one day he called to see if I might want to edit his newspaper—which was going to be called, I kid you not, *The Can-Do Times*. But I still had a job then, so I was brutally honest with him: "Earl, I can't take the job, and I have to tell you, I don't think this is the right climate to be starting a newspaper, anyway." A third-generation Westerner, Earl wasn't a tie-and-jacket man as much as an ironed golf-shirt and big belt-buckle guy. He just laughed at me. "So I should take bid'ness advice from a guy makin', what, fifty grand a year?" It was actually nearly sixty, but I didn't say so. "Look, Earl," I said, "I know you can read stock listings. Newspapers are just a bad bet right now. You might as well be starting a railroad. Or a Pony Express station." This was when media stocks were merely trading down a few points, before "buying media stock" became a synonym for setting your money on fire. But this was also around the time that I was thinking of leaving my job to start a business-poetry website, so I maybe wasn't the best person in the world to lecture Earl on bad ideas.

Over the next year, of course, I went back to the newspaper and quickly lost my job, and Earl's idea began to seem less crazy.

So last week, I called and asked if he was still moving forward with his newspaper idea. He said he was, and he was glad to hear from me because he hoped to be up and running in a year and he still didn't have an editor. And as he talked about his paper, it seemed that he'd been doing his research, because he'd given up the idea of a daily print edition of *The Can-Do Times*. Now, it would strictly be updated online, and he'd only produce one hard copy a week, a slender Sunday night edition—Sunday nights being the cheapest press run in town. This Monday morning howler would feature only the best columns and pieces that had run online all week, and would sit in the offices of people like Richard, my ganja-reefing broker, allowing savvy local businesspersons to feel like they're hitting the week running. I asked if Earl was worried by the hard economic times and he said that a recession was the best time to go into business, just as it was the best time to buy real estate, because, "trust me, the big-dicks ain't hidin' in their panties, Matt," and when Earl gets going, you don't stop to untangle the words, you just go with it; No, Earl added, now was the time to "pull the goddamned trigger, open 'er up like a six-buck whore," whatever that meant.

It wasn't that Earl's bluster totally convinced me, and the thought of writing developer propaganda for him wasn't exactly my idea of a dream job, but if he could at least pay me close to what I was making, say, sixty thousand (I'd gladly take fifty) a year, I owed it to myself and my family to see if Earl and I could make a go of it. And maybe the idea would fail, but it wouldn't be for my lack of trying; I was prepared to give it the best effort I could muster.

Our meeting is 11:30 lunch at a sushi place, which is not as odd as it sounds for a porterhouse like Earl; as my friend Jamie might say: dude love him some uncooked fish. It's something to behold, watching Earl in a sushi place. He has a shark-like single-mindedness, eating roll after gourmet roll, gobbling gobs of sashimi, handfuls of edamame, slabs of seared ahi and maki, full paddies of rice. Every time the waiter passes, Earl orders something else. The last time I saw him, almost ten months ago, we were at this same sushi joint; he killed more fish in two hours than a trawler could in a week.

I walk around the restaurant but don't see him. The only person here is a thin guy who—

"Matt!" calls this thin guy, sitting at a table near the door. He stands. He looks like Earl at the end of an old televised movie shot in CinemaScope, when they have to squeeze everything into a skinny frame to make the credits fit.

"Earl?" I ask.

He is at least eighty pounds lighter. The suburban sprawl that used to spill over his substantial belt has been zoned out of existence, and standing in front of me is a guy in size 33 Wranglers, craggy, gaunt and gray, like one of those aging Grand Ole Opry stars right before they die of lung cancer.

In fact, my first self-pitying thought is that the angel of my recovery has gone terminal on me—along with my prospects for the future—but he says, "Fuck no, ain't never felt better." He had a heart attack, he explains, and his doctor ordered him to lose the weight. "And I don't do nothin' half-assed," he points out, offering me some unsalted edamame. "Doctor says lose eighty pounds, I lose me eighty pounds." He fixes me with a hard stare. "And what's the matter with you? You look ten years older."

I explain that I'm not sleeping well. Or at all.

Another minute of small talk, then Earl says, "Should we get this shit on the table."

Here is the shit Earl puts on the table: he is prepared, right now, to offer me the job as editor of *The Can-Do Times*. At first it will just be me, but eventually he wants a staff of six, made up of three part-time entry-level people, two college interns and possibly one other mid-career person like myself.

"That'll all be your call," he says. "I'm gonna stay outta the kitchen. Not that I won't give you my opinion, but shoot, you can feed glue to a horse an' it'll look like he's doin' algebra. No, only thing I ask—" and his skinny index finger points at my nose "—is that you give business in this town a fair shake and a voice for once. But this here's your deal. I ain' about to piss in the whiskey barrel."

And suddenly I love Earl. I love his belt buckle and I love that country-lisp-whistle in his voice that cuts the ends off words and makes a word like *whiskey* sound cool and I love a man who can simply *will himself* to lose eighty pounds and I love his business sense and I love *Can-Do* and I love this man's courage, and his balls (metaphorically) and I especially love this homespun way of his, in fact I vow to start using phrases like *piss in the whiskey barrel* in conversations. I think I'll have it burned onto a wooden sign for Earl, the kinds of signs people put at their lake cabins, and I can even imagine—although I'm not stupid enough to bring it up right now—that once we're off the ground and I've introduced the extraordinarily popular feature *The Fiscal Poet* to *The Can-Do Times*, I'll write a sonnet in Earl's honor, fourteen rhyming lines breaking into four heroic couplets featuring Earl's own homespun wit, ending with his lyric motto:

. . . Man who could feed glue to an upright horse
Make it look like the animal's talkin'
Could throw a fastball a hundred-n-four
Knock down batters even when he's balkin'

Earl who can eat bone and drink marrow
Ain't gonna piss in the whiskey barrel.

The business plan calls for one tech person and one advertising person on staff, he says, but this could also take a while. Everything will take a while.

"Fine," I say, and my cell phone rings—it is my Drug Dealer Dave—but I click it off because I'm not about to fuck up this meeting and just then the voice in my head starts in, that awful *Matt-this-is-all-too-good-to-be-true* voice. I don't want Earl to see that things have been going so badly for me recently that I would distrust his offer, but the voice tells me: *distrust his offer* and so I start down the mental list of what I might be missing. The obvious thing is pay, but I feel the need to circle around to that: "Benefits?" I ask. "Health insurance?"

"This is a start-up, Matt," he says, and shrugs. "I have a plan for the people in my construction and real estate offices, but this here's more like my restaurants. I could let you buy into the plan at a pretty good discount, certainly better than anything you can get out in the world, but I can't match or go employer-based. I mean, you can't give a virgin the biggest bed in the whorehouse, right?"

Whatever. Still love this guy. I take a deep breath. "And pay?"

"I gotta pay you?" He smiles, then makes a face. "Nah, this here's a start-up, Matt. Ain' no one gettin' rich. I 'spect my ranch-han's to put in some sweat equity, 'specially in the first couple-a-years. In exchange, you'd get real ownership shares, which—let's be hones', neither of us knows if they'll be worth the paper they're shit on."

Yes, this is exactly what I was afraid of. "Look, I understand that, but I can't work for free, Earl. And I can't just work for stock. I've got a family."

"No one expects you to work for free, or jus' for shares." He looks genuinely pained. "But this bird, she ain' gonna fly weighed down by salaries. In the beginnin', I'm sorry but I could only pay you fifty, Matt."

Fifty? I pretend to have to think about it. Fifty!

Love this guy!

"Look, I know it's significantly less than you was makin'," he continues, "but I've crunched the numbers and if we don't keep payroll at a bare minimum, this thing's gonna go like the salt block at a slaughterhouse."

No idea what that means!

"You'd have to supplement your income elsewhere . . . maybe even jus' do the job part-time at first, but it's the only way."

Fifty grand? Part time? Love this guy! Don't look too eager, I tell myself. I wish I could call Lisa right now. "Don't suppose you could go to sixty," I say.

He wrinkles his mouth. "Fifty . . . five?"

Love! Him! Fifty is what we need to basically support our lives . . . to tread water . . . at fifty-five, we can slowly start to chip away at our debt. "How about fifty-eight?"

"Aw screw it, what's a few hundred bucks," Earl says and sticks out his hand. "You got a deal, my friend. Fiftee' thousan', eight hunnerd."

I laugh. "That's funny."

"What?"

"It sounded like you just said fifteen thousand eight hundred."

He stares. "That *is* what I said."

"But you meant fifty-eight thousand, right?"

"Fifty?" he says. "You sayin' fifty? Fu-u-uck." And then laughs. "Shoot, Matt I can't pay no fifty. No, I said fiftee'. *Fiftee'-eight!* Fiftee' thousand, eight hunnerd."

"But . . . earlier you said fifty. Then I said sixty."

"I said fiftee'. Then you said sixtee'."

"Wait. Fifteen thousand dollars? A year?" And now I hate this country shit with his stupid country-lisp-whistle that cuts the last letter off every word so that fifteen actually sounds like fifty. "I can't live on fifteen thousand a year, Earl."

"Well, hell Matt, I don't know why you took this meeting then. I tol' you it was gonna be sweat equity early on. That it might even be part time. Hell, you're the one been telling me for years they ain' no money in this shit."

"But . . . fifteen?"

"I got no problem findin' people will work for that."

And the awful thing is that I have no doubt that he does have journalists who will work for fifteen grand a year, for ten dollars an hour, there are so many out of work, and I also have no doubt that I can't entirely afford to walk away without at least considering this offer.

"I got people will gimme shit on the Internet for free," Earl says apologetically. "An' I ain' so sure it's any worse than the crap I'm payin' for."

And I think this is likely true, too. I sigh. Look around the restaurant, then down at my cell phone, which is displaying Dave the Drug Dealer's text message: "1 hour . . ."

"I don' t . . . know if I can," I tell Earl. Deep breath. "I might have to do something else." I rub my brow. "Look, can I get back to you?"

"Fine," he says. "Sixtee'. But that's as high as I can go, Matt. I want you. We both know I like havin' you on my side. But I pay any more'n that . . . I'll jus' be shittin' in my own soup."

CHAPTER 12

You Will Need

(A̲LL PRESSURE-TREATED STOCK)
18 eight-foot four-by-fours
to build the side walls and
30 more for the floor,
6 three-and-a-half footers
for the fort's side door
(Foundation underpinnings
are 16 four-foot boards)
and 6 two-footers more, for
the other fort door
16 one-footers for top cops
and spacers for the door
12 four-foot galvanized spikes
(although you may need more).

This list, along with the requisite tools—circular saw, fram-
ing square, twenty-eight-ounce framing hammer, measuring tape
and heavy-duty drill with various bits—constitutes, according to

my new friend Chuck, crowned prince of Lumberland, Duke of cuckolding, Earl of Homewrecker, the basic raw materials for the simplest tree fort I can build, Frontier Fort #2, a tree fort so simple it doesn't even require a tree.

"So wait, it just sits on the ground?"

He looks up from the book? "Hmm? Yeah. It just sits on the four-bys. That's why you gotta make sure the wood is treated."

So . . . Chuck is a *Hmm-er,* one of those people who hears you but pretends he doesn't, says Hmm, and then answers your question. Lisa is going to hate that after a few years. She's going to say, *Why do you say Hmm, if you heard what I said?* And he's going to look up from his newspaper in *my* living room and say, *Hmm?*

It's only a beginning, but I am starting to find weaknesses in my opponent.

After the disastrous meeting with Earl I still had an hour to kill before meeting Dave the Drug-Dealing Lawyer. I couldn't bear taking a meeting with Noreen my unemployment counselor, who would no doubt encourage me to take Earl's $16,000-a-year job so she could scratch me off her list of unemployables. So I canceled and came once more to the mystical land of lumber for a bit of recon behind enemy lines.

Chuck stands while he types at a plastic-covered computer. This seems unfair to me. I had really hoped to tower above him. As Chuck goes back and forth from the tree-fort book and his computer, I whistle a song I downloaded earlier today. He doesn't react to it. My whistling is a bit rusty, so the song may not be immediately recognizable, so I try the chorus, which it pains me to sing: *"She's sweet/and oh-so vulnerable/a man's wet dream/or his worst nightmare."*

Chuck doesn't say anything. He just runs his finger down the list of supplies I need and then switches back to his computer keyboard.

"You know that song?" I ask.

His brow is wrinkled up in a difficult math problem. For a second, while he calculates, he looks right at me, but it's as if he doesn't recognize me, or is looking through me. There is a low hum of space heaters in Lumberland, as all around us men are gathering the materials to build things; it's what we do at Lumberland. *We come get stuff to build stuff.* In this way, over time, men like us built all the stuff in the world. "Hmm?"

"The song I was just singing? By the band, Blue Eyed Jesus? You know them?"

Chuck's lips are still moving as he adds my lumber purchase in his head. When he's done, he jots down a number. "Hmm? I'm sorry. What?"

"Oh. This band I heard. Supposed to be coming to town? Blue Eyed Jesus? I really like 'em, but I can't find anyone who has heard of them. I was just wondering if you knew them."

"What was it again?"

"Blue Eyed Jesus?"

"No," he says. "I don't think so."

This proves, of course . . . nothing. It could be that the concert is simply a cover story for their rendezvous and so Chuck wouldn't know the band. It could also be that he's pretending to not know the band because he's figured out who I am. Or it could be that Lisa really *is* going to the Blue Eyed Jesus concert with Dani. It could also be that Jesus really did have dreamy blue eyes, just like Chuck's. Maybe Chuck *is* blue eyed Jesus, Prince of Peace *and* of Lumberland. Maybe Chuck is the emperor of ice-cream. Or maybe life is an illusion, an image shadowed by fire onto a cave wall.

Chuck hits print and when he bends over to pick up the printout I am finally given a gift, the kind of thing that makes me thank Jesus' blues, the kind of vision that makes me believe that I can turn around this long losing streak, the first sign of light in a very dark tunnel:

Chuck has a bald spot!

The genre calls for me to go coin-size with my estimate—quarter, fifty-cent piece, silver dollar—but it's hard because Chuck's bald spot isn't exactly round. (Who ever heard of an irregular bald spot? Cancer, I think, before the burgeoning Catholic in me scolds with self-directed guilt; after all, the man *does* have children, and anyway, I've never heard of scalp cancer. Okay . . . how about just an acceleration of this uneven hair loss?)

And then it comes to me: Chuck's bald spot is roughly the size and shape of a fried wonton. "I don't suppose there's any good Chinese food around here?"

"Hmm?" Then, still bent over, reading my printout for the treeless tree fort, Chuck tells me the name of a place nearby.

"They have wontons?"

"I don't know," he says. "Probably."

I have, I should point out, a luscious head of hair. Cut short now, up over my ears, my hair is nonetheless thick and healthy and free of dumpling-shaped islands of skin. The wonton is turning, my friend, decaying Prince of Lumberland, balding boy-wonder of woodwork, male-pattern ninja of wife-thievery. I run my hand through my hair; it bristles like windblown wheat.

And when Chuck straightens up with the printout, I see that the triangular-shaped hole has two allies I didn't notice on either side of his head: a couple of little lots just being paved on either side of those dreamy Jesus blue eyes. (This is the thing about dreamy eyes; like red paint on a car, they cause buyers to overlook a lot of other problems.) Looks like some very real hair-care disappointment ahead for the blue-eyed Prince of Pine.

"Here you go."

I look down at the invoice, eyes going straight to the bold

number at the bottom of the page . . . "Eleven hundred bucks! For a kid's tree fort! Christ on a bike! How much would it cost if it was actually in a tree?"

"I'm sorry. I said it's the easiest, not the cheapest," Chuck says, and he wrinkles his forehead and takes back the estimate and I can see the condescension creep into his face (*this jerk's wasting my time; he was never going to build a tree fort*) and it pisses me off—are you really looking down on me, wife-stealer? You can't possibly be looking down on me, *baldy*—and my face flushes, and I ball up my fist to smack this asshole and that's when I notice the phone is buzzing on my waist and I look down at the number, it's Dave the Drug Dealer, and instead of punching Chuck, I have what can only be called, in the religious sense, an epiphany—

More than a good idea, I *see*, as clearly as if it's right in front of my sleep-hungry eyes: a stack of boards sitting on my front yard, the Stehne lumber invoice stapled to it, Lisa walking up, bending over, reading, her eyes going wide (*What?*) looking toward the neighbors (*Do they know?*) typing furiously on the keypad of her phone (*Did U send this wood?*) getting his response (*That's UR husband?*) and then her typing back (*U think he knows?*)

Yes. I know. I can't control the smile that crosses my face. "I'll take it." I snatch the paper back from him. "When can you deliver it?"

"Monday?"

"I need it tomorrow."

"Our driver's off tomorrow."

"Well, that's when I need it. My wife's going to a concert this weekend and I'm apparently going to have a lot of time on my hands."

"I could maybe get it there . . . on Saturday?"

"That's too late. Look," I say. And I hold up my buzzing phone like a time bomb—*deliver my lumber or I blow this little wooden king-*

dom to hell. "I have to take this. Now can you deliver my lumber tomorrow? Or should I go to a different store?"

"Okay." He shrugs and gives me one of those idiot-customer-is-always-right sighs that must come from a lifetime of working in the family business. "I may have to deliver it myself, but I'll get it there."

CHAPTER 13

On the Spiritual Crises
of Financial Experts

T HIS ONE ADMITS TO being a lifetime
    proponent of deregulation
but now, on NPR, he doesn't know what to think—
I however, think of Mother Teresa, who at the end of her life
admitted she'd had a crisis and had
    stopped hearing God's voice
decades earlier, which had to be a bit of a relief, I'd think—
hard enough to live a perfect life without
    being hectored about it
—give away everything, feed the poor, don't forget to love
the lepers!—but back to this disillusioned expert who says
you could go to any business school in the country and learn
the same lousy things he believed during those wasted years
—those Brooks Brothers days of strippers and Town Cars—
which is that financial systems are equilibrium-producing
engines and it takes random or external forces to derail them

that our entire economy is based on this simple principle—
that left alone markets will chug mostly in a straight line
that they will mostly do what is in their own best interest—
Balance risk with reward.
Throw out bad paper.
Make money.

But this crisis, the broken expert sadly explains
belies all of that, defies everything everyone ever
believed because it wasn't caused by famine or hurricane or
by war, by OPEC raising prices or by
      some third-world country
bailing on billions in loans while its epaulet-happy despot
bags the humanitarian aid and raids the banks—no
the ultimate cause of this global crisis
in our financial system
is our financial system.

This problem is endemic to the faulty machine it exposed
and contrary to the news, it wasn't caused by poor people
being allowed to borrow one hundred percent
of inflated home prices with nothing down, not really—
and it wasn't even caused by traders inventing questionable
derivative side bets against those same bad loans, not really—
(that's like saying a cold is caused by a cough
that your pneumonia came from a sneeze)—
no, the root cause of this global crisis
in our financial system
is our financial system.

And here is my real issue with financial experts
the whole time they're advising you what to do

with your retirement accounts, or your kids'
college funds, or when you happen to catch them
on TV (all fancy cuffs and high collars)—
they all sound so smart. They all sound so right.
Their true currency is surety and they're so sure
of their surety—but wait, the bull and the bear
can't both be right, how can the liquidity position
and the long-term hold both be sure bets, and yet
these guys are always so sure—and this sure expert
says if there's a flaw in the mechanics, dare I say—
his voice begins to quaver—there's surely a flaw in our
entire system of lightly regulated capital generation
and investment, which would mean there's surely a flaw
in nothing less than humanity itself—and here
the financial expert's voice breaks even more
and he has to clear his throat and—surely he is crying,
surely we've let him down, we humans, and he's
sure sobbing, devolving into a socialist, a fiscal atheist
right before our Dolby-sure-sound public radio ears.
And that's when I hear the unsure voice of Mother Teresa
praying to the God Who So Selfishly Refused To Speak
To Her (the god of angry middle school girls
the deity of ladies who get stuck with lunch bills
the lord of stubborn brothers and jilted lovers
the petty pouting feuding god of hurt feelings)
and I say, in Teresa's rat-infested, leper-loving lilt
this wise, weary prayer—"Dear Father, if you're out there
and if you can hear me, protect us from
        harm and by all means
comfort the weak and the poor, the wageless and
homeless, hungry, foreclosed, wandering, woefully
afflicted, but if you get just a minute after that

could you please please please
spite the living fuck out of this asshole—I mean it
go old-school Job on this rich fat fuck
this expert who apparently slept through
history class, through every relationship
anyone was ever in, and through the entire
twentieth century, this sure dickhead who
has only now discovered that there is
a goddamned flaw in us all."

CHAPTER 14

On the Spiritual Crises
of Drug Dealers

THEN BEA KISSES ME.

And how did I get here, on this front porch, among strewn leaves and half-hulled chestnuts, endangering fifteen years of mostly solid marriage by accepting a sweet kiss from a tall blond drug dealer's moll? A quick retrace of my steps doesn't exactly illuminate (took senile dad to doctor; got soul-crushing job offer for sixteen grand a year; went to Chuck-the-wife-thief's lumber store; erratically purchased eleven hundred dollars' worth of wood; got a call from Drug Dealer Dave suggesting I meet him at Bea's apartment; drove here listening to infuriating financial expert on NPR; rang Bea's doorbell, small-talked about her cool English major bookshelf; came outside with her so she could smoke; found myself telling her that she shouldn't go out with Dave the Drug Dealer because, well, he's a drug dealer; went on to add that she should find a nice sensitive poet boy rather than . . .)

Bang. Bea leans over and kisses me.

She pulls away and touches her mouth. Giggles. "Sorry," she says. "I kiss people. It's like . . . my thing." Her mouth is lovely, sitting in a narrow cat-like jaw beneath that roof of blond hair. We've just had a short, sweet kiss and I don't even know if there was anything sexual about it except that it was on the lips and her hand was on my jaw when she delivered it. No, it was definitely an in-between kiss, not exactly mustached-Aunt-Martha-at-the-train-station, but probably not meant to be erotic either; and probably because of that, it's incredibly erotic, and I flush like a teenager and gulp and swoon and feel in every other way achingly heartbreakingly young—which is all any of us can ever hope to feel from a kiss.

"You're sweet," she says, "Jamie's right about you." And then she puts her cigarette out on the stoop and long-strides over to a garbage can to toss the butt. Her skirt swirls as she walks—my god, she's got to have four feet of legs under there—and when she turns to face me her eyes are red and teary and I can't imagine what I've said that's made her tear up. "I'm not going out with Dave."

"Oh. I assumed—"

"I know he wants to," she says, "but we're just friends. I was having money problems and Jamie introduced us, and he agreed to pay part of my rent if he could have his meetings in my place. Dave's paranoid. Thinks his house is bugged."

"Oh." And I'm so smitten it's all I can do to not offer her money right now, to get her out of this arrangement with Dave the paranoid Drug Dealer, but I have no money to give that isn't already tied up in drug deals or in treated lumber.

She gives a wry, half-smile. "And there aren't nearly enough sensitive poet boys."

That's when Dave pulls up, in a Nissan Maxima exactly the year and color of mine. This makes me feel creepy in some way I can't quite name.

I wonder for a moment if Dave was parked down the block and saw the kiss, or if he can simply tell from my flushed face that Bea has kissed me. Maybe we'll go for a drive now and Dave will whack me, or, being a *lawyer* drug dealer, sue me. Or maybe this was all a setup and Dave has been taking pictures of Bea kissing me and will use them as blackmail. If so, the joke's on him: I'm not sure my soon-to-be-straying wife will care.

"There he is." Dave is wearing his tieless suit again. "How you doin', Slippers?"

"Good." I stand and we shake hands.

"Isn't this a beautiful fall day?" Dave asks.

It is, I have to admit, beautiful: crisp and sunny and the edges of the world seem sharpened by the depth of the sky. This fall is achingly clear.

Dave looks over at Bea, who has lit another cigarette. "How's school?"

"Fucked up."

"Doesn't matter. You make it to classes anyway."

She flips him off.

"Lovely. Everyone's so cynical these days." Dave walks over, grabs her cigarette, takes a long, flaring drag and hands it back to her. She's taller than he is. When did girls get so tall? Dave says, in smoke: "Whole world's cynical." Then he stares up at the white edge of the horizon. "I was just listening to this refreshing investment banker on NPR—"

"Hey, I heard that guy."

"Wasn't that great? Amazing to hear one of those guys be so honest and real, just say, 'Man, we messed it all up.' It made me feel . . . I don't know . . . hopeful."

"Really?" I ask. "It made me mad."

"No, I thought it was cool. I sat there thinking, shit, what am

I doing? All of this striving? Worrying? This shit with the bar? What does any of it mean if I die tomorrow?"

Great. My drug dealer is getting religion. Hopefully not before I get my dope. "Here's what I thought," I say. "Here's some guy who made millions off what he now admits was a corrupt financial system, probably spent twenty years living on champagne and strippers, and now, when the whole Ponzi pyramid falls on the rest of us, he gets religion? Why do people never get religion *before* the champagne and strippers?"

Dave stares at me. "You're even more cynical than she is. You guys are quite a pair."

I can't tell if he's teasing me, or if he knows about our kiss. I look over at Bea, who leans against the garbage can, her chin pointed down disapprovingly. Her mouth makes a little pink heart, the mouth that just kissed me . . . and again, I feel the teenage flush but when—

My waist starts buzzing.

"You ready, Slippers? We gotta go pick Jamie up first."

I glance down at the buzzing phone on my waist. It's the boys' school. Someone must be sick. Of all the stupid omens . . . "Uh . . . I might have to postpone."

CHAPTER 15

Good Choices

MY KID'S TEACHER IS such a hot lusty
ball of blond, even the worst boys behave.
But if I were in her class, I'd get me
some of that time-out—that's what I crave:

Ms. Bishop sitting my spanked bottom down:
young man, here we use our inside voices;
you sit still 'til you're ready to rejoin
the rest of your class and make good choices.

"Good choices"—this is the constant refrain in Franklin's
second-grade class: *Marshall, was that a good choice? April, we make
good choices in second grade. Parents, I'm just trying to teach the kids to
make good choices,* and I know exactly what goes through the minds
of the other fathers (and not a few of the mothers) as they listen to
nasty lovely sweet Ms. Bishop of the pouty mouth and black-lined
eyes, because it's exactly what goes through my mind: *Oh, you
hot minx of an elementary school vixen, there are some bad choices I could*

make with you right now. On conference night, you have never seen so many fathers haunting the halls: smartly dressed, cologned, they pace and pretend to contemplate child-art and Popsicle stick dioramas, eager for a glimpse of Ms. Bishop's famous paint-on skirts tracing her perfectly symmetrical and round a—(*Stop, bad choice!*) For me, a true Bishop connoisseur, it's not the tight skirts (so obvious, unrefined) but the blouses, and it's not the eye-catching fronts—these are for Bishop neophytes, with their V-cut, cleavy, gravity-defying peakage. No . . . my Bishopiphany came on Open House Night a few years ago, when she turned to the chalk board during a school open house and I caught a glimpse of the symmetrical small of her lovely back. It was as if, weary from riding all night, my horse and I had come upon this gentle, narrowing valley, smooth, gracefully tapering down from her shoulders, and there I saw it, this small, quiet place . . . an easy place . . . a place where a man could rest his head after two hours of extremely questionable choices.

Teddy was in Ms. Bishop's class then, three years ago, and it was Lisa who noticed how, after we got home from school events, she and I couldn't keep our hands off each other; it was as if Ms. Bishop were some sort of fertility goddess. After ice-cream socials and candy sales, pizza parties and school auctions, Lisa and I would fall off each other in bed, sweating and breathing deeply, and it was lovely Lisa who first said it: "Wow. Extremely good choice." For a while, in the good old days, it became our code in front of the kids: "I'm thinking of making a good choice tonight." "I hope you're planning on making good choices later, young man."

This, however, promises to be a less-than-erotic meeting with Ms. Bishop.

I've rescheduled my desperate wollie purchase (now I not only have to pay off the mortgage and private school tuition, I also have to cover eleven hundred in lumber I just bought from the guy

Bishoping my wife) to come to school and talk about frail little Franklin, who is accused of making an unprovoked attack upon a defenseless playmate using as his weapon the little wooden blocks he was supposed to be clacking together primitively in his music class.

Every father—whether he admits it or not—is gripped by two opposing thoughts immediately upon hearing that his child has been in a fight: first, the hope that no one was hurt, and second, the deep fear that your kid might not have won. *(The art of losing isn't hard to master.)* Two days after punishing Teddy for slapping a classmate in the third grade, I found myself surreptitiously teaching the boy how to make a fist, how to keep his left up, jab, jab, cross with the right. (Speed, boy: stick and move, stick and move!)

"It's just not like Franklin," Ms. Bishop says.

"No," I say helpfully, "he usually makes such good choices," and the Pavlovian reaction to that phrase causes me to cross my legs. Franklin is cooling his heels in the office while I talk to his teacher, the rest of his class in Afternoon P.E. as Ms. Bishop and I sit alone in her classroom, surrounded by penguins and thick cursive letters and easy math problems, wedged into little chairs, and while this is serious stuff, our legs nearly brush and it's all I can do not to *look* at Ms. Bishop, because then it will all be over, and I will not be able to affect the serious parent I need to be. My unemployment and Lisa's recent flirtation with affairing has cut into my sex-frequency—it's been nearly a month—so this is not a good time for me to be dropping in on women like Amber Philips and Bea and Ms. Bishop (whose jersey has long ago been retired from the delusional list of women who secretly long to sleep with me).

"No, it's not like Franklin at all," says Ms. Bishop. Franklin is the frail one. I fully expect Teddy to get in fights, but Franklin? His teacher shakes her head; she's in a plaid skirt and buff-colored blouse that clings to her as if she's just come in out of the rain.

"That's what's so disappointing," Ms. Bishop says. "That Franklin would make such a bad choice." She crosses her legs with a sweep of fabric and a glimpse of toned, muscled leg and I clear my throat to cover the sound of the whimper I feel in my chest. I stare at the ceiling, hoping it looks like I'm taking the details of Franklin's assault especially seriously: apparently, in the middle of music, while they were learning the concept of keeping a beat, Franklin snapped and, without provocation, swung his clackers and hit his friend Elijah Fenton in the face. Elijah curled up. Franklin fell on him, crying, then hit him twice more before Ms. Bishop managed to pry the clackers from his cold dead fingers. *(Clackers don't kill people; people kill people.)*

"Do we know," I ask, "what precipitated it?"

"Some teasing, apparently, although Franklin wouldn't tell me what it was about. I told him it doesn't matter. The children know that nothing excuses physical behavior like this."

(There's some physical behavior I'd like to . . .)

"Franklin knows that violence never solves anything," Ms. Bishop continues. "I told him that if he's being teased in the future, he needs to come talk to me or to you or to Mrs. Prior about it." (Who? Oh, right. Mrs. Prior. My wife. Bad choice.)

Ms. Bishop walks with me down to the office, where Cool Hand Frank is stewing in the hole, principal's office. (My boy can eat fifty eggs!) I stare straight ahead, but the sound of Ms. Bishop walking nearly does me in. (What's happening to me? Irrational, passive jealous reactions? Swooning over stoop kisses? Dizziness in the proximity of attractive women? I am officially fourteen again.)

Outside the office, Ms. Bishop explains that the school has "a set of violence and aggression protocols that Franklin has now accessed" and she sounds like my old editor, the nonsensically evil M— and I find myself wondering when the business jargon people took over education, or maybe it was the other way around. According to the violence and aggression protocols Franklin has accessed, my little offender gets a one-day suspension for the first act, a week of suspension for the second and expulsion for the third. Because Franklin has never done anything like this before, Ms. Bishop says, she and the principal have agreed that if he writes a note of apology to Elijah, he will not be suspended, but this will count as his first act of violence. Any more acts, though, and he will be suspended for a week. I thank her. "Nothing is more important than providing a safe atmosphere for learning," Ms. Bishop says.

In the principal's office, poor Franklin is sitting with his head in his hands. "Come on," I say. He moans. Thirty minutes later school is over and the boys sit in the backseat while I drive home. Franklin sniffs as he stares out the window. Teddy works like an old reporter, trying to get information about the fight.

"What kind of noise did it make when you hit him? Was it a slapping sound or a thumping sound?"

"Enough, Teddy."

Another sniffle from Franklin.

"Elijah Fenton is kind of a jerk, Dad," Teddy says. "It's not the worst thing in the world that Frankie hit him."

"I don't think that's true, but even if it were, you know it wouldn't matter, Teddy," I say. "It's never right to hit people."

Teddy asks, "What if they're gonna kill your family with a grenade?"

"Elijah Fenton carry a lot of grenades, does he?"

"He probably said something really bad," Teddy says. "He swears a lot."

"It doesn't matter. We don't solve problems that way. No matter what someone says."

"What if they *say* they're gonna kill your family with a grenade?"

"Let's stop talking about grenades and think about how Elijah feels."

Another moan from Franklin.

"He was playing kickball after school," Teddy says. "He's fine. Can't I just ask what Frankie hit him with? Please. Let me ask that one question and then I'll be quiet."

"No." I'm stuck behind someone turning left; I miss the light. Traffic is hateful.

"Please."

"No!" I snap, then, realizing I've overreacted: "The wooden blocks from music."

"Clackers! You hit him with clackers. Wow!"

Franklin moans.

"Teddy, that's enough."

I pull into the driveway. Inside, Teddy and Franklin retreat to their rooms. I try the Providential Equity prefixes again, leave voicemails all over their phone system. Since Lisa mysteriously claimed to have something to do this evening, I make dinner—chipped beef. Dad comes in from the TV room, sets his remote on the table, wrinkles his brow but doesn't say a word about what I've made. It sits on bread on his plate, covered in white-gray septic gravy.

"Chipped beef, Dad."

"Gravy looks funny," he says, but he eats it, fork clacking the plate. The boys herd the food around. Dad gets seconds without a word. We're a stoic breed—Prior men.

When he's done, Dad pats his chest for a missing cigarette, then grabs his remote, gives a sigh and marches into the TV room. Plops down in his easy chair. The boys pick at their chipped beef, give me plaintive looks. I give them an extra scoop of ice cream for dessert.

Dark settles in. I help the boys with their homework, avoid doing dishes, and another night bleeds away (where the hell is she?). I drink a cup of coffee alone at the table (maybe it's too late . . . they've run off together), check on Dad, who remarks that playing quarterback in a beard would be tough ("Itchy?" I ask), tuck the boys in (have I lost her?) and lean over Franklin in his twin bed, finally ready to have a talk with my little ultimate fighter.

"What did Elijah say that made you so mad?"

"I don't want to say."

"Sorry, pal, you have to."

The covers are at Franklin's chest; his too-small Shrek pajamas ring his neck. "He called Ms. Bishop a bad word."

"What word?"

"I don't want to say it. I'll get in trouble."

"I'm giving you a mulligan, Frankie. Bedtime amnesty."

"What's that?"

"Means one time you won't get in trouble for saying it."

"He said Ms. Bishop was a slut."

"How do you know that word, Franklin?"

"Elijah always says it." And then, possibly thinking I don't know the word, Franklin adds, "It means a girl who kisses lots of people. Elijah says Ms. Bishop kissed his dad, and that his mom called Ms. Bishop a slut. I said she isn't and he said she is and then . . . I got real mad. And I hit him."

But it's the earlier news that I can't process. *Elijah Fenton's dad kissed Ms. Bishop?* Bullshit. *Carl Fenton?* No way would that tool have a chance with Ms. Bishop. Not possible. Although . . . if a tool like Carl Fenton can get in there. . . .

"So you just . . . hit him?"

"I kept saying she wasn't a—" he looks at me to see if his amnesty is still in effect . . . "—slut, that she was nice. Elijah said that

I must love her too, and I probably want to kiss her. So I hit him." His eyes tear up again. "When he said I liked her, it made me so mad."

"Maybe . . . because . . . you do like her?"

"Da-a-d." He looks at me like I'm crazy. "Come on. Have you *seen* her?"

And as much as I empathize with him, this is a lecture I must deliver. The highpoints: (1) Violence is always wrong, except in rare instances of self-defense, or to protect those who can't protect themselves. ("Like grenades?" Franklin asks, echoing his older brother. "Sure.") (2) While it was certainly wrong of Elijah to say those things, stacking a wrong on top of his wrong just makes a higher pile of wrong. (3) Next time, Franklin should tell me or tell his teacher, even if it's embarrassing. (4) It is, however, perfectly natural to have a crush on a teacher. (Especially your teacher, my God, that taut little guitar string . . .)

Franklin sighs and promises he won't hit anyone with clackers ever again. (I imagine his next defense: *you never told me not to use shakers.*) I kiss his forehead and he grips my arm one more time. "Do people have to sleep even when they're old?"

"Yeah," I say. "They do." More hypocrisy from me: king of the sleepless.

Franklin falls back in bed. The world is so incomprehensible to him, so difficult; he must imagine there is some other world after dark that he can fit into. This is the kid I have to worry about, I suddenly see, the one most likely to land outside a convenience store.

Downstairs I check on my own father, who is staring warily out the dark window, ignoring the television in front of him. He turns to see me in the room, and it takes a second for him to remember who I am. Pats his chest. "Know what I miss?" he asks.

I pray for *Rockford Files*.

"Chipped beef."

Back to the kitchen, I scrape shit and shingles, wash, stack and stare at a second cup of coffee. Clock ticks. Mail sits on the counter, waiting for Lisa, a stack of red-lined bills and rustic catalogues that I consider throwing away. I get nervous whenever Lisa picks up a catalogue; since her binge, she's seen them as cruel taunts, news from the outside. Even before her recent trouble, of course, Lisa had a complicated relationship with shopping and with money. She grew up an only child, spoiled for the first decade of her life by her oft-traveling car-dealer father—although, as it turned out, she wasn't spoiled as much as the kids in his *other* family. Lisa was twelve when Walter McDermott died of a heart attack and this odd bit of truth came out: not only did Walter have two McDermott Dodge dealerships in two states . . . he also had two wives in those states. In court, it was established that Lisa and her mother were actually Walter's second family—he'd never divorced Wife #1 (nor had he told Lisa's mother about her), so the entire estate went to the first wife, and to Walter's three older children. Lisa and her mother ended up with nothing. To hear Lisa and her mother talk about this period, you'd think it was the siege of Leningrad, them boiling shoes and eating tree bark. Finally, when Lisa was fifteen, her mother found a responsible, older man to support them and pay for Lisa's college (this was her advice to Lisa, obviously ignored: go for a wealthy man at least a decade older than you). The surprising thing for me was how Lisa continued to idolize Walter. The unsurprising thing is that she grew up so conflicted about money, security and men—and that her deepest anxieties remain where those three things intersect. I remember being a little scared when we'd just started dating, and Lisa dragged me into a shop that had a belt she'd been scouting. I flipped the price tag: $280. I said that all of my clothes together didn't cost that much. She was mad for two days, angry at me for humiliating her (and for letting her down), but irrationally angry also at the store for the affront of stocking clothes she couldn't afford, and at the world, for excluding her from its best things. This was before I realized that Lisa would always take issues of wealth and poverty personally, before I understood that, while she loved me, Matthew D. Prior didn't exactly allay her deepest fear about being stuck with a breadwinning failure . . . (or, perhaps she fell in love with me because of that, because I remind her of dangerous old Walter).

Maybe we are drawn to our own destruction, pulled into our own 7/11s.

Where is she? The clock on the kitchen wall says five minutes to ten. I look out the window, past my tiny reflection, into the black backyard. I knew two years ago that this would be a difficult time for Lisa, watching me quit my job to venture into something as unlikely as a financial poetry website. But how could I know the economy would go this far south, that I'd get laid off from the job I scurried back to, or that our house would lose nearly half its value. Or maybe I didn't care (. . . we *are* drawn to our destruction). I recall once watching Teddy, when he thought no one was looking, staring at a cup of milk on the edge of the counter. Inexplicably, he gave the cup a little nudge. Or it wasn't inexplicable . . . these cups sit on the edges of counters and sometimes you just can't help yourself.

Finally, a few minutes after ten, headlights come down the alley. I watch the garage light come on. And three minutes later, my cheating wife comes in the back door.

She's wearing a plaid skirt, too . . . must be in style. And even if her legs lack some of the tone of Ms. Bishop's, they are great legs, and they are the legs I'm married to, legs I'd wrap around my waist if they'd have me. She's also wearing a red, wool beret. The cap is not something I've ever seen Lisa wear and the sight of it breaks me a little, as if she's on her way to becoming someone else, top-down.

A gift from Chuck, maybe? As if reading my thoughts, she sets the cap on the counter.

"Thanks for putting the boys to bed." Lisa looks through the mail: But she seems too nonchalant, even as she flips through the catalogues, as if even they have no power any more (in love maybe?) her good mood pissing me off. "Any news from school?" she asks.

And I realize this is exactly what I've been lying in wait for, and I try not to sound too pleased with myself as I lay out the whole while-you-were-out-doing-God-knows-what-I-had-to-deal-with-keeping-this-family-together clacker incident, and maybe it goes on thick, maybe even embellished—the ferocity of Franklin's attack, severity of the school's reaction, passion of Franklin's crying afterward—but I'm feeling desperate and I hope that ten logs of pure-grade guilt will shock Lisa out of this thing that she's on her way to doing to our family. Indeed, she covers her mouth and shakes her head as I tell the story.

"My God, Matt. Why didn't you call me?"

I shrug. "You said you had plans tonight."

"And . . . you didn't think I could take a phone call?"

I give another passive, wounded shrug. "I didn't know what you were doing. I didn't want to interrupt if it was something important to you."

It is this *to you* that I hope will sting. I look down at the table.

"Interrupt . . . what . . . what do you . . . *interrupt*?" She stares at me in disbelief. "You knew what I was doing. I told you a week ago. I was at Karen's candle party!"

Candle party? And now that she mentions it, I do remember something about candles . . . I quickly look for refuge from my own guilt, something to be mad about: those candle parties always start at seven, which doesn't explain why she wasn't home for dinner. "All night?" I ask desperately.

Lisa turns away. Hands shaking, she pours herself a cup of coffee, but throws it in the sink, cup cracking in the basin. "It was a fucking candle party, Matt!" She turns to me, eyes red and teary. "You want me to feel shitty about going to a candle party?"

I open my mouth to say something, but nothing comes.

"Because I do! Okay? Happy? I feel awful. I felt awful sitting there with all those women ordering candles and drinking wine and talking about where they were going for the holidays. I could feel their pity, Matt! They were sitting there feeling sorry for me. And do you know why? Because they know I can't even buy a *fucking candle*, because . . . because—" She covers her mouth and cries silently. I sit at the table, staring into my coffee.

We both know why she can't buy a fucking candle.

My mom used to describe Lisa with the best praise she could ever heap on another person. Matty's wife, she would say, now there's a woman who is *put together*. To my mother, the best men were "real gentlemen" and the best women were "put together." Oprah Winfrey? "Put together." Hillary Clinton? "Really put together." My oldest sister's mother-in-law? "Likes to *think* she's put together." And while my dad would scoff (his stripper friend Charity, now there's a woman *put together*, surgically so), Mom merely meant by the phrase that a certain woman was successful, sure-of-herself, composed. All those things Mom believed she wasn't; all those things she wanted to be.

When Lisa went back to work and couldn't find a job, I thought about Mom's pet phrase. And I thought about it again almost a year ago, when—in the fog of *poetfolio.com*—I happened to get the mail and saw a bill from MasterCard. It wasn't the URGENT stamp on the bill that got my attention; while I paid the mortgage, Lisa took care of the monthly bills, and I knew she sometimes mugged Peter to pay Paul. It was the fact that we *didn't have a MasterCard*. We had

Visa. As it turned out, we had both now, and Discover, too, and all three were maxed out. I went out to the garage, where the boxes had been piling up—investments, Lisa called them—and I started opening them, porcelain dolls and commemorative plates and limited edition plush toys. After five or six, I stopped. None of this was secret. I'd seen the boxes. And she'd tried to tell me about the online "business" she'd read about—buying collectibles on eBay, holding them for a few years as their value increased, then reselling them on craigslist (or maybe it was vice versa). Deep in my own delusions, I'd only *pretended* to listen, so I missed the desperation and envy in the way she described people who made a living buying and selling such crap online, and I completely missed the fact that my wife—who, an hour later stood in front of me, weeping *(it just got away from me, Matt)*—was suffering deeply, unsure of her place in the world, of her value, pathologically afraid that the solid man she'd married was morphing into her irresponsible father—and that she felt she needed to do something immediately to take care of herself.

Here's the thing: if you're put together, you can also come apart.

Now Lisa stands in our kitchen, leaning on the sink. She sets her face, shakes her head without looking at me and leaves the room. In the TV room, she offers a flat "Hi Jerry" to Dad, whose voice cracks raspy and urgent, like a man dying of thirst: "I miss chipped beef!"

"I know that, Jerry," she snaps, and then, softer, "I'm sorry." And then Lisa goes upstairs, and after a minute, I hear her gentle, sweet voice in Franklin's room—just a low hum, I can't make out any words; this goes on for several minutes, punctuated a few times by Franklin's voice, first frantic and then high, then low, easier—muffled jazz horn of comfort. Lisa won't make more of this than she should. She's good that way, good with them, a genius of perspective and calm. I know Franklin must feel better, and I feel another rush of jealousy. I want that comfort, that voice. Then I hear her feet pad across the floor upstairs and the toilet flushes and there's more padding and the door opens on the office—my eyes tracing her movements in the lines in the ceiling, as if I could see through the floorboards to the world where Lisa lives now, and then I hear the first, faint clacks of computer keys. *(U will never guess what he did now. . . .)*

I know I should go up there and talk to her. And what? Apologize? Confront her about Chuck? Wait for her to confront me? What do I say? We're in a perpetual blind stalemate here; lost. I can see how we got here—after each bad decision, after each failure we quietly logged our blame, our petty resentments; we constructed a case against the other that we never prosecuted. As long as both cases remained unstated, the charges sealed, we had a tacit peace: *you don't mention this and I won't mention that,* this and that growing and changing and becoming everything, until the only connection between us was this bridge of quiet guilt and recrimination. I don't bring up her insistence on remodeling and her online shopping binge and she doesn't stare across the dinner table and say, *with all due respect, Matt: financial fucking poetry?* And on and on we go, not talking—all the way to the incriminating cheating and weed-dealing mess we're in now.

We're not husband and wife right now; we are unindicted co-conspirators.

It's almost as if Lisa and I *deserve this.* Or believe we do. And I don't think we're alone. It's as if the whole country believes we've done something to deserve this collapse, this global warming and endless war, this pile of shit we're in. We've lived beyond our means, spent the future, sapped resources, lived on the bubble.

Economists pretend they're studying a social science, and while the economy *is* a machine of hugely complex systems, it's also organic, the whole a reflection of the cells that make it up, a god made in *our* image, prone to flights of euphoric greed and pride, choking envy, irrational fear, pettiness, stinginess, manic euphoria and senseless depression. And . . . guilt. Embarrassment. Somewhere a genius economist is factoring the *shame index* into this recession because we want to suffer, *need* to suffer. Like the irritating talk radio host who's been giddily predicting economic collapse for five years, and now is more than I-told-you-so self-satisfied. He actually seems aroused by the specter of soup kitchens and twenty percent unemployment; I'm telling you, the man has a recession boner. Politicians and TV analysts put on leather stockings and whip their own backs like self-flagellating end-times Christians, slathering for payback for profligate spending, for reliance on debt, for unwise loans and the morons we elected, for the CEOs we overpaid, the unfunded wars we waged. We are kids caught lying and stealing: guilty, beaten children of drunks; give us our punishment so we can feel loved, so we can feel *something*.

And Lisa and me? We constructed our trouble, for better or worse, richer poorer, built it out of mistakes and arrogance and yes, at some level, we *deserve* this . . . bottoming out. No other explanation. She deserves an unemployed pothead husband. I deserve a distant, cheating wife.

I stare at the ceiling separating us. She's up there.

I hear the low buzz of the TV in the room next door. Dad sighs.

I could still go upstairs. And what will I see? Lisa on the computer? Or lying in bed, texting him? Is there the slightest chance she'll lift the covers and say, *Matt, don't go out tonight?* Or the awkward silence, avoiding eyes, me shifting my weight, making my lame excuse and Lisa simply shrugging when I say I'm going out for milk for the third time this week?

There are always moments in which a person can stop, cross-roads where you can change course . . . there are those moments . . . until there aren't any more.

I grab my keys.

CHAPTER 16

Welcome to Weedland, Haiku #2

I WANT MY DEALERS
To be smarter than they are;
Welcome to Weedland

"Wake up, Slippers," says a voice I don't recognize. I snap awake.

"Welcome to Weedland!" Jamie says from the backseat. I look out my window and then over at Dave the Drug Dealer, who is driving.

"You have a nice nap?" asks my sidekick Jamie.

"How long was I out?"

"Half hour."

It was oddly relaxing, riding in a car with someone else driving, even if that someone was Drug Dealer Dave and his car was disconcertingly just like my own. We met at Bea's, and since I hadn't slept in days, I started feeling my head bob as soon as Jamie began a story about "this dude in my math class who wants to get an operation to make himself into a chick, but dude says he ain't gay and I'm like, what the fuck you mean you ain't gay, but he insists he ain't gay, he's, like, a woman, and I'm like, 'Dude, until you're a real woman, you are totally a ram-banger, yo,' and he's like: 'But if I've never had sex with a man, how can I be gay?' and I'm like, Dude, whoa! That is kinda freaky . . ."

And the next thing I knew Dave was saying, "Wake up, Slippers."

And I snapped awake here in . . .

. . . Weedland, which exists in the last place I would've ever guessed, a small farming town an hour from the city, on a little road behind the main street of this endlessly dying wheat and mill town—a town which fell on hard times so long ago the people there are actually nostalgic for the *old hard times*. These new hard times? Boring. Wimpy. Back in the old bad days, they ate dirt. But they were happy!

I don't tell Dave that I've been to this little town at least five times before, back when I was a reporter. Off a nowhere, two-lane highway, this little shitburg is close enough to the city that it was one of five or six trusty small towns that served the newspaper staff whenever we needed "rural reaction" to stories. We came to Weedland fairly often (without knowing it was Weedland, of course) to write about *this* agricultural bill's failure or *that* wheat embargo, or *this* local politician's pandering run for office. Sometimes a story just calls for a random quote by some craggy old farmer and there was always a craggy old farmer to quote here, the sons of other craggy old farmers that my newspapers quoted in the hard-times 1970s, the grandsons of old crags we quoted in the hard-times 1930s. Legacies.

Dave parks along a street of plain clapboard houses, just behind the town's main street, which is, appropriately enough, called Main Street. The house we walk toward is situated behind a couple of unlikely Main Street businesses—a camera and watch shop and small engine repair. There are a dozen houses on this block, six on each side of the street. We park behind a red Camaro *(so much depends on a red Camaro)* and I follow Dave and Jamie between piles of leaves up the sidewalk to a simple two-story with a pitched dormer, a hot tub on the side of the house and an old RV with an electrical cord leading to the back door.

Dave rings the doorbell.

A shortish, roundish, twentyish guy in a backward ball cap answers the door, chattering away on a cell phone ("No way . . . She did not . . . Come on . . . Just my brother's friend and some cop . . . No way . . . Come on . . . No way . . .") and after opening the door he steps back without really acknowledging us; he just keeps talking, into infinity ("No way . . . Come on . . . She did not . . . No way . . .") as he pushes through a door and disappears.

"Don't worry about that guy," Jamie confides. "Fat fuck thinks everyone's a cop. I hate that guy." Jamie is wearing his skullcap again, along with a knee-length black coat and a disarming pair of black glasses (he explained that he's out of contacts and his mom switched insurance companies to one that has *totally worthless vision benefits*).

Jamie says again, "Fuckin' *hate* him."

And I haven't known Jamie all that long, but I'm surprised to hear him say he hates anyone. Maybe all skullcaps simply hate all ball caps, some kind of Red America/Blue America, India/Pakistan thing.

I look around the living room of this old house. There are a couple of beer posters and a big map of the world, a bad oil painting of a house in the woods, a couch, two old easy chairs, a TV, a set of World Book encyclopedias and another bookshelf of Reader's Digest Condensed. The carpet is well-worn beige. But for the beer posters, it could be your grandparents' house, everything where it should be, yet there's still something . . . I don't know . . . wrong about it . . . something forcedly random, as if it's been put together for a family melodrama by the set designer of a local theater.

Dave the Drug Dealer bounces on the balls of his feet as we wait for the person we're meeting. Dave's hair is freshly trimmed and gelled and he's wearing a beautiful worsted wool overcoat. I have a wool overcoat almost like it and again, something feels off about that—my drug dealer sharing the same car, same coat? A drug dealer should drive a low-rider Monte Carlo, and wear shark-skin or black satin or velour sweats or something. I officially don't like having a lawyer for a dealer.

We stand a minute longer and, finally, into the room comes the man we've been waiting for . . . and again he's not at all what I expected—even though I don't recall expecting anything. This guy is round and heavy, in his thirties, with a baby face and puff-ball cheeks, thinning blond hair. He's wearing the largest parka I've ever seen, zipped to his tree-stump neck. He's a walking Quonset hut, this guy. Then Big Parka and Dave do an awkward handshake hug thing—heads tilted back, using the soul-shake as a buffer be-tween them.

"How you doin', man."

"Good. You?"

"Oh, you know."

"So." Dave backs away from the hug and . . . presents me. "This is the guy."

I put out my hand and Big Parka takes it with his squishy wet mitt. He gives me a damp handshake and I look up into his ruddy, gentle face. "Nice to meet you, Guy."

"Uh . . . no." I glance over at Dave. "My name's not Guy."

Big Parka looks back at Dave. "You said, 'This is Guy.'"

"No. I said, *the* guy. 'This is *the* guy.' His name's Matt."

"Oh." Big Parka looks sort of horrified at this dealer faux pas. "I thought Guy was like . . . short for Matt."

"How could Guy be short for Matt?" Dave asks. "Who short-
ens a name by going from four letters to three?"

I feel bad for awkward Big Parka, who is in full blush now.
I actually think he might cry. "But . . . it could be a nickname,
right?"

"Dude's nickname is Slippers," Jamie says.

"Oh," says Big Parka. "Look, Slippers. Is it okay if Dave and I
talk alone for a minute?"

I say that of course it's fine. Then Jamie and I sit on the couch
while Dave and Big Parka rumble off to talk in low voices in the
kitchen.

On the couch, Jamie says, quietly, "Dave grew up around
here."

"Really?" It's not that I'm that surprised Dave is from this
town; I'm just surprised that Dave is from any town. Of course he
has to be from somewhere, but you don't expect to end up in the
old neighborhood of your drug broker.

Jamie goes on, sotto voce: "Big dude in the coat's named
Monte. He went to high school here with Dave. Played football to-
gether. You imagine those dudes playing football? Shit, I should've
lived in a small town. I'd have been fuckin' all-state. Definitely
wouldn't have gotten cut in eighth grade. After they graduated,
Dave moved away, went to law school. Monte stayed around here.
This is his grandpa's house."

"Where's Monte's grandpa?"

Jamie makes a kind of bug-eyed face that makes me think
either Monte's grandfather has gone crazy and is in an asylum or
that Monte and Dave have choked him to death.

"Monte got popped on a possession couple of years ago. Dave
got him off and they been workin' together ever since." Jamie nods
toward the kitchen. "Asshole on the cell phone? Monte's brother,
Chet. Real prick. Leeches off Monte, stupid motherfucker. Me 'n

him are gonna go one day. And I can't wait, yo. I'm gonna lay that punk-ass bitch *out*."

Even though this sounds like empty bluster coming from Jamie, I contemplate giving him my effective four-point nonviolence lecture, a version of which I delivered to Franklin earlier (. . . (1) Except in rare cases of self-defense involving hand grenades, violence is always wrong, even against stupid motherfucker punk-ass bitches . . .)

Jamie looks around the living room. "So . . . you're like a businessman *and* a writer?"

"I covered business for the newspaper for eighteen years."

"And you write what, poems and shit?"

"Mostly shit."

"So how'd you get into that? You get, like . . . a degree in it?"

I've been sitting next to Jamie on the couch, but now I turn to face him—gaunt cheeks, straight, dyed-black hair, a stud through his nose and another through his lip and that tattoo wrapping partway up his neck, and at the top, a pair of downturned eyes. My drug dealer sidekick is like any kid venturing a tentative question. He blushes.

I can't help smiling. "You want to be a writer, Jamie?"

He chews his lip nervously and looks down—unsure if my smile means I'm making fun of him. He's embarrassed to aspire to something as low-rent as being a writer.

"I don't know," Jamie says. "I'll probably end up in sales . . . or law enforcement . . . or, I don't know . . . I might be in a band? I'll definitely have to do something else to make some coin." He shrugs. "But yeah, I always thought I'd be a good writer."

Sadly, our career counseling session is interrupted when Big Parka Monte comes back in the room alone. I don't know where Dave has gone. "Come on, Slippers," Monte says. "I want to show you something."

Jamie and I follow him through a rustic kitchen—an open pizza box with half-a-veggie on the Formica table (stoned stock analyst side-note: Domino's Pizza's time-tested delivery platform and low price-point make it a solid recession buy)—to a padlocked basement door. Big Parka produces a janitor's key ring and unlocks the door and we descend (Jamie: "Watch your head, Slippers.") into a paneled rec room with two small window-wells. There's an unlit pellet-burning stove in one corner and a ceiling fan moving the warm air around. It is surprisingly hot down here, stuffy even. On the other side of the room an air hockey table is pushed up against the wall. Big Parka grabs one side of the air hockey table and Jamie grabs the other and they pull the table away. Then Big Parka Monte takes a putty knife and wedges it into a seam in the paneling, pries away a door-sized section, sets the paneling against another wall and steps away to reveal a narrow, yellow-glowing hallway lit with strung Christmas lights along its dirt floor.

"During Prohibition, there was a still down here," Jamie tells me. "Monte's great-grandpa was a rum runner."

I follow Monte down this narrow hallway. It's warm. No windows. There are three small doors off the hallway, each one padlocked. A slender yellow strip of light burns beneath each door. Monte uses his key to open the first door and steps aside as I look in.

Dave is nowhere to be seen; everything he does seems planned in advance for some later testimony: *Mr. Prior, did you ever see my client in the grow room itself?*

I step into the narrow doorway.

I'm not entirely prepared for what I see.

The room is small, maybe ten-by-ten. It's almost unbearably bright. There's a low gurgling hum, the sound of water moving through pipes. Hanging from the ceiling are three banks of hooded lights, like a photographer might use, and the walls are papered in reflective Mylar. Space heaters line the bases of the walls, and temperature and barometer gauges are on the wall nearest the door. In the center of the room, beneath the lights, are what we've come here for: four rows of chest-high counters, each with a pot and rows of large cubes that look like steel wool, each of these cubes connected by plastic water pipes, and rising from each cube of steel wool, like rows of patients on IV's, three dozen of the most glorious dark green hydroponic marijuana plants anyone has ever seen, their stems bursting into ferny leaves and sitting on top, like dirty Christmas tree toppers, gorgeous bursts of purple-green, scuddy buds.

"Wow," I say. There are rows and rows of these top-heavy, budding, dark green plants, and more plants hanging upside down to dry and I recall the old gray ragweed my friend Donnie used to grow and it's like the difference between thoroughbreds and burros. And even though this is what I've come for, there is something vaguely unsettling about this room, like one of those chicken farms where the birds are kept indoors and given steroids to grow their breasts. And the low gurgle of hydroponic tubes connecting the plants makes it seem even creepier, like one of those body-snatcher movies, or the nest of dead bodies in the *Alien* movies. Monte puts a hand on my shoulder. "Come on."

The next room is similar, but with buzzing sodium lights and what Monte tells me is a carbon dioxide generator. And rather than growing in "rock wool," as Monte calls the cubes I saw earlier, these stems emerge from a whitish-gray stuff that looks almost like packing material.

"Shredded coconut," Monte says. "It works great for this kind of plant, but you really have to watch the aphids. I lost a whole crop to aphids one year."

"I see," is all I can think to say.

In the next room, the lights are fluorescent and the plants grow out of a mixture of soil and sponges. "This is incredible," I say. "You must have a botany degree or something."

From the rec room behind us, Jamie calls: "No way, yo. Monte's self-taught. Dude's like a genius, somethin'."

Monte shrugs shyly.

The short hallway ends at a tiny iron door, like the hatch of an old coal furnace. Monte opens it and I peer into a crawl space leading to another glowing passageway. "This tunnel leads to my neighbor's basement," Monte says. He tells me that three basements in this block are connected by these tunnels, that each basement has a secret panel leading to other grow rooms. There are twelve grow rooms in all in his little underground maze.

I think about the craggy old farmers I used to interview about falling wheat prices—and I wonder if any of them lived in these houses with moonshine basements converted into marijuana tunnels. Perhaps they've been growing pot in this maze of basements for decades.

Monte tells me that his brother Chet lives in one of the houses. The other is a rental that he owns and the renters are friends who aren't allowed access to the basement, which is boarded up and padlocked. Monte keeps the rent low and pays the renters' high electrical bills. Every electrical appliance in the houses is the highest efficiency and all of the houses have empty hot tubs or RVs parked outside, in case someone starts sniffing around about the high power bills. Managing power bills is the key to the whole industry, he explains. Drug agents routinely look for big surges in the power grid to find grow operations, so Monte disperses the power bills not only between the houses on this block, but also to the two businesses behind his house, on Main Street: the small engine repair place and the camera and watch shop—both of which can hide higher power bills easier than a residential property.

"So you own those, too?" I ask.

"No, no," he says, "they're just friendly businesses. We run power lines from their shops to a few of the grow rooms. In exchange, I pay double their power bill every month."

"Monte keeps them businesses alive," Jamie says from the doorway. "Dude's like the last industry in town."

Monte's high round cheeks instantly go red; this amateur botanist drug kingpin is so easily embarrassed.

The whole operation is fascinating to me, and yet there's something about all of this that is bothering me, too—and not what *should* be bothering me, that I'm matter-of-factly taking a tour of a sophisticated, *illegal* grow operation. No, I can't help wondering something else.

Monte looks back down the dark hallway. "Come on," he says. I follow him and Jamie back into the rec room. Then Monte closes up Weedland, and we move upstairs.

Dave rejoins us and we sit around the Formica table—Jamie and me on one side, Monte and Dave on the other. Monte's chair strains beneath his considerable weight.

Chet circles back in, still on his phone, and opens the refrigerator again. "Bullshit . . . Come on . . . Not possible . . . It's bullshit, that's why . . . Come on."

I glance over at Jamie, who is glaring at Chet through angry, squinted eyes, like a dog about to pounce.

"Chet!" Monte calls. "What's the matter with you?"

Chet turns to his brother, and shrugs. Then he closes the fridge and moves out of the room onto an enclosed back porch. "Bullshit," he says on his way out. "Come on, no way."

When the door closes, Monte smiles. He rests his big red-raw steak-slab hands on the table. "When Dave and Jamie told me about you, I wanted to meet you right away. Nine grand is an impressive first buy."

"'Course we did a background check on you—make sure you weren't a cop," Dave says.

Monte shifts nervously, as if afraid that I'll be angry at this invasion of my privacy. "We Googled you is all," he says.

Drug Dealer Dave shoots a glance, perturbed at Botany Monte for popping the illusion of an intensive background search. These guys are worse than Lisa and me, with their glances back and forth, their miscommunications, halting awkward affection for one another. "Anyway," Monte continues, "we're excited by your contacts, the new markets you might open up. We've always thought there was a . . . a . . ."

Dave finishes for him. "A demographic we weren't reaching."

Monte glances at Jamie. "I mean, the people we use now are great, but Dave and I always thought there were people outside the usual smokers we know. Older people, people with good jobs and money, people who used to smoke and maybe would again if there was a safe place to buy it. And you're just the kind of guy Dave says would know 'em: Respectable. Not flashy. No criminal record, no reason for the police to suspect you of anything, no tattoos or drug habits or unsavory associations—"

As much as I wish I could stop myself, I can't, and at the words *tattoos, drug habits and unsavory associations*, I glance over at Jamie. He is chewing gum, his neck tattoo twitching at every chomp. He pushes his glasses up on his nose and smiles at me.

"—Like I told Dave, if you can come up with nine grand for a first buy? That's a guy we should be in long-term business with."

"I appreciate that," I say. This all seems oddly formal. "But I should tell you: I'm only going to do this a little while, until I get a few things paid off, get back on my feet."

"Sure," Monte says. "Sure. But—" And then he leans back in his chair and the legs on the chair splay just a bit, gritting on the old linoleum floor. I worry the old chair is going to snap. "Dave, do you want to—"

And with that, Drug Dealer Dave leaves again. This must be when I get my dope.

Instead, Monte hands me a small pipe and lighter and I fire one up, feel that first hot burn in my throat and then the sweet smoke. Ah yes. There it is. Two hits and I set the pipe on the table. I feel better already.

Monte holds out his hands.

I take the envelope of money from my pocket—and feel a tug of regret (there it goes). Monte doesn't count it. The money just disappears in his coat. Then Monte rises, goes to a kitchen drawer, opens it and takes out a quart Ziploc bag (Stoned stock analyst side-note: Watch for SC Johnson and Sons—makers of those popular Ziploc bags—to go public) with a big cigar-sized roll of rich green buds in the bottom. He also removes a baby scale, which he puts on the kitchen table. He sets the baggie on the scale and I see that it's three ounces. Then he hands me the baggie and takes his chair again.

"I need a little time to get the rest of it together," Monte says. "You can't just pull two-and-a-half-pounds off the shelves. And I needed to make sure you actually *had* the money." He shrugs apologetically. "Tomorrow night, you pick Jamie up, come out here and get the rest. That's a little taste. Three ounces. I'll take it out of the two-and-a-half."

"Just enough for your glaucoma," Jamie says, and laughs.

I'm a little confused, and feel stupid that I let them take my money. I wonder if that's why he had me smoke first—to loosen me up. And why'd they have me all the way out here if they were only going to give me three ounces? Why couldn't I wait and pay him tomorrow? I shift . . . there's a hole in my side where that big stack of money sat.

Monte holds the pipe up. "You good?"

I say that I am and he puts the pipe away in that giant file cabinet of a parka. "Put that away," Monte says, and so I put the three ounces of weed in my messenger bag. Then Monte yells, "Dave!" and Dave comes back in with his briefcase again and I think, Oh great, more contracts, but instead he pulls out an envelope that is red-stamped *Confidential*. He slides it across the Formica table to me. "I trust you'll keep this between us."

"What is it?"

"A kind of . . . prospectus. A business plan. The real reason we wanted you to come out here tonight. Now, obviously, you can't take this with you. You have to just read it here."

A prospectus? What kind of drug dealers have a prospectus? I glance over at Jamie. He is unflappable, never looks confused, but also never seems to entirely grasp what is going on around him. Maybe he *should* be a writer.

I look at Dave, and then back at Monte, who has that same tentative, eager-to-please look on his round, red face. He runs bratwurst fingers through his side-parted hair. "Everything you'd need to know is in there."

Then, as I'm still trying to understand, Chet comes back through the room, eternally talking on the phone: "No fuckin' way." He opens the refrigerator and grabs a beer.

"Chet!" snaps Monte again.

"You gotta be kidding," Chet says into his phone, waving his older brother off. "No fuckin' way. You gotta be kidding." And then Chet is gone. I'm actually starting to wish Jamie *would* crack his skull.

I turn back to Dave. "Why do I need a prospectus to buy weed?"

Dave pokes Monte in the big parka. Nods at him.

"There's something I'd like you to consider," Monte says. And

he looks at Dave again. "I'm looking for someone . . . I mean . . .
Ask yourself this: why go on buying milk when you could have
your own cow?"

I look from Dave to Monte. "Because . . . I don't want a cow?"

Dave puts a hand on Monte's arm. "What Monte's trying to say
is that you should think about buying the farm."

I laugh. But they're serious. I look from Monte to Dave, to
Monte again. Yes. They are serious. "I really just want a little milk.
I don't want a cow."

Dave shakes his head. "Look, that wasn't the best analogy. But
you really should consider this . . . it's a once-in-a-lifetime offer."

And I don't know what makes me ask this, maybe the bowl I've
smoked, maybe simple curiosity: "How much?"

"Well," Monte says, a little embarrassed. "I'd like to get four
million."

"Dollars?" And I laugh again.

Dave sits back, crosses his arms. "I don't think you're taking
this seriously, Slippers."

"No," I say, "I'm certainly *not* taking it seriously. No way I'm
going to buy a four-million-dollar drug business."

Monte looks hurt again, those cheeks venting pink. "It's worth
a lot more than that."

And, as I'm thinking of the falling value of my own home,
Dave taps the prospectus in my hands. "After costs, Monte nets
upwards of a million a year. You'd recoup the entire purchase price
in four years. With his old buyers, you increase the market even a
little? You could do two million a year . . . pay it off in even less
time."

I have no idea what to say. What do you say to an offer like
this? You go in to buy a Chrysler and they try to sell you the whole
lot, the whole company? "This is why you had me out here? To try
to sell me your drug business?"

"The four million includes equipment, property, plants, every-thing," Monte says. "And two weeks of transition and training."

"And you're not just buying a business." Dave says. "You get all of Monte's knowledge, his accounts, access to markets. You get an experienced lawyer—me. And Monte will agree to a noncompete clause so you don't have to worry that he'll just go start up another operation somewhere."

I stare at them. They're serious. "Look, guys. Even if I *was* interested, which I'm definitely *not*, I don't know what makes you think I have four million dollars sitting around."

Dave has a quick answer for this. "Monte would carry the contract. I'd arrange it through a foreign bank. You put some-thing down as good faith, say fifteen percent, and after that, Monte gets a percentage of your sales until you pay it off. It would be like making payments, like any home purchase, except rather than paying your mortgage off in thirty years, you could pay if off in four or five. And make a sweet living in the mean-time. Tax free."

"If it's such a sweet living, why is he selling?"

I think Monte might cry. He shoots a quick glance at Dave and then says, "I'm tired," his voice cracking. "I've been doing this six years. It wears on you. It's a young man's game."

Dave puts a hand on Monte's arm. *Don't mess this up.* "It does wear on you . . . but while you're enduring the stress, you can make a lot of money. We've managed to put away well over a mil-lion dollars for Monte's retirement."

It's quiet in the kitchen, long enough for the irony to register: I've been working in the "legitimate economy" for twenty-some years and my retirement amounts to four hundred bucks in the bank and the two-and-a-quarter pounds of knock-off weed I have to come back here tomorrow to pick up.

Monte nods. "I'm going to Mexico. I'm freaked out by the direction of the country. I think we're headed toward global social-ism. This isn't the America I grew up in."

I just stare. The high is descending on me like drawn curtains. I smile. What do you say to a drug dealer afraid of socialism?

Monte shifts in his big parka. "I want to spend the money I've made but I don't want what I've built to fall apart. I'm proud of it." He looks at the door. "Chet wants it, but he'd be in jail two weeks after I left." Monte leans forward to confide in me. "He's kind of a moron."

Jamie laughs.

"Why me?"

"Monte has wanted to get out for a while," Dave says. He shrugs. "He has some stress issues, anxiety attacks."

"I can't sleep anymore," Monte says, and his eyes tear up. "I had a nervous breakdown."

Perfect business for me.

Dave goes on: "So when Jamie told us he met a businessman who could buy real weight, we talked about it, and I said, 'Hey . . . maybe this is our guy. He seems perfect for it.'"

It makes me realize just how low I've sunk in my unemployed funk, that it's actually flattering to hear that I'm perfect for some-thing, anything—even a drug operation. "First of all, I'm not a business*man*. I was a business *reporter*. Look, I never made more than sixty thousand a year in my job."

Monte and Dave look at one another; slight winces.

"And I don't even have a job right now."

"You'll find something," says Jamie. "You're smart."

I laugh and rub my brow, sort of touched by Jamie's confidence in me. "Shouldn't you guys . . . I don't know . . . sell to crimi-nals?"

"You can't just look up the Russian mob in the Yellow Pages," Dave says. "And you can't put something like this on craigslist.

And most of our customers—" He glances at Jamie "—aren't the kind of people who could come up with that kind of money."

I look from red face to red face. Fat Monte: confused, a little paranoid, flushed. Pocked Dave: intent, brewing, scheming. Jamie: chewing gum.

And I think of . . . Lisa. She loves to shop for houses we can't afford. On weekends she used to like going to open houses for two- and three-million-dollar homes. We'd park down the block so they couldn't see we were driving a Nissan and we'd try to look like BMW people, and then we'd walk through these big, grand homes and pretend to be considering whether the indoor lap pool was big enough for our kids (when they came home from boarding school); whether the subzero refrigerator and double Viking commercial oven would work for the gourmet meals our staff prepared for dinner parties with our country club friends. (I'd occasionally crack from the pressure and say something stupid: "I like the double oven; we could put fish sticks on one side and crinkle fries on the other.") Lisa was the master at looking these shit-for-sure real estate agents in the eye, conveying, *You bet your ass we belong.* In fact, she always looks like she belongs. Maybe I just miss her, but I find myself wishing she was with me on this conversation, helping me seem as if I can afford a four-million-dollar grow operation.

I don't know whether I'm afraid of endangering my drug purchase, or hurting the feelings of my sensitive dealers, or whether I want to be the successful businessman they mistook me for—or I'm just high again—but I find myself feigning interest. I pull the two-page prospectus from the envelope. The first thing I see is a kind of quarterly report, including a graph with three bars—sales in blue, gross earnings in black and net profit in green. As a business reporter, I saw enough of these to know a real winner when I see one. That green bar rises above the skyline like the Sears

Tower. I flip to the next page . . . see assets dwarf liabilities and expenses. The return on investment is insane.

Dave leans in over my shoulder. "I know what you're thinking."

I look up into Dave's acne-scarred face.

"You're thinking, too bad we can't take this public."

When he thinks I've had enough time, Dave takes the prospectus from my hand. "Slippers, this is the kind of opportunity that comes once in a lifetime. Ask yourself this: 'Who gets to buy a potential two-million-dollar-a-year business for four million?' You think Jack Welch wouldn't jump at this? Or Warren Buffett?"

And this is when I finally crack . . . go all fish-sticks-and-crinkle-fries . . . burst into laughter. The idea of Warren Buffett owning a grow operation gets me. I can't do the Lisa-at-the-mansion feint, can't pretend this makes sense. I'm too high, too tired, unraveling and I simply don't have it. "Guys, I appreciate you thinking of me, but even if it wasn't crazy . . . fifteen percent down is still, what, six hundred thousand? Look, that nine grand I just gave you, Monte? That's all the money I have. In four days, they're coming after my house. Which bank do you suggest I go to for this? Which bank specializes in half-million-dollar loans to homeless guys looking to buy hydroponic grow operations?"

Monte looks stung. "I know it seems like a lot." Again those cheeks flush. The man is so vulnerable. It's heartbreaking. He is Piggy, Drug Lord of the Flies. "Dave said it might be hard to raise that kind of cash in this economy. Dave thought you might be able to, you know, put together a—" He glances over at his high school buddy "—a contortion?"

"A consortium," Dave says weakly, to his shoes, embarrassed by Monte's slipup.

"Right," says Monte, "a consortium."

I am sitting in front of the most hapless drug dealers in the world. "A consortium," I say, full of sympathy, and again, strangely flattered that—to these guys—I look like the kind of person who could put together a bowling team, let alone a four-million-dollar consortium. "Look guys. I'm going to be absolutely clear with you here. There is no way I'm going to buy a four-million-dollar grow operation—"

"Okay, okay," Dave says, and for the first time I see something else on his face; thin-lipped and arms crossed, he is pissed off. "We get it." He stands and shoves his chair toward the table. And then he turns back. "Three-point-eight?"

CHAPTER 17

In Monte's Fields

In Monte's fields the sweet weed grows
On a basement farm where row by row
    Water courses through plastic tubes
    Feeding unlikely dreams of rescue:
Roughly four million dollars in B.C. bone

Who knows what it is that causes the world to seem benevolent: you rise in the morning and it just feels like something has lifted, some weight. Everything that yesterday looked terrifying today seems benign, maybe even munificent. There's a certain slant of light, or the turning of those red leaves . . . or it could be the last of a good buzz or simple brain chemistry; hard to say. Whatever it is, I sit up on the basement couch curled beneath an afghan—I can't say that I wake, really, since I only slept an hour or so—and my eyes land on a small painting that Lisa and I bought years ago at a little gallery, and for the first time in weeks I feel . . . hopeful. Clear. The painting is the style that Lisa and I both like—not quite abstract but not overtly figurative either, in between: there appears to be a couple standing near a road, and I don't know why I missed it before, but now it's obvious to me: the man in the painting is reaching for the woman.

I walk over and lightly touch one of the squalls of paint on the dry warm canvas—all reds and oranges and browns—and then I climb the basement stairs and glance outside; it's beautiful out there, trees emerging from leafy cover like the bones of an old ship. Dad stirs on the living room hide-a-bed, and I hear Lisa and the boys upstairs, getting ready for work and for school and it sounds so wonderful, so sweet; is it possible to fall in love with your own life?

It's not that I've caught up on my sleep—other than the thirty-minute nap in Drug Dealer Dave's car and a quick hour this morning, I haven't really had any. It just feels as if there has been a slight turn in events, a gentle shift in my direction . . . a clearing, so that I get a glimpse of the other side of this storm.

It certainly isn't Lisa's reaction that cheers me; she turns away on the stairs, as pissed off as I've ever seen her. I was hoping that she'd assume my "sleeping" in the basement was a way of giving her some respectful space. But Lisa is seething—greedily anticipating more space between us. I volunteer to make pancakes for the boys and she wordlessly heads back upstairs to finish getting ready for work. I try to catch her eye as she leaves, to give her a short shrug of apology for ambushing her with guilt last night. She wants no part of me.

And it's not Franklin who turns my mood, either, because he's pretending to be too sick to go to school. "You know what I think?" I ask, pulling a 98.8 digital thermometer from his down-turned mouth. "I think you're worried about seeing Elijah, or that Ms. Bishop will still be disappointed in you. But listen, you have to face your fears, Frankie. You have to look them in the eye and say, 'I can handle you.'" Franklin gives me the first of what will likely be thousands of rolled eyes, and heads upstairs to brush his teeth.

Dad doesn't exactly spread rays of sunshine from his ass, either, when I force him to take a shower and he comes out of the bath-room naked, insisting that someone has stolen his clothes.

No, the evidence of a shift in fortunes isn't there, but I feel a shift anyway. And when Lisa leaves with the boys—still without a word—I stand at the window and watch her back out of the drive-way. She glances up, and this might be the only opening I'll get today, and so I give her a slight nod and a tip of my coffee cup, just a beginning, a first entreaty, and even though my move is firmly unreturned (she looks away) I feel better.

I feel better, because today my long road to comeback begins, because today, rather than just taking all of this shit I have a plan of action. Today, I settle all family business *(so don't tell me you're innocent, Carlo)*.

Today I: (1) Go out into the world and sell the three ounces of weed in my messenger bag to Richard and Amber, and (2) get some names from them and begin compiling my pyramid of future customers. (3) Watch a load of lumber get unloaded in our yard—a clear message to my drifting wife that tomorrow night's "concert" is off, and that, hopefully, no more need ever be said about Chuck Stehne. (3a) (Afterward, I'll call and have the lumber taken back . . . it is not to my liking.) (4) And tonight, go back out to Weed-land with Jamie to get the rest of my dope, so I can (5) get to work pulling my family out of debt.

My phone rings. I look down at the number. Earl Ruscom: "Look, Matt. I'm sorry to call so early, but I felt shitty about our meeting yesterday." Another good thing about Earl: the man loathes small talk. "Offerin' you fiftee' when you expectin' fifty? Sup'm like that'd make me feel like a neutered dog in a bitch fac-tory."

"It's okay, Earl. In this economy . . . starting any kind of busi-ness, especially a publication . . . I really do understand."

"Well, I don't want my editor feeling like a failure on day one. So I ran the numbers again, tightened some shit up . . . and I know it ain't much, but I can go to twenty."

Yes, a very subtle shift . . . "That's very generous, Earl—"

"Naw," Earl says, "it's shit and we both know it. But it's all I got, Matt. Look, even if you just think of it as a thirty-hour-a-week job, if this thing somehow takes off . . ."

I tell Earl that it's still not close to the amount of money I'd need to live on, but "I think I'll probably take you up on it," and he whoops and that's when I get another call on my cell. I hold the phone away to see the number but don't recognize the area code. "Earl, I got a call coming in. Can I get back to you?"

He's still whooping and in the middle of some homespun inanity about kicking one's own ass with someone else's boot when I click over.

A woman's voice. "Mr. Prior?"

Yes.

"This is Joy Addison, with Providential Equity? Gil West asked me to look over your file, and to give you a call." Wait—

Is it possible
that my long-lost lapsed lender
has contacted me?

As lifesaving news must often be, this phone call is simple, matter-of-fact. Joy says that I've been identified as a strong candidate for their mortgage modification program. In the coming days, I'll get an application packet, and then an account specialist will contact me about setting up a new payment plan, with a new rate. In the meantime, if I am found to be eligible under one of several federal assistance programs—if for instance, I've suffered some catastrophic event, say, I've been laid off—Yes, that's me!—

and as long as I have a decent credit rating and no active criminal record—again, me!—then I might also qualify for an interest-free loan so that I can bring my account current and resume making payments. And the payments on that interest-free loan can even be deferred. Of course, I'll still owe what I owe, but with the payments flattened and delayed, I can hopefully get back on top, says Joy Addison. After that, it will be up to me. And if I default, Providential might still have no choice but to file a deed-in-lieu-of-foreclosure.

"Sure," I say, and "No, no, obviously," and "Of course, of course," and "I just want a chance, that's all."

"We all deserve a chance," Joy says and I want to kiss her. I want to kiss Gilbert West. Want to kiss every person at Providential Equity, every person in Benicia, in California, in the United States of America, on Planet Earth.

"I was getting sort of worried there," I say. "Four days . . . you people really know how to take it down to the wire."

Joy ignores this, tells me that a packet will be arriving in the mail, and that I am to fill out the forms, sign them, have them notarized and send them back. And she gives me her direct phone number in case I have questions. I thank her. We hang up, and I immediately call right back and when she answers, "Joy Addison," I pretend that I've accidentally hit the return-call button on my phone, but I'm pumping my fist in the air because *I have my lender's phone number*! Take that, Terminator mainframe! I'm back, baby . . . back!

I stick my head in the living room. "We're gonna make it, Dad!"

He holds up his remote control, bares his old yellow teeth and points at the woman on TV. "How'd you like to plow *her* road?"

"Only if she's got a friend for you, Dad."

He laughs.

"You an' me? There gonna be some world-shakin', boy!"

And I bound up the stairs to our bedroom. Hell, I didn't need sleep. I just needed a break. One or two little things to go in my direction. I can see the way now. I take Earl's job offer and work part time while I augment my income by selling weed. And with the house temporarily safe from foreclosure, I can talk to Lisa, tell her that everything is going to be okay, that the boys can even stay in private school. I can begin the process of winning her back. This is what I've been waiting for, the tiny opening I needed, a message I can send in her *love language*—as our couples' counselor called it. After Lisa's shopping binge, I was mildly resentful about what I saw as her obsession with money and stability. I saw those boxes in the garage as a kind of punishment, a rebuke for quitting my job (and in the process putting our family in danger). I was angry with her, and, frankly, I was terrified that I'd married a shallow, materialistic woman.

Then we saw this couples' counselor, a big sensitive bearded guy who diagnosed us as "two people with very different love languages." Many wives, the counselor explained, share Lisa's love language: the way they feel *most loved* is when their husbands work hard to take care of them, to make the family secure and safe. "And tell me Lisa," the counselor asked, "what's Matt's love language? What makes him feel loved and special?"

Without hesitation, Lisa said, "Blow jobs."

"Many men measure love through physical affection. That's their love language," the unshakeable counselor said. "So, Matt, can we agree that Lisa's desire for financial and familial security is no more a sign of shallow greed than your need for sexual love is a sign of depravity? We're just made differently, don't you see?"

Oh, I see all right.

I glance over at the made bed, Lisa's side slightly rumpled, mine untouched. Jesus, I am so close to getting back in there. Who knows . . . maybe this will be a good thing for us . . . this trouble. Maybe we'll come through this better than before.

On the way to the shower, I stop at the window and allow myself a little math daydream. Let's say I somehow keep turning a fifty percent profit on my weed: roll my nine grand into thirteen five, and roll that into just over twenty and roll that into . . . I take Earl Ruscom's job and this opens another vault of thought: the money that Earl no doubt has sitting around, and just then I glance out the window to see an industrious squirrel doing a little last gathering for his chestnut 401K, and I think that as long as we move we are alive; by hustling, that squirrel and me, we can survive even the hardest winter. And as I start for the shower, for just the briefest moment, the old healthy greed returns, and I wonder if maybe I might not even be *under*selling the potential of this thing. . . .

CHAPTER 18

My Consortium—A Villanelle

How much capital does a consortium need
(I've got four hundred in the bank)
To buy four million dollars in weed?

A thousand jobless reporters give money to seed
(At four hundred per out-of-work hack)
How much capital does a consortium need?

Say a homeless photographer begs ten on the street
(Assuming he doesn't blow it on crack)
He could help buy four million in weed.

A sexy ex–copy editor goes to work on her knees
(At forty-a-hummer and twenty-a-yank)
How much capital does a consortium need?

Newspapers everywhere are dying, indeed
(Even the *Times* reclines in a red bath)
Let's go get that four million in weed.

Success for my syndicate would be guaranteed
If there was just one journalist decent at math
To figure how much our consortium needs
To buy four million dollars in weed.

"I think you're considering it," Ike says, one corner of his mouth going up.

"What? No, I'm not considering it. Who considers something like that? I'm just saying . . . you should have seen this prospectus. I've never seen numbers like that."

"You *are* considering it."

"I swear. I'm not considering it."

"Well . . . maybe you should."

Everyone needs a confidante, that person you tell about the crazy shit you're thinking of doing—as Lisa apparently did when she confided in Dani her plans to go out with Chuck tomorrow night. But I think these confidantes should be the kind of people who talk you *out* of big mistakes, not into them. You have to choose such people carefully—better than Lisa and I apparently have.

My own confidante seems too depressed to be good counsel. "I'm just saying, where else are you going to make that kind of money? Not in newspapers." It seems my old paper has just announced another round of layoffs. It's cruel the way they do it, not whacking people all at once, but every three months—picking us off a few at a time, like kids in horror movies. The cuts this time came all the way up to the reporter hired six months *after* Ike, which means if there's another layoff—and there's always another layoff—he'd be next. "Those of us left," Ike says, "are like survivors in a cancer support group."

"I'm really sorry, Ike," I say, and he looks up at me. Of course, if the cancer support metaphor carries through, then I'm a ghost.

"No, *I'm* sorry," Ike says. "You're the last person I should whine to about this."

"It's fine," I say. We're back at The Picnic Basket, where the morning crowd curls over maple bars and lattes—and where the baristas are two striking women in their early twenties. These girls have no demonstrable skill in espresso-making; they alternate between scalding the lattes, foaming them into oblivion and serving them tepid, but they have two qualities that men our age find unbearably attractive: (1) They are somewhat exotic, with their ratty, box-dyed-hair, their belly-rings, nose-studs and back-tattoos that peek over the low waistbands of their tiny jeans, and (2) they are stunningly uninterested in us.

Ike claims that the owner Marty once told him that the baristas at The Picnic Basket are all former strippers and prostitutes, that Marty's wife Beth has a soft-spot for such women ("and Marty has a hard-spot," Ike added unnecessarily). While it sounds apocryphal, we can't help glancing over when one of them delivers a coffee to the table next to us. Ike sighs.

"You think becoming a weed dealer is such a good career move," I tell Ike, "then let's do it together. What do you say? Want half a grow operation?"

"I would if I didn't have asthma."

"We'd be selling it, not smoking it."

"Yeah, but people are gonna want to try it and you know how I get."

I do know about Ike's debilitating asthma. I also know that he is allergic to wheat and to pet dander and to peanuts and dust and is, all in all, a shambling mess of a man. Our nickname for him in the newsroom was always Bubble Boy. In the old caveman days, we'd have pushed him out of the pack and let the wild dogs get him. Today, Bubble Boy wears the requisite uniform of a news reporter, the outfit of small town city councilmen and strip-mall

insurance agents—reluctant business attire—khaki pants, mis-
matched jacket, a short-sleeved button shirt whose lumpy collar
rejects the badly looped tie like a drunk rejects a liver transplant.
Still, it makes me wistful, seeing—in uniform—a soldier from my
old decimated unit.

"It *is* . . . you know . . . illegal," I tell Ike.

"Yeah, but is it . . . *illegal*-illegal? Isn't it more like wink-wink-
nudge-nudge illegal?" He shrugs. "It's just pot."

"I'm pretty sure running your own grow operation is *illegal*-
illegal. Besides, I don't want to end up paranoid like these guys,
Ike. You should see them. The lawyer's creepy intense. And the
grower? I thought he might start crying at any minute."

Ike swirls the dregs of his coffee and throws it back. Sets his
cup down. "So . . . what *are* you gonna do?"

"For now . . . stick to my original plan. First, go sell this." I
hold up my messenger bag, which is on the chair next to me, and
which contains a baggie with the three ounces I got from Monte
last night. "Tonight, go get the rest of my two pounds. Sell that.
Buy more. Keep going until I'm on top of my debts."

"How long will that take?"

"I made sixty percent on a few hundred bucks this week with-
out even trying, so assuming I can keep selling, even at a fifty
percent profit . . . spread the word . . . keep using the money to
buy more weed . . ." I grab a napkin and sketch out the numbers
for him. "At fifty percent—say I roll my original investment over
four times—nine grand becomes thirteen-five becomes twenty
becomes thirty becomes, what . . . forty-five thousand? That's all
I'd need. Show me another 300 percent profit I can make in a few
weeks."

Ike spins the napkin to see the numbers: 9, 13.5, 20, 30, 45.
"How much is that?"

Below those numbers, I write: 2, 3, 4.5, 6.75, 10 pounds.

He adds it up, scoffs. "You're gonna sell twenty-six pounds of pot?"

"I think so, yeah. From what I've seen, there's no shortage of buyers. I'm telling you, Ike, this thing spreads virally—everyone knows a weed-smoker who can't find any, who doesn't want to buy lawn clippings from his kids' friends, or risk going to jail." This is true. I've already gotten extra orders from friends of both Amber and Richard. "Then, after a month or two . . . I quit with my forty-five grand. Get caught up on the house, pay private school tuition."

"Then what?"

"Then . . . I'll go back to work. I got a job offer . . . sort of . . ."

"From who?"

I say into my coffee cup: "Earl Ruscom."

Ike winces like someone who has just heard that Earl Ruscom had offered his friend a job. "Not his stupid *good-news*paper."

"He's done his homework this time. Problem is, early on, he can't pay much."

"How much is not much?"

"Twenty."

"Twenty?" Ike, on deck for the next layoff, gapes. "Is it that bad out there?"

I channel Earl: "It ain't rainin' silver dollars."

And then a yawn overtakes me and something about it bothers me . . . it's like a deep crack in the plaster . . . and I begin to worry: what if this good mood, this seeming good fortune, the clarity with which I can finally see my way through this trouble, what if it's all just a further sign of my deterioration, some trick of sleep deprivation. . . .

"You okay?"

"Yeah. I'm just tired. Haven't been sleeping much." Or at all—

Ike checks his watch. "Shit, I gotta go." Ike stands wearily. "I'll say this about your new life, Matt. You're the only person I know who has anything to talk about right now other than budget deficits and layoffs and the death of newspapers."

Ike nods at one of the stripper-baristas on his way out; she makes his day by continuing to ignore him. Then Ike sticks his head back in the kitchen, where Marty is making pies and sandwiches for the afternoon rush. I can hear Marty's gravelly, light East Coast accent: "Hey paperboy. How's the news business?"

"Insolvent," Ike says, and with that, he's gone.

I should get going too, but it feels like something is caught in my throat (why should it be so troubling, a simple yawn?). I swirl the last of my latte, drain it and—

"Mind if we join you?"

I look up. Two tall guys loom over the table, the bright ceiling lights behind them. I have to squint to see their faces. One guy is my age, balding, wearing glasses, a sports coat and open-collared shirt. The other guy is younger, with hard-parted brown hair, and a leather bomber jacket over a sweater.

"No, I was just leaving. You can have the table." I start to gather my stuff.

"We don't want to drive you away." The younger guy smiles. "Why don't you sit down with us for a minute, Matthew?"

Oh shit. Shit, shit. Cops. Anyone who ever worked as a newspaper reporter can spot cops. Especially when there are two of them; in pairs, they give off a vaguely threatening Kafkaesque civil servant vibe.

No, I tell myself, don't be paranoid. They're not cops. It's this season of paranoia, that's all. No reason to think they're cops.

They sit and I get a better look at them. The older one—shiny head, half-smile and glasses, the toughest accountant at the firm—slides a card forward. The card has a shield on it.

Yep. Cops.

Shit shit shit.

They smile.

I clear my throat. Pick up the card. Greg Reese. Lieutenant. State Police. Coordinator, Regional Drug Task Force. Shit shit shit shit.

The younger guy is one of those people who smiles for no reason. He picks up the napkin I have set down. He shows it to the older one. "Ten pounds? Of what?"

"Concrete," I say. My face flushes. "For my driveway."

"Come on." Lt. Reese frowns. "You're paving a driveway with ten pounds of concrete?"

"Patching it."

I nonchalantly reach over to my messenger bag, on the chair next to me, and lower it to my sweating, twitching feet. Inside that bag, next to the empty journal that I began *not* writing in when I lost my job, sits a Ziploc baggy with three ounces of what I hoped would be the first blocks of my pyramid of wealth, my recovery, my last hope, three ounces of recently harvested grade-A knock-off B.C. bud. I slowly scoot the bag away with my foot.

"Hey man, you okay?" asks the bald one, Lt. Reese. He must be the good cop.

"Fine." Okay, think: (A) They would need a warrant or something, wouldn't they, some kind of cause before they arrested me? (B) And how could they possibly know? (C) They can't just search people (can they?). (D) Don't panic. (E–I) Deny, deny, deny, deny, deny. (J) Yes, nothing to worry about. (K) Don't give them permission to search your bag. (L) Don't panic. (M) Stop panicking.

"I'm gonna get some coffee," says the younger one, still with that inane cult smile. "You want some, Matthew?"

"No. Thanks." My heart beats in my temples. "I gotta get going."

Most suspects make their mistakes in the first five minutes. Be coy. Quiet. Reserved. Wait, did I just think of myself as a *suspect*? Shit, shit—

"You don't remember me, do you?" Young Cop asks.

(N) Don't talk unnecessarily; guilty people ramble.

I shake my head no.

"You work for the newspaper, right," he says through those perfect white teeth. "I was media liaison officer for the SWAT Team. We busted this big meth house and burglary ring a couple years ago? You interviewed me. I think you must've been working a weekend shift or something. You wrote it up in the Sunday paper. My mom has the story framed on the wall, that's why I remember. I can still see your byline. *By Matthew Prior. Staff Writer.*"

"Oh . . . yeah . . . sure," I say, even though I don't remember.

And a wave of relief washes over me. That's why he called me Matthew. My old byline. (For a while, it was all the rage in my newsroom to add an initial, *New York Times* style, to the front of our bylines, I was R. Matthew Prior.) Of course! These guys aren't here to arrest me—how could they possibly know what's in the bag? They're just cops in a donut shop, that's all. They've just recognized me from my reporter days. I smile.

Still, this close call, this scare, has taught me a lesson. That's what my yawn was—a gentle warning. So that's it for me. I'm done selling pot. Too scary. I take a deep breath. Smile like the young cop. "So . . . how did I do on your story?"

"Oh, you did great," the young cop says. "Got everything right. You still at the paper?"

I can feel myself relaxing. "No, I took a buyout."

"I read about the layoffs there. It's crazy, what's happening to newspapers." Young cop shakes his head again and turns to older cop. "Can you imagine a world without newspapers?"

"Happily," says the older cop.

Then the young smiler turns back to me: "So what are you up to now—"

"Other than being a drug dealer," interjects the older, bald one, Lt. Reese. His voice is flat, chilling. He is staring at me. No . . . he's staring *through* me.

"Wha . . . what?"

Lt. Reese leans forward. "Maybe we should look in that backpack you keep pushing away with your feet . . . *Matthew*."

I feel my jaw trembling.

"You sure you don't want some coffee?" the younger guy asks.

And all I can think is: Huh, so they really *do* play good cop/bad cop.

So young cop gets me coffee. And for the next few minutes, I try not to vomit as I listen to gruff old state cop, Lt. Reese, and grinning young city cop, whose name turns out to be Randy Martinez, explain that: (A) For the past four years, they've worked together on a federally funded drug task force charged with infiltrating and breaking up the pipeline of British Columbian marijuana that has flooded the West. (B) Near the end of this very successful four-year tour, they arrested a suspect who, hoping to avoid prosecution, became a CI—a confidential informant—and told them about a quaint little farming town where a local grow-op wunderkind and his skeezy lawyer friend managed to shave off a slice of the legitimate smoke market with their home-grown knockoffs. (C) And while it's not in the task force's direct mandate to break up baby grow-ops like this—they would normally just turn such information over to local police—this one was big enough to warrant their attention.

"So here we are, all ready to make a case against this farm," says young Randy, "and who should come along?"

I'm pretty sure it's me, but my voice is too weak to contribute to this conversation, and anyway, I'm still half-afraid I might throw up if I open my mouth. My hand twitches around the coffee that Randy has gotten me. I just shake my head.

"Some asshole takes a verbal shit all over our wiretap," says old Lt. Reese, "bragging that he can sell weed to middle-class fat-fuck hypocrites like himself."

I don't remember bragging that, but I'm not really in the position to deny my middle-class fat-fuck hypocrisy.

The young cop reminds me of someone as he puts out his hands soothingly. "Here we've been working four years to bust a bunch of kids and . . . what? Now their parents want in?"

Lt. Reese's turn: "I just wanted to sweep you up with the other losers, but Randy here says, wait a second, I know this guy. He's not a bad guy."

I look gratefully at Young Randy: No! Not a bad guy! Good guy! If only they could get to know me . . . I used to give so much to United Way.

"Here's what I said," Randy jumps in. "Lieu, this guy, he's no drug dealer.' "

I shake my head no. I'm not.

"I said, 'In fact, maybe we should talk to this guy. I think he has goodness in his heart.' "

I do. Good heart. Goodness.

Old cop rolls his eyes. "Tell me something. You got kids, Matthew?"

Before I can answer, young cop asks, "What ages?"

And for the life of me, I can't remember. "Uh. Ten? And, uh . . . the little one . . . eight?"

Old cop: "Boys? Girls?"

Young cop: "One of each?"

Me: "Boys?"

Young cop: "Bet they're cute."

Wait. I know this one. Nod.

"I don't know." Old cop, sighing, turns to his partner: "I gotta be honest, Randy. I'm not feelin' it. You sure you wanna give this asshole a break?"

Yes, please. Break. Break, please.

"Lieu—" Randy starts to plead my case. Even when he frowns he smiles.

But Reese wants none of it. "It's fucked up, Randy. This is what's wrong with our country, this lack of responsibility. Drug dealer dads? Cokehead in the White House?"

Randy looks at me apologetically. "I don't think Mr. Prior here is interested in our political views, Lieutenant."

Lt. Reese turns back to me. "Matthew, you have any idea how deep a pile-a-shit you're standing in?"

I look down at my feet to see the shit and my messenger bag.

Randy puts his hand on Lt. Reese's arm, maybe trying to lighten him up. "What've you got in there, Matthew, two ounces?"

"Three." My voice is a low death-rattle. Wait—what happened to B. through N.: coy, quiet, *deny, deny, deny, they have to have a warrant? Be quiet.* Wow. I'm bad at this.

Both cops sit back, maybe a little embarrassed. It's probably not supposed to be so easy.

Lt. Reese shakes his head. "It's the hypocrisy. That's what's so offensive."

He's right, of course. I look down. It's the same move Franklin makes when he's in trouble, and I picture myself in handcuffs, my boys watching the police haul their father away. My head falls into my hands.

"Hey," says Randy. "It's gonna be okay."

"Give me a break," says Lt. Reese. "We're fifty fuckin' miles from okay here, Randy. Don't sugarcoat it for this delusional fuck-stick."

Delusional fuck-stick—right. Amazing, how you can misjudge everything, how blind you can be to the truth. The ways you fool yourself. Believing something has shifted, that the world can be benign. No, this is what it means to come apart—not gently unraveling, but blowing out, a tire on the freeway.

I have been wrong about everything.

For instance, I was so sure the older one was going to be the good cop.

CHAPTER 19

Ah Yes, Now It's All Coming Together—Haiku #3

STARTING TO SEE WHY
Monte wanted to sell me
His bammy business

The Regional Drug Task Force office turns out to be within walking distance of the coffee shop, behind a door marked "R. Thomas—Clinical Social Worker/Therapist, MSS, LICSW," on the first floor of a nondescript downtown office building overlooking the river, across the hall from an insurance company. We sit in a conference room that looks like it recently hosted a corporate brainstorming retreat, a white board covered in various numbers in columns below the phrases "Potential Funding" and "FY '09-'10," and I think this white board could be from any business strategy session, but of course, it's not. It's a task force set up to arrest drug dealers.

Like me. My coy strategy gone now, I spill it all . . . how I've been under financial stress, how I found myself getting high for the first time in years, bought a little, then realized I knew other people who would buy weed, how I went out and visited the farm and gave Monte nine thousand dollars, but didn't get my pot, how Monte tried to sell me the whole operation. The cops don't say much, but nod approvingly a few times. Then I open my backpack and—hands shaking—remove the three ounces of bud and hand it to Randy, who goes off to weigh and photograph it. I watch him take a small sample, which he seals in a Ziploc baggie; then he puts the rest of my weed back in my messenger bag. During this, Lt. Reese has me initial some sort of requisition form that I probably should read before signing.

"So much paperwork," I mutter.

"I suppose that shithead had you sign his stupid contracts," Reese says. "He knows we're closing in. More nervous he gets, the more worthless contracts he prints up. That's probably why you only got three ounces yesterday, because Eddie was there."

I think: who's Eddie?

Randy says, "He's doing everything he can to keep this in state court, keep the feds out."

I shrug. No idea what any of this means.

Lt. Reese is getting tired of explaining things to me. "Three ounces? Well within the state limit for medicinal use? See, you'll never get weight with Eddie around. The medicinal dodge is bullshit, but it'll give his lawyer something to argue."

"Who . . . is Eddie?" I finally ask. "Do you mean Dave?"

Lt. Reese spews contempt. "You have no idea who you're dealing with, do you, fuck-nuts?" From another file, he hands me a photocopy that includes a mug-shot of Drug Dealer Dave, identifying him as "Edmund David Waller Jr.," AKA "Eddie Waller" AKA "Dave Waller."

My mouth goes dry. Dave is an *Also Known As*? I tend not

to have a lot of dealings with aliases. "He . . . he said he was a lawyer."

"He *was* a lawyer. For about an hour. Worked for an old hippie firm defending drug dealers. But the bar tends to look down on psychopaths with multiple convictions."

Psychopath? Multiple convictions? My eyes drift toward the Arrests and Convictions part of this rap sheet. Indeed, Eddie-Dave has two convictions—misdemeanor possession of a controlled substance almost a decade ago and misdemeanor assault—but he's been charged two other times, once for intimidation seven years ago, a charge that was dropped, and another charge that, according to this sheet, is still pending—vehicular manslaughter?

Drug Dealer Dave? Assault? Intimidation? Manslaughter?

Lt. Reese sees me swallow. "You think this is the fucking PTA you're dealing with?"

I say, weakly, "He did ask to look up my ass."

Randy and Lt. Reese make uncomfortable eye contact.

Lt. Reese takes the file from me. "The assault charge was on a twenty-two-year-old female. The intimidation came about when he tried to . . . convince someone . . . not to testify against him."

"And the manslaughter charge?"

Lt. Reese hands me a black-and-white photograph . . . a roadside somewhere . . . with a lump of clothes . . . or—

"Is that . . . a dead body?"

"It ain't a pile of leaves. Dave doesn't like leaving anyone around to testify."

I think I'm going to be sick. "Wait. He ran over this person to keep them from testifying? Is that what you're saying? Why . . . why wasn't he charged with murder?"

Lt. Reese rips the photo from my hands. "Eddie's a lot of things, but he ain't stupid."

My head's swimming. "What about Monte?"

"Oh, *he's* stupid," says Randy.

"No, I mean, is he dangerous?"

Lt. Reese leans in. "Wake up, fuck-stick! Who do you think these people are?"

"Come on, Lieu," Randy interrupts. Then to me: "Monte has no violent priors."

After a second, Lt. Reese sits back and nods. "Yeah, Monte's a tool. Mildly autistic. Does whatever Eddie tells him to. Parents died in a car wreck when he was fifteen, lived with his crazy old grandfather, raised that dipshit little brother of his. This whole deal is really Eddie's; he uses poor Monte like a shield. That's what Eddie looks for—people to insulate him. Everything's in Monte's name. Monte does all the work, takes all the risk. But now he wants out. That's why Eddie wants you in. 'Cause he needs a new shield."

Randy steps in. "When we finally arrest him, Eddie will try to pull out his contracts and claim he never was around more than the medicinal amount . . . that he never had it in his possession, that he simply worked as Monte's lawyer."

I look back at Eddie-Dave's rap sheet. "I had no idea."

"See, this is what pisses me off!" Lt. Reese stands up, his face red. "You old pot-head baby-boomer shit-bags thinking, *it's just marijuana. No one gets hurt. Let's smoke a reefer and go bomb the ROTC building!* Well, fuck you!"

I start to say that I wasn't going to bomb anything, but before I can—

Lt. Reese waves me off and stands. "I gotta get some air." He storms out of the room, although something about his eruption seems vaguely Arthur Miller-ish.

"Okay," says Randy quietly. He leans forward, and I think maybe his smile means no more than a dog's does. "Let's figure out how we're going to get you out of this."

Wait. I know this: Mark Akenside, the salesman at the Nissan lot! Lisa and I had gone in to buy the more modest Altima but Mark kept glancing over at the sleek, gunmetal Maxima, with its sunroof, spoiler and heated seats. We can't afford that, I said. Sure, Mark said, and *why should you spend more . . . after all, the Altima's a great little car . . . but what if I could get you the top-of-the-line Maxima for virtually the same price?* Then Mark wrote a number on a sheet of paper that was definitely *not* the same price as the Altima. *But,* I said, *that's a much higher price* and Mark turned the paper toward himself and wrote a slightly smaller figure, and he kept doing this, coming down a few hundred bucks each time, saying, *Work with me here* and *I'm doing all I can for you here* until *here* was only two thousand higher than the Altima and Lisa and I would have confessed to being domestic terrorists to get out of that room. I said, *Fine, we'll take it,* and Mark dragged us into a room with his manager, whose job was to close the deal as Mark went out *for some air,* just like Lt. Reese did—though less angrily—and the manager did everything he could to pump that number back up (thus my redundant service contract and winter floor mats) and we left having paid more for the Maxima than the first number Mark wrote down.

Randy slides a piece of paper in front of me. It has a seal and a chart and what appears to be a mission statement on it.

"We are a federally funded task force working in conjunction with the DEA," Randy says in perfect loan-closing voice. He takes the page back before I can read it. He replaces it with a page that has a graph with FEDERAL SENTENCING GUIDE-LINES. "Because of that, our mandate is a little different than, say, your local drug unit. We're about big fish, so our focus is on intelligence-gathering as much as enforcement and prosecution. But that doesn't mean we turn our backs on dime-bag buyers. Make no mistake about it; we *will* take down the little fish. Like you?" He runs his finger past the steeper crimes and sentences until

he arrives at mine. "Three ounces? Intent to deliver? You're look-
ing at a year and a fifty-thousand–dollar fine. But sometimes . . ."
He pretends to look up to make sure Lt. Reese isn't in the room.
"We can let a little fish wiggle off a hook if it means getting a
bigger one. Now, you're probably thinking . . . what constitutes a
big fish?"

I nod as if that's what I was thinking.

He points a few slots up the sentencing guidelines to 100 kilos
or 100 plants. Then his finger goes to the mandatory sentence:
twenty years. "I'd guess right about now you're thinking: Gosh,
these guys have me over a barrel. Well, ask yourself what would
happen if we'd waited and arrested you tomorrow, when you had,
what, two pounds?" He points to a column that ends with five
years in prison and a $100,000 fine. "So ask yourself, why would
we do that? What do we gain by keeping you from becoming a
big fish?"

Small fish make better bait?

Then a new page appears, a spreadsheet that reminds me of
Monte's business prospectus. "You were a reporter," Randy says.
"So I'm gonna be straight with you. There's an institutional side to
all of this." He points to the bottom line, the *operating budget* on this
spreadsheet: $1.18 million. "We're at the end of a four-year bud-
getary period, and the lieutenant and I are charged with coming
up with a budgetary proposal and rationale for why, with all the
cuts we're facing, regional drug interdiction remains a priority.
We're setting goals for the next biennium, and our primary target,
the trend we're seeing out there . . ."

And now he looks at me. ". . . is indoor domestic grow op-
erations. So you're probably thinking, 'That's all fine, Randy, but
where do I come in?'"

I don't mind someone telling me what I'm thinking. It's nice.

Randy's budget disappears and taking its place is a flow chart of drug prosecutions for the last two years, in both state court and federal court.

"Those big fish I talked about, they end up in this pond." He points to federal court. "The little fish we just turn over to local police and prosecutors. That puts us in a unique position. We can . . . overlook some of these cases. See, Matthew? We're not compelled to turn over all of our little fish." He holds up my file folder. "These files can remain sealed. They can even just . . . go away. Do you understand what I'm saying?"

I nod.

He smiles gently. "Good." He takes a deep breath. We are apparently through some number of steps. "Now, it probably feels like you don't have any choice here."

I nod.

"I hate that. I always ask the Lieu, why do we back people into a corner this way?" He shakes his head, as if he's sorry for all of this unpleasantness. "I mean . . . what's the point if we don't give people a choice? By the way, I like that name . . . Matthew. It's Biblical."

I nod. Don't tell him I'm named after my dad's drunk-a-day brother.

"Listen, Matthew," Randy says. "Do you know Jesus feels the same way, that he doesn't like backing people into corners either?"

"Jesus?"

Randy nods. "Why else would He give us free will? He could make us robots. But He wants us to *choose* to be good. Our good works are empty if we don't choose them." Then Randy looks up at the door, to make sure his lieutenant hasn't come back into the room. It occurs to me that he might be off-script here. He speaks quietly: "Remember, before, when I talked about big fish and little fish? Do you know who else was a fisherman?"

I take a stab: "Jesus?"

The Up-With-People smile returns. "That's right, Matthew. Metaphorically, Jesus was a fisherman. And his disciples were *actual* fishermen, many of them plying the seas of Galilee. They all came to work for that great fisher of men, Jesus."

Oh. My good cop is a born-again Christian. Sure. Randy nearly whispers: "Matthew, have you accepted the Lord Jesus Christ as your personal savior?"

"Well," I say weakly, ". . . I've been thinking of becoming Catholic."

Randy looks stung. "I'm afraid that's a false doctrine . . . not His true church." He puts his hand on his heart. "But at least you're looking for something deeper. If your heart is genuinely open, Jesus will find His way in. Don't worry. Now watch closely. I want to show you something."

And he suddenly raises the slender criminal file he's created on me—the sample of weed and whatever form I just signed—higher and higher it goes above the conference table . . . and then he tosses the whole thing into a garbage can, which I hadn't seen before, but which seems perfectly placed for this display. "Those are your sins, Matthew. How does that feel?"

"Uh . . ." I stare at the garbage can. "Good?"

"Did you know it can be as simple as that?" He leans in, practically whispers. "Jesus doesn't want anyone in heaven who doesn't want to be there. And we don't want anyone on our team who doesn't want to be *here*."

I stare at my file in the garbage can. For the first time in my life I understand the power of religion. What if you could take all of your trouble, put it in a file folder and throw it away? Maybe the Catholics have a big sin Dumpster outside the Vatican.

"Matthew, don't you want to choose to do the right thing,

on your own, without being motivated by the threat of punish-
ment?"

"Yes?"

"Excellent. So tell me, which do you choose? The darkness?
Or the light?"

"The . . . light?"

"Yes." He smiles beatifically. "Good," he says. "Good. I thought
you might say that. I told the Lieu I had a good feeling about you."
And then he pulls my file from the garbage can, smiling—as if
we both know he couldn't *really* throw my file away. He puts the
folder on top of the conference table, and he pulls out a little tray
and a sheet of paper from below the table, and says, "Welcome to
the righteous side, Matthew!"

Randy takes my hand and pushes my thumb down on the desk
between us, and I imagine this is some bizarre rite of initiation,
but of course he's just fingerprinting me. "Just in case," he says,
and he winks, and I think, *just in case*, what? Just in case I decide
not to cooperate, or I do it wrong and they have to prosecute me,
or just in case they need to identify the hands that Eddie-Dave the
legalistic and brutal drug lord has whacked off after discovering
that I'm a snitch? "And let's keep your pending salvation between
us," Randy says, and he winks.

Then Lt. Reese comes back in with another round of paper-
work for us to fill out; these appear to be more like employment
contracts. All in all, they are extremely efficient, smiley righteous
Randy and shit-heel Reese. This whole scare-the-poor-bastard-
into-working-for-us (and-save-his-soul-while-we're-at-it) process
has taken just over an hour, less time than it took me to buy my
car, or my house, less time than it took to meet with Drug Dealer
Eddie-Dave the first time. And not once has anyone tried to look
up my ass.

My shattered nerves begin to calm. Maybe this is one of those classic good news-bad news situations. Good news: I have a job! I am a confidential informant. Lt. Reese explains that there are two kinds of CIs—(1) lifelong criminals who get arrested and charged and who cooperate to eventually lessen their own long sentences (these CIs tend to make imperfect witnesses because of their long criminal records and penchant for lying) and (2) basic non-criminals like me, who tend to make better witnesses because they tend not to have . . . oh, for instance, killed someone. Some CIs even get a taste for it and work as paid contract agents, like professional undercovers. "You can even get paid," Lt. Reese says.

"How much?" I ask, a little too eagerly.

Lt. Reese admits that it's not much—there are federal guidelines governing it—but that agencies are allowed to award bonuses after successful prosecution. My new handlers explain that as long as I'm honest with them, do what they say, follow the rules—I'll be the latter sort of CI. They'll try to get me paid and no one need ever know how my employment came about.

And the bad news? Lt. Reese holds up the file that was, until a few minutes ago, safely in the garbage can. "Fuck around on us one time, you shit-sack, and we'll charge you with possession with intent to deliver." During this part, I notice, Randy won't meet my eyes.

Then Lt. Reese explains that the paperwork I've just signed stipulates that I have agreed to: (A) work as a CI, infiltrating domestic grow operations by posing as the point man for a consortium planning to purchase and run said grow-ops (B) continue purchasing and selling marijuana in this grow-operation for a period of two (2) years as a part of the task force's program, Operation Homeland (C) meet once a week with my handlers, Randy and Reese, advising them of what I've learned and any new targets of the investigation, including all of my unsuspecting bud-buying friends, or as Lt. Reese calls them, "fat-fuck hypocrites like your-self."

So tired. My head bobs. "So I'll be wearing a wire?"

Randy and Lt. Reese make eye contact. "Yes," Randy says. "We'll eventually put a trap-and-trace on your phone, maybe a wire in your car." And then he proceeds to lecture me about some-thing official-sounding, but I'm having trouble following it, and pick up only snippets, random phrases: "Title Three . . . Omnibus Crime Control and Safe Streets Act . . . wiretap warrants . . . our mandate . . . the transportation of narcotics over international bor-ders . . . wiggle room under The Patriot Act . . ." And then Randy holds out a box. "In the meantime—"

I take the box. Open it: wristwatch. "Retirement gift?"

Stern look. And I think of something Lisa said once—"It's not that you're not funny but your timing is so awful"—after my sister got divorced and I asked for the wedding present back.

"This is a self-contained unit," Randy says, "safer than a body wire. Has one gig of memory, twelve hours of recording time. It's voice activated, so that when it's on, it kicks in as soon as someone speaks. When it's recording, this backlight is on. See? When it's not, it's dark. Easy. You know how I remember?" He holds up the dark watch. "Darkness . . ." Then he presses the button so that the faint backlight comes on. ". . . and light."

Lt. Reese looks at the ceiling.

"Most of the time it should be off," Randy says, "so just hold the knob down for two seconds and it'll go dark." I put my wrist out and Randy slides the watch on me. "It has a wireless transmit-ter, but we haven't figured out how to use that yet, so for the time being you'll need to drop it off and we'll download the files and reset it."

He slides a business card to me: R. Thomas—Clinical Social Worker/Therapist, MSS, LICSW. "You tell your friends and family you're seeing a therapist every Tuesday afternoon. If it's an emergency, you call this number, you'll get a voice saying this is Dr. Thomas's office. You say you need an appointment. Got any questions?"

I have so many. . . . "When do I start?"

"Wake up, fuck-chop," Lt. Reese says. "You started the second you unzipped that backpack. Now get out there and buy us that grow-house."

Randy nods apologetically. "The number we're assigning you is OH-2. On all reports, all contacts with us, you use that number, CI OH-2. Can you remember or should I write it down?"

"CI . . . OH-2."

"Good. From now on, you only use *our money*. We'll requisition the cash and you bring back whatever you have left. On Tuesdays, we'll inventory whatever cash and drugs you've got, take your reports, and send you back out for the week. The most important part of this job, like most jobs, is record keeping."

Lt. Reese steps in again. "And listen, jack-stick, if we catch you with more pot or more money than you've recorded . . . you're goin' to jail. Mess up my record keeping, leave anything out, steal five cents, misplace one fuckin' bud, you're going to jail."

"Okay."

"And no more smoking that stuff," Randy says quietly.

Ouch. I nod. Stand. Sigh.

The detectives lean back in their chairs, big men after a big meal.

"Right now, this must be hard to stomach, but I hope you feel proud," says my grinning born-again handler Randy, kindly assuager of hurt feelings. "You're working for the good guys now, helping to protect kids like yours—"

Then Lt. Reese, sensei of hard reality, interrupts: "—from drug dealers like you."

CHAPTER 20

Stopped by Wood on My Front Lawn

W<small>HOSE WOOD THIS IS</small> I think I know
Blocking the path to my front porch
Sent by the asshole stealing my wife
Sure it is, of course, of course.

Oh, I'm done. I slump against the steering wheel. The world looked so clear this morning, so warm. But it's the same cold, hard world. I pull out the card Randy gave me. I know there is some debate over the effectiveness of various types of therapy, but I'm not a fan of my psychologist, Dr. Thomas's methods so far. I suppose I'm not really in a position to bargain, but I wish I could get a little real therapy from my phony therapist.

I feel feverish. Sick. Tired. Think I'm losing my mind. What do you do when you can't even put your various soul-crushing crises in any rational order? Is it: 1. I'm now a drug-dealing snitch sent out to entrap my friends? 2. My marriage is crumbling, my wife about to have an affair, (2a. And my lame response is to order the material for a tree fort from her boyfriend.) 3. I'm unemployed, broke, and even with the short reprieve on my house, deep in debt. Or is the order: marriage crumbling, drug dealing, going broke. Or broke, drugs, marriage.

I suppose it's a judgment call. And now, paralysis seems to have set in. Where would a complete physical breakdown fit in with my various crises? I sit in my car, arms dead at my side, leaning against the wheel, mouth slack, staring at the eleven hundred dollars in lumber on my front yard. It looks small from here; amazing how little wood you get for a grand these days.

Maybe I should go inside and see if I can smoke myself to death on three ounces of marijuana. Can you OD on pot? Maybe I can get so high I choke to death on a Dorito. I picture Lt. Reese showing my corpse photo to the next poor sap they arrest. *It ain't a bag of leaves.*

My cell rings. It arrives at my face in a quivering hand. Amber Philips. Here we go. Amber must want her weed. I put my thumb on the answer button. But it makes me sick, getting poor Amber in trouble like this. Is this really what I've become? I look from my phone to my dark super-spy watch. Okay, undercover operative— what now? I try to remember . . . Randy said something about protocols . . . warrants . . . cell phone traps. Do I answer the call? I suddenly feel so unprepared. Wish I'd paid more attention.

And then, through the windshield, I see the front door of my house open. And out comes my senile old father, staring suspiciously at the pile of wood. These days, Dad doesn't like any change in his physical environment. He edges over nervously. He's wearing his pajama bottoms and a Go Army sweatshirt. He has his battle-ready remote control in his hand.

I set my buzzing phone down and climb out of the car. It's cold outside; steam leaks from my nose and mouth. "Hey, this all goes back, Dad. This lumber, it was a big mistake."

Dad says nothing, simply pulls the work invoice from the top of the pile, where it's been stapled. It's in a plastic envelope, along with the folded plans for the tree fort. I gently take the invoice from him. There's a signature from the delivery driver, but it's not LumberChuck's. Great. I didn't even get Chuck to deliver my tree-fort wood so that he could see the home he's wrecking. Christ, what's a mad genius to do when none of his mad plans works?

I look up at my father, who has his own mad-genius thing going—wild, gray hair, vacant eyes. I think of asking his advice, but even when he was sharp, Dad wasn't exactly an expert in the advice department. He almost always deferred to my mother for pep talks, lectures and philosophical discussions. He'd probably be the first to admit that cheering up his children wasn't a particular parental strength for him—like when I was thirteen and got cut from the eighth grade baseball team. It's okay, I remember my mom saying; over and over she said this: *it's okay, it's okay, it's okay.*

"But it's not *fair*," I cried.

"Damn straight!" I heard a gruff voice, and looked over at the table, where my dad had set down his newspaper. "What do you say we go kick the ass of whatever sorry son-of-a-bitch told you it would be?"

My father did pass on plenty of wisdom, of course, a lot of it incidental, like other men from his generation, hints and clues glimpsed through his unfailing work ethic and his refusal to ever complain about anything. No matter what happened, the man soldiered on—got up every day and put on that tie and went to a job he knew was beneath his abilities—and anyone who thinks there's anything more profoundly inspiring than that is fooling himself. I wouldn't mind talking to that old clear-eyed Sears tie-and-coverall father of mine again. Or better, I wish I was five again, that he'd take my little hand and pull me up on his lap. But we stopped hugging at the time Prior men have presumably stopped hugging for hundreds of years, right around ten or eleven. Teddy, for instance, is out of the embrace business. Franklin: still in for another year or two. I wonder why I can't hold Teddy, why my father and I can't hug.

My dad used to be bigger than me but I'm standing next to him and I'm looking down on that wild hair. His shoulders are thin and drawn in.

"Dad," my voice cracks. "I need . . . help. I'm falling apart here." And my dad turns and looks at me—and I hear his clear old deep voice, *Damn straight*—and a kind of epiphany begins to form in my mind—

It's all connected, these crises—marriage, finances, weed dealing—they are interrelated, like the physical and mental decline of my dad, and my own decline, like the housing market and the stock market and the credit market. We can try to separate them, but these are interrelated systems, reliant upon one another, broken, fucked-up, ruined systems.

It's the same world, the same clear, cool place I woke up to—both sunny and cold.

And just like that . . .

A plan. "Hey Dad?"

He turns.

I laugh, probably a little crazily. "Think it's too late to go get the sons-of-a-bitches who told me the world would be fair?"

Dad shows me his remote. "Can we do it after *The Rockford Files*?"

CHAPTER 21

Agent CI OH-2 Goes Rogue

CHUCK TAKES A STEP back and
   looks at me like I'm crazy.
Oh I'm crazy, all right! A crazy man
   with a crazy glowing watch!
Fans whir; warehouse breezes blow through Lumberland.
"I'm sorry, but this is just . . . kind of weird," Chuck says.
"Yeah, I know," I say, "but I felt awful about yesterday—"
"Look, it's really fine," Chuck interrupts me.
"This seemed like a good way to apologize—"
"Really, it's not necessary—"
"So much stress with this economy—"
"I promise you, it's just fine—"
"I'm telling you, this is really good stuff—"
"I'm sure it is, but I'm not interested," Chuck says sternly.
Come on . . . "It's a great price—"
"Look, I don't mean to offend you, but I don't smoke pot."
My watch glows with failure, picks up my insane laugh.
"Never too late to start!" I practically yell.
I cannot buy a break in this life.

CHAPTER 22

A Good Old-Fashioned Newspaperman

So the Chuckholder wouldn't buy any pot and impli-
cate himself in a drug-buying conspiracy. Fine. I knew it was a
long shot with a stiff like him. And toward the end there, I was
probably flirting with entrapment anyway. But still my mission to
Lumberland wasn't a total failure. Chuck *did* agree to send a truck
tomorrow morning to take back the lumber I can no longer afford.
And he also agreed to give me a full refund on the lumber, to only
charge me one delivery fee, so that's good.

Then, with all of the pot-selling weirdness still in the air,
Chuck was doing the paperwork for my refund (I stared daggers
into that pot-sticker bald spot) and Chuck *finally registered my name
and address*. And I swear his bald spot turned red. He looked up,
slowly—into my mad, grinning face, and he gave me the most
gratifying double-take, went pale, coughed, excused himself for a
minute (long enough to leave a phone message for Lisa, perhaps?)
and then he came back looking awful. So I accomplished one of
my goals—showing my enemy the face of the man whose life he
would destroy. Of course, I didn't let on that I knew anything about

him and Lisa. And before I left, I apologized for trying to sell him pot, and asked him to keep the whole thing between us. "My wife doesn't know I'm selling pot," I said. "It would kill her." Chuck stared at the ground. And right there, in the cold, high aisles of Lumberland, my enemy Chuck Stain finally saw the anguish of the man on the other side of his harmless little flirtation. Even better, he saw the overlapping layers of stalemate and mutually destructive conspiracy here, the untenable situation we are all in.

In the car now, I laugh again. It always seems strange when maniacal movie villains laugh for no reason, but I'm finding that when you're in the grips of mania, you really do laugh maniacally. What can Chuck do . . . tell Lisa? "Hey, your insane husband came in today and tried to sell me pot." What's Lisa do then? Confront me? If she does, I'll just say, "How did you find out about that?" It would be like admitting the affair!

No, I've drawn Prince LumberChuck into our stalemate now, and depending on how fast his mind works, I bet he won't even tell her. Out of self-preservation, he might think, I do not want to be in the middle of their shit. I imagine the odd, halting conversations going back and forth between them and I get a strange mixture of nausea and glee, my skipping heart about to leap out of my chest. Is this mania? An anxiety attack? A euphoria that precedes death?

Whatever it is, I am driven by it, and by my epiphany; for the last hour I have known exactly what to do. I am on the righteous team, Randy. And yes, I screwed up my plan with the Prince of Lumber, but Chuck's refusal to buy weed does not change my mission: I will be a narco–Robin Hood. It's the only way out: if I'm going to be a snitch, secretly taping people buying drugs, then I'm only going to sell to people who deserve to go to jail.

I will be the arbiter of guilt and innocence in this messed-up world.

First order of business, I call the HR department of my old newspaper from a phone booth. "Sorry," I tell innocent Amber Philips, my watch sitting dark and harmless on my wrist. "I couldn't get any weed after all."

"Aw, it's probably okay," she says, and then she tells me that she and her boyfriend have decided to call it quits anyway. "And I mostly only smoked with him."

I hang up, happy with my first pardon: Amber Philips doesn't deserve to go to jail.

And yet, *deserve* is such a difficult concept to define. Take money-man Richard, for instance, he of the Mexican Shipping Bonds and commissions on eighty percent losses . . . does he *deserve* jail for that? Even as I call him, I wonder if incompetent is the same as guilty.

"This is Richard Blackmore."

No. Being a bad financial planner is not a crime. Watch remains dark. Heart racing.

"I'm sorry," I say to Richard. "I couldn't get any more weed after all."

"Yeah?" Richard asks. "That's okay. Honestly, that shit was kind of strong for me anyway. I didn't get a thing done yesterday. Fine for you, but I still *have* a job."

God, he really is an asshole. I fight the urge to sell to him after all.

After I hang up with Richard, I call the number I've been planning to call ever since this idea revealed itself to me . . . the moment I asked my father if we could still get the sons-of-bitches who told me the world would be fair.

M—'s secretary answers. I tell her it's Matt Prior. And although it kills me, I tell her to say that I've called to apologize. Just as I expected, the Idi Amin of newspaper editors can't resist contrition from someone he's tortured. I stammer, shuffle, swallow my pride and offer this ass-bag my (God, this is hard) apology. "I'm sorry," I say, "I shouldn't have said what I said."

"I appreciate that, Matt," he says, and the worst part is that I've given him the chance to sound magnanimous. "And I understand. I think we're both victims of this economy."

"Yes," I say through gritted teeth. "It was wrong to blame you. I hope you'll accept my apology. I've been under a lot of stress."

"Sure," M— says. "This has been stressful on us all." Just the sound of his voice makes me strangle the steering wheel, as he explains that it's been hard on him too, laying off so many people. Turns out he isn't sleeping well at night. (Yeah? Day Four for me, asshole.) "It can't be easy to be laid off, but at least those people only go through it once. I've had to go through it over and over again."

Thankfully I'm not driving or I'd have to veer into a telephone pole to make it stop. The poor assassin—all those beheadings! Noisy crowds . . . guillotine cleanup . . . constant blade sharpening . . .

"I don't mean to suggest that it's not hard on people like you," he says.

"No, I hear you," I say. And then, when my hatred is strongest, I gently release the line into the water. "And I know what you mean about stress. I got a prescription for medicinal marijuana."

"Did you really?"

"Yeah. It's the only thing that helps."

"You can get a prescription for that? For stress?"

"Sure," I say. "It saved my life. You should try it. The pot they grow these days, you can't believe it. It's amazing."

"Yeah, I keep hearing that." He laughs. "But it's been years for me. Those days are long behind me, I'm afraid."

Circling . . . "Yeah, that's what I thought, too. I hadn't gotten high since college." And I give a little hum. College. (Introduce nostalgia and the carefully chosen word: *high*.) "Man, we used to tear it up back then, didn't we?" Wait, wait. And how do I know that M— smoked in college? He graduated in the 1970s from a state school and went into journalism, the home for authority-questioning slackers; if he didn't smoke pot, he was the only one.

"My roommate was from Hawaii," M— says. "You don't have to tell me."

I laugh nonchalantly. Then: "Hey. You know what? I ended up getting way more than I can use . . . I mean . . . I could sell you some, if you want. You should just try it. Amazing stuff."

"Oh," laughs M—. "No. I don't think so."

"It's perfectly legal," I say. "I have a prescription."

Quiet for a moment. Wait. Wait.

"Oh, I don't know."

Wait. Don't speak. Wait.

He laughs. "You know what? That actually sounds good. I'd like that."

"Yeah? Okay. I could bring it down today if you want."

Just like that. Easy. Maybe I've found my calling.

I meet M— in the parking garage of the newspaper. I don't have a parking pass anymore so I have to walk in. M— is waiting by his car, wearing his fey 1940s newspaper editor uniform, gray suit, suspenders, fedora. He has a small twitch in the corner of his lying mouth, which is perfectly framed by his pencil-thin beard. M— looks around the parking garage and makes a Deep Throat joke. I pretend to laugh. It's cold and gray all around us. He holds out three fifties even though I told him two hundred. Is he really low-balling me? Guy's an asshole to the end. Still, I give him one ounce in a sandwich bag. I'd sell at a loss to get this asshole. He closes his eyes, smells it. Smiles.

I collect the money with the hand wearing the bright watch.

"I'm looking forward to this," he says. "My first newspapering job, we got high in the darkroom every afternoon. Everyone got high then." And then, perhaps worried that I'm judging him, he adds: "Nobody had kids." Shrugs. "It was the seventies." Smiles wistfully. "It was a different time, wasn't it?"

"Yeah." God, I want out of there. I feel sick . . . can't spend another second near this guy. "Call me if you need more." My hands are shaking.

"I might do that." The pot disappears in his coat. "I'm going to have some time on my hands. Have you heard? I'm leaving, too. I quit rather than be a part of this any longer."

"No. I hadn't heard," I say, though I have heard, of course. And I also know that he's really being forced out. But unlike the scores of people he slagged, M— gets to go out on his own terms, probably with a bonus. A guy like him saves the suits a few hundred grand by marching good people into the wood chipper, then gets to pretend he quit in indignation (even though he stuck around to do the layoffs *first*, protecting his Vichy loyalists to the end) so he can save face and go around speaking in front of college classes and journalism groups, eventually getting another job ruining some other newspaper.

M— nods, and seems to take my silence for sympathy, which I'm in no danger of actually feeling. "I'll be okay, though," he says. "I can always teach. And maybe there are still papers out there looking for a good old-fashioned newspaperman."

With his last ship still listing in the bay, Queeg wants another one. I suppress a scoff.

Meanwhile M— is warming to our postwar camaraderie. "So you're out there . . . in the world. What's the job market like for old ink-stained pros like us?"

Us. "I don't know . . . if you're willing to work . . . there's always something. In fact, I picked up a little freelance work today."

He smiles wearily and I think his eyes rim with tears. "That's great, Matt. I'm happy for you."

I have to look away to keep the sympathy from welling up in me.

"I don't mind telling you, I'm a little bit scared," M— says, and tightens his scarf. "Fifty-six? And no job?" He wipes at his eyes. "What if it's . . . you know, the end?"

I don't say anything.

"Well." He pulls the bag of weed from his coat and smells it again. "Thanks for this, Matt. I think it's going to help." And then he puts his pot away again and considers me seriously. "It's too bad you and I didn't spend more time together."

"Well . . ." I twitch and shudder, glance at my glowing watch and hear myself laugh maniacally again. "Never too late to start!"

CHAPTER 23

OH-2 *The Vengeful*

I AM OH-2 THE VENGEFUL
Wiretapping angel of fury
Be prepared to meet your maker
Or at least a federal grand jury

The guy who talked me into refinancing last year, John
Denham, no longer works for the mortgage company in the mini-
mall next to the tanning salon. In fact, John's mortgage company
is no longer a mortgage company but an empty storefront—as is
the tanning salon. In fact, this whole mini-mall appears to be on
its way to becoming surface parking.

Mark Akenside, sly salesman who bait-and-switched us into
the more expensive Maxima, also escapes CI OH-2. He no longer
works for the Nissan dealer, and neither does Dodsley, his old
manager, the capo who dry-sold us winter floor mats. "It's been a
bloodbath this fall," a surviving car salesman confides, staring out
at a savannah of starving sedans.

Fine. There are others. Always others. It's Friday, so I find our old phony Aussie real estate agent, Thomas Otway, running an open house on a foothills cul de sac.

"'Ello, mite," he says when I come into the blond-wood foyer. "I 'ope you're ready to see the house-a-yah drimes." He sweeps his arm toward a living room tastefully appointed in French Colonial furniture, with a grand staircase and a completely updated kitchen.

"Oh, it looks like a dream all right," I say. And then I smile and explain that we already bought one dream from him.

"Oh?" Thomas doesn't remember me. In fact, he doesn't seem to register people at all, any more than a reef shark notes the kind of fish it's eating. But he does remember the house when I describe it. "Ah, yeah. A tudah, on almost a half-acah. Go'geous home. Only drawback was the neighbah-hood school if I remembah roight."

Oh, you remember roight.

Thomas Otway's skin is perfect. He has longish, soap opera styled hair, light brown with crazy yellow highlights, and besides affecting more accent earlier in the sales process, he apparently frosts his locks, too, and I begin to imagine a system for determining who I'll entrap, giving points for various crimes against humanity: Real estate, or any kind of predatory salesmanship, is four points. Fake or affected accents? Two points. Frosted hair? Four points. Right away, without even knowing if he beats his kids or fails to stop at red lights, the bastard's at ten, which will be the threshold for incurring the wrath of CI OH-2.

No, I'm not bad at this. For one thing, it's easier to bring the subject up than I thought it would be. The key is patience. So I let Thomas show me around the house, pretending to be interested in the lush runner carpets on the wood-floor hallways, the limited edition lithographs on the walls, the horrid Chihuly blown-glass chandelier. I think the transcribed wire in this case could be used to train other informants:

CI OH-2: It's certainly bigger than it looks from the outside.

Suspect 2: Mite, this house has 3,600 square feet on two floors.

CI OH-2: Wow. And does that include the basement?

Suspect 2: No, bisement's unfinished.

CI OH-2: Good, because I have big plans for the basement.

Suspect 2: Pehfect for a home gym, roight?

CI OH-2: Actually I might put a grow room down there.

Suspect 2: What? You serious?

CI OH-2: Serious as a bloody reef shark. Why, do you smoke, Thomas?

"Sure." Thomas smiles out one side of his mouth. "I used to," he says.

"You should try this stuff I have. It's killer."

Thomas stares at me for a long second before shaking off the temptation. "Nah. I'm try-ning fur a meer-athon. I'm a runnah. That stuff . . . bad for the lungs, roight? But listen—" He looks around, then leans in close. "I don't suppose you can get your hands on some coceene?"

Side-note for my handlers, Randy and Lt. Reese: you have *got* to get me some coke.

I check my glowing watch as I drive out of the cul de sac, through the splotches in my exhausted eyes. School's almost out. Work's done for the day.

I never thought I'd like working in sales, but it is strangely satisfying getting people to do what you want. And I'm not *just* working; Randy says I'm doing something for society and maybe I am, in my way—ridding the world of parasitic, layoff-happy newspaper editors and asshole real estate agents, home-wreckers and tailgaters and people who speed on residential streets, all the phonies and villains and fuck-sticks in the world. As Righteous Randy might say, I am the Light *and* the Dark.

From now on I will answer every phone call from a telephone solicitor with purpose—No, I don't need a new long distance provider, but would you like to buy a spliff? I think of the assholes I meet every week—snooty waiters and people who park in handicapped spots and all the arrogant, selfish, lying cheats. I can bring them all down, one by one.

I'll do my homework: research the most calloused bosses, inept congressmen, corrupt bankers, greedy brokers, predatory lenders. I'll drive my Nissan to Detroit and sell to the auto company CEOs and I'll go to New York and sell weed to that asshole trader I heard on NPR and to the dipshit investment bankers who broke our financial system through their unchecked greed, the lousy ass-ticks who told us all to give them our money, to vote for them, to trust them, guys who said the markets would regulate themselves, that the world was fair.

I sit in revved-up silence in my car, outside the boys' school, my own breathing deafening. Hands shake. I feel flushed. Mind racing, I'm having conversations I can't track with myself, offering justifications and pleadings. I want to sleep, preferably next to my wife, and I wonder what she's doing now. Sitting at her desk at the stupid optometrist's office, staring into space, thinking of . . . *him*? God, I wish Chuck was a pot smoker. How much easier would that be? I happen to look up to see Elijah Fenton's dad, Carl, walking past the line of waiting cars toward the school. The guy wears a softball jacket with the name of his paving and concrete company on it, as if he's taunting jobless losers like me with the fact that he still has a company and that his company still has a softball team—the arrogance of the employed! No doubt made aware of my son's unprovoked clacker aggression, Carl Fenton shoots me what can only be described as a threatening glare. Is there any way the guy really made out with the second-grade fertility goddess, Ms. Bishop? Who knows? All I know is that next week we'll find out if Mr. Carl Fenton wants to buy a reefer. Oh, and there's Nicholas Rowe—he of the T-Ball prodigy son, Caleb—Nick Rowe who famously cut second graders from the second-grade T-Ball team because he feared their lack of coordination might affect his son's draft status a decade from now. (Ten point bonus, that.) A long shot, of course, but perhaps he'd like some weed.

Beyond all these deserving targets, I wonder if I can find my own eighth-grade baseball coach, Mr. Stepney, or Tina Sprat, the girl who refused to kiss me after I spent sixty dollars on dinner before a Sadie Hawkins dance my sophomore year, or the guy in college, what was his name—Yalden!—who sold me that Chevy Luv pickup with the cracked block. Or . . . or . . .

I snap awake.

Was I sleeping?

School is out.

Kids drift to waiting cars.

The doors open. Franklin and Teddy climb in the backseat.

"He-e-ey." I try to not sound crazy but my voice goes up and down the register. I can't stop blinking. "H-h-how was school?" Why is my voice doing that? I'm cracking. Nervous breakdown? Anxiety attack?

"Fine," Teddy mumbles.

"Great!" says Franklin.

"Great? Really?" I turn to see Franklin's big earnest eyes. "What happened?"

Franklin shrugs. "Nothing. It was just a great day. I love Fridays."

I laugh again. And then a whimper, a kind of weep seeps from me, from some deep cavity. I can't say why Franklin's *great day* causes me to whimper—maybe the eight-year-old in me recalls that nothing has to happen for a day to be great. And then it feels as if this broken thing in my chest cracks like an ice dam, and begins sliding up into my throat. I happen to glance down and see the glowing watch around my wrist. Shit. I forgot to press the stop button after my meeting with M——. The voice activation has presumably kicked in.

I imagine the transcript:

CI OH-2: "He-e-ey! How was school?"
Unidentified Juvenile Male 1: (Unintelligible)
Unidentified Juvenile Male 2: "Great."
CI OH-2: "Great? Really? What happened?"
Unidentified Juvenile Male 2: "Nothing. It was just great. I love
    Fridays."
CI OH-2: (Unintelligible, possibly maniacal laugh-cry-whimper
    as if he's snapping, unraveled beyond recognition)

"You okay, Dad?"

I press the wind-button on the watch. The backlight goes out. "Fine, Teddy."

"Elijah Fenton and I are friends again," Franklin says.

"Did you apologize to him?"

"I didn't have to." Franklin shrugs. "He didn't say anything about it."

Something parental I should say here, something about responsibility or contrition, what's the word . . . the other side of forgiveness . . . aw hell . . . I can't come up with it.

So I concentrate on the road. Drive now; parent later.

I squint. It's cleared up again this afternoon, the cool winter fog keeps burning off, leaving no place to hide, and the crisp air throws me; the world is washed out, shimmery. Like a twenty-degree desert. Tree limbs crook accusingly in the wind, and leaves leap at our passing. I can see deep into the cars around me, and it's like looking into people's souls. We round the corner to our house, I'm still shaking, breathing shallow and raspy. We crawl down our block, limp into the driveway.

How is it that I keep forgetting that my front yard is full of lumber?

"Wow," says Teddy. "What's all the wood for?"

"That . . . was a mistake," I say. "They're coming to get it to-morrow. They delivered it to the wrong house."

"The wrong house?" Teddy asks. "That's too bad."

Kid, you have no idea.

"It looks like Jenga," says Franklin.

And this causes me to start crying again. It was Franklin's favorite game a couple of years ago, Jenga. We played every night before I tucked him into his little bed, his feet curled up beneath him. I stare at the beams in my front yard, stacked crosswise, and it comes to me that life is a version of that children's game: pull one from the bottom and stack it on top and try to keep the whole thing from falling. Slide a board out, stack it on top, the structure growing taller as the weight shifts upward, until the base begins to look like lattice, and pretty soon you realize you're holding your breath, that there are no more safe moves, but still you must try, always try, because that's the game . . . so you look for a board to slide, gently . . . slide . . . gently . . . even though you can never win, and it's always the same . . . breathless and tentative . . . the world teetering above your head.

CHAPTER 24

You May Be Experiencing

Slurred speech, stuttering or speaking in monotone
lapses in judgment and trouble with visual recognition
a loss of impulse control, dizziness, nausea and
erratic behavior, along with severe disorientation
all caused by a steep decline in neural activity
which can lead eventually to severe hallucinations
delirium, delusions, manias, even psychotic breaks—
then death—

Then death? Wait. Just like that? Shit. I reread the Wikipedia
sleep deprivation article to see if I missed something. A few days
without sleep and you go from slurred speech to bad decisions to
. . . death? Well, that hardly seems fair. It feels like they left out
a few steps . . . like they skipped second and third base . . . went
straight from kissing to a greasy threesome. I read deeper into the
article: the longest anyone has willingly gone without sleep was
eleven days—some college student in 1965—but because of the
health dangers, the *Guinness World Records* has stopped recognizing
lack of sleep as a legitimate record. Meanwhile, there are all sorts

of folk stories about people going years without sleep. My favorite
is a guy in Vietnam who claims to have gone thirty years.

And then, there's sleep deprivation as torture, of course. It's
one of the oldest tortures there is—relatively clean, no scars—a
big hit at Gitmo. There's an old account by former Israeli Prime
Minister Menachem Begin, who was sleep deprived by KGB of-
ficers in the 1970s. He described "a haze" from which his "spirit"
was "wearied to death."

That about describes it: haze. Spirit wearied. Death.

I put my head down on the desk for a just a second to think
and—

The front door opens downstairs.

I sit up. It's dark outside. Shit, what time is it?

I hear the front door close.

Where am I? Push back from the desk.

She's climbing the steps.

My face feels rubbery. Can't focus.

She pauses at the office door.

She's silhouetted: "I got your message."

"What?" I wipe the spit from my mouth.

Voice quavering: "In the front yard?"

Groggy, I have no idea what she means. What time is it?

Her eyes are strange—unfamiliar. "For what it's worth—"

"Do you . . . know what time it is?"

Her eyes shut. "When did you become cruel?"

I meant it as a question, not recrimination.

"And they're coming to take that wood away?"

Oh, right. The wood. "Tomorrow. Look Lisa, I—"

She walks away. Our bedroom door eases shut.

Then the day comes flooding back to me . . . righteous Randy
and nasty Reese . . . tree-fort wood . . . CI OH-2. Oh, and I have
a watch! A dark, unactivated watch on my wrist! So I know the

time . . . quarter to six. No wonder I'm disoriented; I think I've actually gotten an hour of sleep. I shake my head to clear the static and then walk to our closed bedroom door. I put my hand against the cool wood. So here we are. Now what?

I can't hear anything in there. But behind that door is our bed. (So tired . . .) If I could just somehow get to the other side of this door, climb into that bed, and we wouldn't have to speak, wouldn't even have to face each other . . . I put my hand on the cold knob. I swear, we wouldn't have to say a word, she could just settle in behind me, her knees nestled behind mine, and we could sleep until—

"Dad?" I turn. Franklin is wearing his art hat—a paint-splattered Angels cap that he wears whenever he breaks into his craft caddy.

"Hey pal."

"I need to ask you something."

"Sure." I follow him into his bedroom. Here we go. *What's happening to you, Dad? Are you and Mom getting a divorce? Which parent will we live with?*

In his fussy, cluttered bedroom, Franklin has his easel set up in the center, a big piece of butcher paper clipped to it. He's done a crude painting of Godzilla (Franklin is working through a monsters motif in his art right now, this, a classic interpretation— scales down the back and on the tail, three claws on each heavy foot, fire coming from the gaping jaws.) On top of the painting he's written, "To Elijah. I Am Sorry." And on the bottom, "From Franklin."

"I like this. It's a nice gesture."

But something is bothering Franklin and he looks at me with all the seriousness his earnest little face can muster.

"What is it, sport?"

"I just need to know . . ." He takes a deep breath. "Well . . ."

He sighs; he's just going to go ahead and ask his question: "Who would win in a fight? Godzilla or a tyrannosaurus?"

Christ, I'm a mess—groggy, blubbery, slobbery, easy-to-tears. Crying at the stupidest things: Jenga, Godzilla. I blink away wet salt again. I didn't see weepiness in the list of sleep-deprivation symptoms. Hard to say what gets me this time—the sheer eight-year-old perfection of that question . . . or that he asked *me* . . . or maybe the fact that his little conscience has led him to paint an apology for his antagonist, his Prince Chuck. He stares at me, waiting.

God, they want so little, these shits; they don't care about money, big houses, private schools, darkness and light. All they want is answers. And sugared cereal.

"Well." I wipe at my eyes. "Godzilla would win. You know. Because of the fire."

"The lasers," he corrects. "Yeah." He stares hard at the painting, sighs. "That's what I said. But Elijah said that Godzilla is made up, so Tyrannosaurus would win."

"Well, that's just a lack of imagination," I say. "Some people are literalists. We can't hold it against them. Not their fault, champ."

Franklin nods in agreement. "What's for dinner?"

I glance back across the hall, at our closed door. "I'm thinking pizza."

Franklin's eyes follow mine to our closed bedroom door and he nods.

So I make one phone call, and just like that, we're eating pizza at 6:30. What is this world? You tap seven abstract figures onto a piece of plastic thin as a billfold, hold that plastic device to your head, use your lungs and vocal cords to indicate more abstractions, and in thirty minutes, a guy pulls up in a 2,000-pound machine made on an island on the other side of the world, fueled by viscous liquid made from the rotting corpses of dead organisms pulled from the desert on yet another side of the world and you give this man a few sheets of green paper representing the abstract wealth of your home nation, and he gives you a perfectly reasonable facsimile of one of the staples of the diet of a people from yet another faraway nation.

And the mushrooms are fresh.

I send Teddy upstairs to see if Lisa wants to join us for this tiny miracle. I tell him to let her know that I got fresh peppers and mushrooms on our half, her favorite. She declines. She tells Teddy she doesn't feel well.

"What's she doing up there?" I ask, as nonchalantly as I can muster.

Teddy shrugs. "She's in bed. She's sick." He doesn't meet my eyes.

Dad stares into the winter-black back window as he chews.

"You like the pizza, Dad? Or do you prefer the other place?"

He stares down at the pizza as if he was unaware that it was pizza.

"Pradeep Duncan got Guitar Hero for his Wii," Teddy pretends to tell Franklin. Here it comes—Teddy's regularly scheduled, ten-year-old consumer confidence report, his pointed survey of all the expensive and inappropriate gadgets, games and movies that other fourth graders are routinely being given by their cooler and more loving parents. He gives this quarterly report only to his brother so that Lisa and I can't launch into any kind of lecture about his age, or the fact that we can't afford such things, or how, even if we could afford them, it wouldn't matter to us what other kids have.

"And his stepdad lets him watch the *Saw* movies," Teddy continues.

"No *way*!" says Franklin. Then he shakes his head. "I wouldn't want to watch those."

"Dude, I would," Teddy says. I wonder: where did Teddy learn such indirect communication? And . . . *Dude?* I picture him outside the 7/11—

Above us, the floorboards creak. My eyes go to the ceiling. Up there, the bathroom door opens and closes. After a minute . . . a flush. The bathroom door opens. She pads across the floor. The bedroom door opens and closes again.

My phone buzzes. I glance down at it. Jamie. Another board teeters.

I excuse myself from the table and take it in the living room.

"Hey," Jamie says, and there's a thumping bass behind him, and I hear someone yell, *Fuck you, Larry,* and then there's a burst of laughter, and Jamie says, "Slippers, we're having a rager over at Larry's, yo! You should totally come over, man."

Rub my brow.

Jamie goes on: "We gotta go to Weedland and get our shit tonight anyway, right?"

Jamie has piggybacked a smaller buy on top of mine. Okay, so here we go. I glance at the black watch on my wrist. I suppose there's a certain point where there's nothing more to fear. Once you're not just a drug dealer but a narc, too . . . what the hell have you got to worry about? That is the one good thing about the bottom: at least it's the bottom. "Yeah."

"Cool," he says. "Just come by Larry's and get me, yo."

"Okay. About an hour?"

"Yeah, yeah. I'll just be chillin'." And then Jamie laughs. "Oh, man, Chulo just bit it. He's totally fried, yo."

"Isn't Chulo always fried?" I ask, even though I've yet to figure out which one is Chulo.

Jamie laughs. "No shit, huh?"

I hang up and go back into the kitchen. Dad and the boys are at the table, eating quietly. I slide back into my chair. Here we are. Three generations of doomed Prior men.

Teddy resumes his consumer-spending report: "Tommy Parnell? He's got two Wiis."

"Two? No *way!*" Franklin says. "What's he do with two?"

"One at his mom's house and one at his dad's house."

"No *way!*" Franklin says again.

I could buy five Wiis with the money I spent on treated lumber. Thirty-five with the money I spent on dope. Maybe I can tell Randy and Reese it was all a mistake. I wanted to buy Wiis, not weed.

World teeters. "Look, guys, I gotta go somewhere after dinner. You stay here with Grandpa. Let Mom rest unless it's something important. Okay?"

"Can we watch a movie?"

"Get your pajamas on first, and don't forget—"

"What happened to me?"

Teddy, Franklin and I all look up, across the table at Dad.

"What's that, Dad?"

His eyes narrow. "Why am I here?" He pats his empty pocket for cigarettes.

Veins pop in his forehead. His eyes drill into me. This happens sometimes; all of a sudden Dad will come in sharp, like a distant radio station dialed in on a clear night.

"You just got into some trouble, Dad. It's gonna be fine. Don't worry."

I used to get excited by these occasional glimpses, used to think it meant that *my Dad* was back, and I'd hurriedly brief him on everything that had happened while he was away—as if he'd been in a coma—or I'd try to get information out of him—what did he remember about Charity and her boyfriend? But the station always went away again, and I'd just have to brief him again two days later, so I quit trying to bring Dad up to speed. I've learned to simply stall, make small talk until the clear reception goes away again. It usually takes only a few minutes.

Dad stares at me, waiting for an answer.

"Look, it's nothing we can't handle, Dad. You had a little trouble, but everything is—"

He spits as he says, "Goddamn it, Matt! Will you tell me what the fuck happened to me?"

I look over at the boys—pizza slices frozen halfway to their mouths. Then I look back at Dad. He used to yell at me sometimes like that when I was a kid, but his real anger was directed at my mother. She used to say that Dad didn't yell about anything she *did*; it was her existence that pissed him off. I was twenty-six when he finally left her. Lisa thought my nonchalant reaction odd; but I suppose I expected it, because I never asked for an explanation. From either of them. Mom talked to my sisters about it—she said Dad left because she wouldn't let him smoke in the house. I guess Mom never talked to me about it because she sensed that I would intuitively side with him. Maybe, even then, she saw in me the same unraveling gene.

Dad stares. For once, the sharp eyes aren't going away.

I glance over at my boys, who are waiting along with Dad for an explanation. Sigh. Oh, what the hell. "You met a girl, Dad. In Reno. A stripper. You took her back to the ranch in Oregon. She stole everything, your money . . . credit cards . . . everything."

The boys, of course, have never heard this heartwarming family story. Teddy's eyes are huge. His grandfather knew a stripper? He looks over at the old guy with new-found respect.

Dad nods: go on.

Funny—it never occurred to me to ask my father why he left Mom. If anything, I might've asked why he stayed all those years.

I always felt like he was buzzing with something dangerous, banging against the walls, teetering, and he could just tip over at any time and be gone. To me, it felt like we were only renting the man. All those days he put on that tie and those coveralls; I knew he'd have to leave eventually. The fact that he made it until my sisters and I were gone from home seemed like an accomplishment. He moved to a tiny house on fifteen acres along a dry riverbed in central Oregon, a place where he could smoke all the cigarettes he wanted. In four years, I only visited him there once:

Dry Falls

Dad's land is scabbed and pocked
river channels that forgot not to die
couleed ditches and hard veined cracks
of channeled dust in his razored cheeks
near a broken Case, stranded plow
tooth long lost in an Army row
burns on his forearms from an engine
blown in a falling corral of brown grass
spotted with implements too rusted to name
let alone use—wet nose betraying
disease in his lungs like the fresh pack
in his left breast pocket like the chipped
paint barn its corrugated roof curling
at the edges and a woodstove chimney
jutting through black shingles, fresh pack
in his left breast pocket above a
smoke-choked beater grown over
from neglect, two faint tracks in long weeds
shot up around the burned GMC
the old man still dreams he drives

big right hand on the black shifter knob
fresh pack in his left breast pocket—

And I wonder if we don't live like water
seeking a level
a low bed
until one day we just go dry.
I wonder if a creek ever realizes
it has made its own grave.

Dad stares at me, waiting for the rest of the explanation—*what happened to me.*

"I don't know, Dad. Maybe . . . you were embarrassed that this girl took advantage of you . . . ashamed or something. But you didn't tell anyone. By the time I got there, it was too late."

Mom spent a decade alone, convinced that Dad would someday return—"after he's had his fun." She died without ever speaking to him again, in a sunny hospital room, surrounded by her kids, mumbling in her morphine about terrorists. As far as I know she only mentioned him once, the last day, when she said that she couldn't wait to see him in heaven. My sister said, "But Dad's still alive," and Mom just smiled, as if that was exactly what she meant. That day, hospice was delivering a hospital bed to her house, but she didn't make it home. One of my sisters joked later that she couldn't bear having that mess in her house. I left my crying sisters, went home from the hospital and climbed in bed. We'd just moved to this house. Without a word, Lisa climbed in beside me and nestled in behind my knees. We slept like that for a couple of hours and then I got up and called Dad in Oregon. He answered on one ring. I could hear the TV in the background. He listened, sighed, cleared his throat, thanked me for calling and hung up.

He didn't come to the funeral. After that, Dad seemed to withdraw and I suppose I let him. Life was busy, and then my own collapse began and I looked up one day and realized it had been months since I'd heard from my father. When one of my sisters called to tell me that Dad's phone was disconnected, I drove to Oregon, and that's where I found him—like this—early-onset, post-Charity, un-showered, unshaven, unhinged, disoriented, dazed . . . alone.

"The doctors say you're suffering from early-onset dementia," I tell Dad, "which is just another word for senility."

He leans across the dinner table, nods. Go on. The doctors said that being alone probably hastened his decline; without people to talk to synaptic paths grow over with weeds, and yet, every once in a while, he finds himself on a bare stretch of one of those old trails. Like now.

"The good news is . . . it's not Alzheimer's. Your memory is just . . . well . . . it comes and goes. In fact, I'll probably have to tell you all of this again tomorrow. Or I won't. I'll just say a bunch of stupid shit. And you'll just watch TV and forget you even asked." I try a reassuring smile. "And hell Dad, maybe that's just like the rest of us. Maybe we all forget everything the minute we learn it. I don't know."

Dad sometimes brings the remote control to the table. He always sets it next to his plate, like a fourth utensil, just to the right of his knife. It's the same brand of universal remote that he had at his house in Oregon. Dad was terribly disoriented when he got to our house—until he saw we had a look-alike remote control.

Now, at the mention of the word TV, he picks up the remote and stares at it, as if it contains the answer to this thing he's been trying to understand. Then he sets it down in its place . . . so . . . gently. I don't think I've ever seen my father be that gentle with anything.

He looks up at Teddy, at Franklin, and then at me.

And the light goes out. I can see it in his eyes. The station is gone.

"You know what, Dad . . . it's okay . . . it's all going to be—"

"What kind of man was I?" he rasps. And he pats his empty breast pocket.

"A good one," I say, voice cracking. I look down at my plate; feel the boys' eyes. These people. Are they trying to kill me?

I look up blearily. Dad has picked up his remote control again, and is staring back out the black window. He takes a deep breath, then lifts the pizza to his mouth and chews. He looks over at me like a stranger, this good man who spent forty years losing the people he loved, and then, in only a few months, managed to lose himself. *(We live like water . . .)*

My gaping sons no longer gape at their grandfather, but at me. I guess they've never seen their dad cry before. I wipe my eyes, smile. I don't know what to tell them: Boys, pay attention to your mother; mothers have a million things to teach you. But fathers? We only have two lessons, but these two things are everything you need to know: *(1) What to do* and *(2) What not to do.* I look from the boys down to the dark watch, jutting from my wrist like a tumor. And my bleary eyes drift up to Dad's black window and my own faint reflection in it.

CHAPTER 25

The Last Time I Remember
Crying, Haiku #4

I WAS AN ADULT
When my parents got divorced
Or so I was told

CHAPTER 26

On the Spiritual Crises of
Confidential Informants

THERE IS, INDEED, A rager of a party going on in Larry's fetid apartment and the first thing I see is the answer to why there were pizza crusts all over the furniture and floor the other day. The second someone finishes a slice they are obliged to yell, "Fuck you, Larry," and throw the crust at him. It's a tradition here in low-rent Neverland, where no one grows up and where no one ever has to eat his crusts. For his part, Larry ducks each crust, and says, "Fuck you!" back whenever someone actually hits him, never taking his eyes off the video game he's playing, in which he negotiates dark hallways and shoots zombies on the big screen with another dude, both of them leaning in and working the controllers (Why does a guy making eight bucks an hour have a better TV than me?) and the whole apartment smells like a stale quiche of socks, garlic, sweat and weed—little huffs of smoky clouds surround clustered kids—all clad in tight black or in bright baggy sportswear; the bass whumps, crusts fly, beer bottles tink and I'm not in the door ten seconds when I'm passed a spliff, little wisp of forgiveness curling off the point, and I very nearly hit that shit—but no. Thank you. I hand the joint back.

I do take a warm beer (I am *that* kind of man) and it goes down easy. "Who's got a piece? You got a piece?" asks a red-eyed kid I've never seen before, and at first I think he means a gun, "I need a piece. Anyone got a piece," but then I remember that a piece is a pipe and I shake my head no and the kid moves on, working the room, "Who's got a piece, I need a piece." There are twenty people at this party—including six girls, and I'm happy for the fellas—six actual females at their party—happy for Larry, for the guy with the Festiva whose name I don't know, for Chulo, whichever one he is . . . happy for the red-eyed piece guy who squeezes my shoulder and says: "Damn! Slippers, so you chillin' or what?"

"Yes." This is what I am doing—chilling.

No sign of Jamie, but I spot Skeet, same sweat suit as before, exiting a bedroom, arm on the waist of a dull-eyed girl in a leather coat—and I think, parentally: *you can do better, Skeet*—but he introduces me proudly. "Yo, Lana, this our friend, Matt, he like a doctor, some shit."

"Hey," Lana says, with a tilt of the head.

"Nice to meet you," I say back, and I think of telling her that I'm not . . . like, a doctor or some shit, but what would be the point? Businessman, doctor, unemployed business reporter, failed poet, confidential informant? Really, what's the difference?

"Wish I knew you was gonna be here, yo. I would've brought your loafers."

"That's okay," I say. "Do you know where Jamie is? I'm supposed to meet him here."

"Yeah boy, he hookin' you up, or what?"

Hookin' you up. It sounds worse than I imagined. I look at Lana.

She chews her huge wad of gum rhythmically, turning it every other chomp with her tongue.

Larry calls back over his shoulder without taking his eyes off the zombies, "Jamie went on a beer run, man! Just chill, Slippers, he be right back, yo."

Yes. More chilling. I want to talk to Skeet alone, but I promised myself I'd wait until after Weedland. Whatever I do, it's got to be *after Weedland*. My nine grand. I glance down at my black watch. They're not necessarily parallel paths, of course—what is right and what is best.

A misfired crust hits me in the arm. I mutter, "Fuck you, Larry."

Skeet leans in closer. "Lana'n me got some twenty-fives." When he sees I don't know what he's talking about, Skeet's eyes get big and round. "Some tabs? I could sell you one if you wanna trip, yo."

"No thanks, Skeet. And you shouldn't either."

He laughs. "Right." Silly Dr. Slippers. "So, you just chillin', then?"

I nod. Yes. I am.

Then the door opens and I come off the wall, but it's not Jamie. It's two other guys, and at first I can't place the lumpy kid in the baseball cap until I see he's chattering on a cell phone and it's actually his voice that is familiar, "Yeah, I'm here. Fuckin' lame-ass party though." and I remember—it's Chet. Monte's little brother.

A crust flies. "Fuck you, Larry!"

"Man, this party totally blows," Chet says into his phone. "Ugly chicks. Lame-ass party."

And I have to agree with Jamie's earlier assessment; Chet is an asshole. The last party I came to here, there were no girls at all. We didn't even get to come inside. You want to call that a lame-ass party, fine. But this is Halloween at the Playboy Mansion compared to that.

A couple of minutes and two flying crusts later, the door opens again and this time it *is* Jamie. And he's with Bea. And they're each carrying two cases of beer. In her mouth, Bea has the largest collection of car keys and key rings I've ever seen not on a janitor. She opens her mouth and drops this four-pound key-contraption on a table.

"Beer's here," Bea says and then she sees me and smiles. "Hey, you."

I come off my wall. I am strangely . . . so happy to see them both.

Bea takes off a heavy coat. She's wearing a clingy, old vintage dress that comes to her impossibly high knees. The silky material brushes my arm as she leans in and nods toward the party. "You see any sensitive poet boys here?" Then she brushes my cheek with her lips—*small swoon*—and walks away, grabbing a slice of pizza and joining a cluster in mid-smoke.

I try to catch Jamie's attention but he's going from cluster to cluster collecting for beer. Then Jamie says, "The fuck's *he* doin' here?" and for a second I think he's talking about me—

—until Chet closes his phone, steps into Jamie's face and says, "You gonna tell me where I can and can't go, bitch?"

"Go wherever you want long as I ain't there."

I tense for a fight, but Chet scoffs and walks away, trying to maintain some upper hand in full retreat. He joins Bea in her cluster of smokers, shooting me a dark look on his way past, and Bea breaks my heart a little by kissing Chet on the mouth.

Jamie sidles up to me then, leans against my wall. "Hate that guy," he says.

Before I can start my nonviolence lecture, from the cluster

of smokers comes Chet's amped-up voice—"'Cause I think that dude's a fuckin' cop, that's why."

And I think my heart might stop and I wonder if people can tell just by looking at me. I ease the hand with the dark watch behind my back. And when I look up—

—Jamie is in Chet's face—and that's when everything becomes—wrong. You forget the sound of a fist hitting a head— it's not that deep satisfying *thwump* of a movie punch but a pitiful sound, a wincing red *chuupp*, and when someone really connects sharply—you can just hear the underneath knock of bone—and here's the thing: it's an *awful* sound. Jamie lands two quick deep shots to Chet's soft face and then Chet hits him back and their feet chirp on the linoleum as the clusters of smokers merge like joining cells into a semicircle, and in the center these two young men flail, jab, whirl, and the circle yells and a pizza box flies and maybe three more punches land before I step toward them and people are yelling—"Chill, motherfuckers!"—just as I reach out to help, but the closest thing to me is one of Jamie's pinwheeling arms, so I grab it—forgetting that you *always* grab for the other guy, because I get a piece of one of Jamie's arms and this only allows Chet to connect with a bone-deep fist to Jamie's eye and temple and Jamie's knees crumple, and I feel so bad that I step in and push Chet in his lumpy chest and he swings at me as he falls back—just grazes my chin but that completely pisses me off—so I swing wildly and miss, and someone yells "Old dude's freakin'!" and I suppose I am freaking because I rush Chet, hit him full in the chest and we go down together, air escaping his puffy coat as we fall on that fetid carpet of pizza crusts, cigarette butts and roach ends, and I bring my knee into his gut and we're all flying arms and grunts and that's when the air goes out of the fight like the air in Chet's ski coat—and out of the room too, because once a boxing match becomes a wrestling match it gets boring and even a little embarrassing, *gay*, the fellas would say, and while we snuffle on the ground for a few seconds more, like hogs (side-note: Chet smells like ass), this fight's done. Jamie and Skeet pull me off, but Chet leaps to his feet and wants to keep fighting. "Come on, motherfuckers! I'll take all-a-y'all on!" but then he realizes he's lost something and he pats himself down. "Where the fuck's my phone? Who took my phone? You got ten seconds to give that shit back or I go out to my fuckin' car."

And here's the thing: I have a pretty good idea what Chet means. (I picture him holding it sideways, like they do in rap videos.) Of course, even when you try to make the right move, another board teeters—two minutes ago I was a forty-six-year-old unemployed narc hanging out with potheads, waiting to go to Weedland; now I'm an unemployed narc—who has gotten into a fight with a guy *threatening to go to his car and get his gun.*

There are these lakes in Northern Idaho that are supposed to be bottomless; the Navy used to do submarine training there. They'd think they had found the bottom and then a submarine would find a deeper hole. Of course, the lakes weren't bottomless. In fact, it turns out nothing is bottomless—except the trouble I get into.

But here's the strange thing about the fight. Once it's over, no one says a word about it. The party just goes back to its earlier rhythms—Larry goes back to killing zombies and Bea goes back to kissing people and the other kids go back to drinking bad beer and smoking good weed and throwing pizza crusts and Chet even finds his phone under the couch and then he and his buddy decide to leave—"Lame-ass party"—the door closing behind them—and I try to imagine a party with my friends—say, the old newspaper Christmas party in the company cafeteria—erupting in a fistfight and then just returning to normal five minutes later.

"Sorry about that," Jamie says. A bruise is forming above his eye.

"*I'm* sorry," I say. "I shouldn't have grabbed your arm. You were doing just fine."

Jamie touches his eye. "You ever feel like you're outgrowing your own fuckin' life?"

There's my writer.

Jamie looks at his hand, sees no blood, and shrugs. "Should we roll?"

Bea sees us leaving and asks if she can walk out with us. And while Jamie goes around collecting for the weed he's about to buy, I step on to the cold porch with beautiful blond, blue-eyed Bea, who buttons her heavy overcoat, lights a filtered cigarette and blows slow death at me. "I hate that homoerotic testosterone crap," she says in released smoke and steam. "They should just fuck and get it over with."

We are a foot apart on this landing. I stare past her, over the railing of the apartment landing toward the lights of another apartment building just across the street—they are stacked in this part of town like egg cartons in a grocery store. These kids at this party were born in egg cartons, have spent their lives in egg cartons . . . and I'm fooling myself if I think it's any different in my bigger egg carton.

"Hey. You okay?" Bea asks.

And that's when I have an epiphany, a real, old-fashioned, religious-style epiphany. And my epiphany is this: there are no such things as epiphanies—no moments of revelation, no great reversals of motive and fortune. No stands, no redemptions, no October surprises; everything is inevitable because the world exists exactly as it always has in this moment: the Rahjiv who mops a spilled Slurpee in the tight aisle of a 7/11 is the same Rahjiv who peels back the hair on a cracked skull in a Mumbai ER; my senile old father holds his remote and my five-year-old hand as Lisa talks to her boyfriend in the same bed where she curls up behind me when my mother dies (even as she tells me, *It's okay, it's okay, it's okay*). Creeks flow and run dry, and the last free board teeters and all you can do is reach for it—all you can do is all you can do.

I was going to wait until after Weedland, but I might not see this girl again. So I reach over. Gently take her by the arm. "Listen to me, Bea. You have to get away from Dave . . . he's killed people. Do you understand me? Dave's not even his real name. It's an alias. You have to get away from him. This is all coming apart."

She stares at me as if I'm nuts; I stupidly show her my watch: "I got picked up by the police . . ." Still, I get that uncomprehending look from her—"I'm probably going to jail . . . but if I can keep anything bad from happening to you—I don't know . . ."

"You ready, Slippers?" Jamie interrupts, comes out onto the landing.

"Yeah," I say, and I let go of Bea's arm.

And so Jamie and I start down the landing, on our way to Weedland. But I stop after a few steps and my eyes are drawn back up to the landing and that's where I see her, watching me, mouth slightly open—a distant, implacable look in her blue eyes, not at all what I expected—not gratitude, but something else—as the world teeters.

CHAPTER 27

Transcript, 36-Ounce Buy, Operation Homeland 11.15.08: 23:31—

Monte: (UNINTELLIGIBLE)

CI OH-2: Monte, I—

Monte: Good timing, I just finished bagging it.

CI OH-2: No, listen—

Monte: Each of these zips is a quarter. Eight is two pounds, ninth makes two-and-a-quarter, minus what you already got. So, do you want to weigh 'em or—

CI OH-2: Would you listen to me, Monte? I'm trying to tell you: I don't want this anymore. I'm quitting. I want my money back. I'm—

Monte: That's funny, Slippers. So you give any more thought to buying this place?

CI OH-2: No, I told you. I'm out.

Monte: I thought you was looking into one-a-them (UNINTELLIGIBLE)

CI OH-2: Consortium, Monte. The word is consortium. Now listen carefully to me. That's not happening. You can't sell this place. You need to just walk away while you still can. Give me back my money and quit . . . you too, Jamie—

Monte: That's why I need you to buy me out so I can—

CI OH-2: No, you don't understand—

Monte: I know what you're saying, Slippers. I knew that shit was high. It was Dave's idea, starting at four. I wanted to start at three, end up around two-eight, right? So how about that? Two-eight? That sound better?

CI OH-2: Listen carefully, Monte. I am done. I just want my money back.

Monte: What the fuck you—money back?

CI OH-2: This whole thing . . . the cops . . . they (UNIN-TELLIGIBLE) . . . you guys . . . Jamie, you need to get fifty miles away from here. Away from Dave. He's—

CI OH-1: Come on, Slippers. Stop talking shit—

Monte: What the fuck is he (UNINTELLIGIBLE)

CI OH-1: Nah, don't listen to that shit, Monte. Dude's just freaking out is all. Slippers all paranoid and shit—

CI OH-2: —see this watch?

CI OH-1: Come on, Slippers. You'll feel better out in the car. Get your shit and let's go.

Monte: Wait, I want to know what he means—

CI OH-1: What he means? Dude don't mean shit. He's just freakin'. I told you—

CI OH-2: No, listen to me—

CI OH-1: Shut the fuck up, Slippers! Get your weed and let's go.

(UNINTELLIGIBLE YELLING, A DOOR SLAMS.)

Monte: What are you doing here? We're moving this shit.

Eddie: Ask him what the fuck I'm doing here.

CI OH-2: (Unintelligible)

Eddie: What have you done, you snitch fuck?

(UNINTELLIGIBLE YELLING)

Eddie: What the fuck are you smiling about?

CI OH-2: I was just thinking—who would win in a fight, Godzilla or a tyrannosaurus?

Monte: Is it a real tyrannosaurus?

CI OH-1: That's easy, yo. Godzilla . . .'cause of the lasers an' shit.

Eddie: You think this is fuckin' funny?

(UNINTELLIGIBLE)

CHAPTER 28

Eddie's Anger—A Limerick

THERE ONCE WAS AN Eddie named Dave
Whose deep loathing he heartily gave:
    "What am I supposed to do
    with a snitch prick like you?"
As his own ass he endeavored to save.

Fear leads to the lowest of poetical forms. And it's fear that I
feel right now, fifty meggies of it, as Eddie/Dave looms over me,
his face red with rage. I've probably been punched all of twice in
my life until tonight. I've already matched that, and tonight's not
even over.

I'm lying on the foot-worn carpet of Monte's living room, be-
tween a La-Z-Boy and the *World Book Encyclopedia* set—I glance
over and see that S and T are switched and fight the urge to switch
the books back; I remain curled up, covering my swelling eye as
Dave looms over me in his seething rage.

"I'm sorry, Dave. I didn't—"

"You're fuckin' sorry?" Dave turns to Monte. "He's sorry."

"For what?" Monte asks innocently, miles behind still.

"I know," I mutter. "What kind of man was I?"

"What's that mean?"

I start to sit up. "Rhetorical question."

Eddie/Dave kicks me in the side and I feel the air go out of me and I fall again.

"What . . . fuckin' rhetorical question? What the—Do you have any idea what you've done?"

Jamie stands beside Dave, arms at his sides, strangely subdued. I sort of thought he might help me, but maybe not. For his part, Monte is red faced and sweating, eyes going back and forth from Dave to Jamie to me. He looks like he's going to explode in his parka—like a burrito left too long in a microwave. "W-will someone please tell me what's going on?"

What's going on? Okay. Well, Monte—(1) Apparently Bea has called Dave and told him that I warned her to get away. That's something you can never judge—another person's loyalty. (And maybe I'm just weak for tall and blond, but I'm not that disappointed in Bea. After all, she did know Dave first, and there is a certain chronology to loyalty.) And (2) Dave has driven out here, smacked me in the face and, now, seems to want to kick me to death.

Then, with my side aching and with Monte's *what's going on* still in the air, and because the shit apparently isn't deep enough yet, the front door flies open again—and I think once again of Monte's living room as the set of a play, because, in a hot stampede of rash fat, in comes the character of Chet. As played by Chet.

"I fuckin' told you!" Chet yells; for the moment he seems most furious with Dave.

So here we all are, in Weedland: me, Monte, Jamie and both of the guys who've punched me today, in a less-than-circular circle, me on the floor of the living room of a four-million-dollar grow farm, surrounded by my angry colleagues (at least one of whom I suspect carries a gun in his car), these four guys who now understand that Slippers is a snitch.

Or three of them understand: "Will someone tell me what's going on?" Monte asks.

Chet ignores his brother. "What do we do?" he asks Dave.

Then Chet and Eddie/Dave make dark eye contact and I see, maybe for the first time, that this can get worse, and I think of Lt. Reese and his well-timed aint's—*he ain't stupid*—and the lump in the photograph that he showed me—*it ain't a pile of leaves*—and all of my cute, sleep-deprived faux-brave responses just leak right out of me—Godzillas and limericks and *What-kind-of-man*—and all that's left is fear, more fear than I thought was possible—like a heightened version of the terror you feel during a rough landing on a jet . . . and then, this unwieldy thought: I desperately want to see my kids again. And Lisa.

Lying on the floor, curled up—this is why I no longer believe in epiphanies, in profound revelations, because how stupid is the one I'm having: *I don't want to die?* How inane, "realizing" the thing you always knew, from your first breath, that you'd prefer to live, to see the people you love? What sort of pointless realization is that?

"I told you not to trust these fuckers!" Chet says again.

"Don't look at me," says Jamie, hands in the air.

"You're the one who brought him here!" Chet says.

"How was I supposed to know?"

And this is when Monte finally arrives at the party. "Wait. Is Slippers a cop?" His cheeks fill with blood and he looks over at Jamie. "Jamie?"

Jamie simply shrugs, looks at his shoes.

"You're so stupid, Monte," Chet says. "He's not a cop. He's a fuckin' narc."

Then poor Monte doubles over and retches, and this might be the most remarkable thing in a remarkable day—that, in that vast gut of his, Monte apparently has nothing but stomach acid, because he heaves and heaves, but nothing comes out except bile and an acrid smell, which joins with the other smells—faint whiff of weed, musty house and a lot of scared-boy sweat—to make me feel like I might get sick too.

Bent over, his hands on his knees, Monte looks up at Jamie. "Did you know about this?" Jamie just stares.

"He didn't know," I say.

"Now look what you've done," Dave says to me, and he helps Monte to the bathroom, calling over his shoulder to Chet. "Put this fucker downstairs while I figure out what to do."

That word . . . *put* . . . seems so much harsher than: *Take* him downstairs.

"And get his phone and his keys," Dave says.

Chet holds out his hand. I hand over my phone and keys. I think of turning on the recorder on my watch, but don't want him to see. Chet follows me through the kitchen and down the stairs. The basement is warm, overhead light on. The air hockey table has been moved aside and the paneling removed. The corridor to Weedland is open. I can see down the short, narrow dirt-floor hallway, and the three lines of bright lights that glow beneath the grow rooms. Monte must've left it open. I sit on the hard carpet next to the pellet stove, lean against the wall.

Chet points a thick index finger down at me, in warning, I guess, and then tromps back upstairs. And for the next few minutes I hear footfalls and low voices, a steady hum, Chet's voice occasionally rising above the rest—"*What the fuck does that do for us?*" and "*Why do I have to do it?*" More footfalls. Doors open and close.

God, it's warm down here. I look around. There's nothing on the paneled walls, not even a beer poster. If I had bought this place . . .

Jesus, what am I thinking? Across the room, that dark hallway leads to short beams of light beneath the closed and locked doors.

There's more talking from upstairs, the low voices, more doors open and close, and finally . . . footsteps on the stairs. I look up and see business loafers. Eddie. Dave.

He takes the last of the steps, turns and walks slowly toward me without meeting my eyes. He stands above me, staring darkly down. I look for the trace of a handgun in his wool coat and pressed slacks, but I don't see one. He looks like a lawyer after hours, like an extremely angry lawyer.

I sit up a little. My neck and side are killing me. "Look, Dave. I don't blame you for—"

He holds up a hand to interrupt me: "Are you wearing a wire now?"

I ease the watch off my wrist. Hold it out. "It's not a wire. It only records. They don't monitor it. It isn't even on unless the backlight is lit."

Dave reaches down, takes the watch and turns it over in his hand. I glance past him, to the stairs, wondering . . . if I made a run for it . . . is Chet waiting for me up there?

Dave looks confused as he turns the watch over in his hand.

I take this opportunity to rise off the wall, so we're both standing. I'm so sore. "They wanted me to pretend to buy this place," I say. I glance past him, to the stairs again. God, I want to be up there. Down here, it's just Dave and me—and suddenly the low ceiling and the dark hallway on the other side of the room make me think of a grave.

Dave is staring at my feet again. "Did you tape our conversations?"

"No . . . I just got the watch today. . . ."

"Tell me exactly what you told them."

"I didn't tell them anything. They knew it all. They're the ones who told me about you."

"What did they say?" Dave's voice is barely a whisper. He still won't look me in the eye. I'm not an expert in these situations, but this fact doesn't seem to be in my favor.

"Well. They said your name was actually Eddie . . . that Dave is an alias . . ." No reaction. "And they showed me your record . . . you know . . . which was . . . well . . . I mean, we all make mistakes, right?"

He is shaking with anger. He says something so low I can't make it out.

"What?"

"Bea said . . ." He looks up. "They told you I killed someone . . ."

"Yeah," I say. "That was a little alarming."

Then a deep, guttural noise comes from Dave's chest and he starts to move on me and I put my fists up . . . and in that moment I think of the boys and of Lisa—and I understand something about myself, that to see them again I will scratch and kick and bite, I will kill this son-of-a-bitch with my bare hands if I have to, and anyone up those stairs who gets in my way, too and the adrenaline courses and I tense for what comes next—almost eager for it. But Dave simply shoves me against the wall, spins away, staggers and walks toward the dark hallway, enters it, throws his face and arms against a wall and begins wailing.

"Fuck, fuck, fuck!" Dave yells. "I can't believe this!"

I look from Dave to the stairs—freedom—and then back at Dave, who is pressed face-first against the wall in the narrow corridor leading to the grow rooms, a drying plant hanging near his head. Dave cries, blubbers, moans through his nose . . . not crying like Franklin when he doesn't want to go to bed, but wailing like Teddy the time he rode his bike into a parked car, broke his wrist, split his head open and saw his own blood for the first time.

And I find myself at the door to the grow rooms, the staircase just to my right—

"It's so unfair!" Dave sobs over his shoulder. "That they'd tell you I killed someone! It was a fuckin' car accident!" Dave wipes at his eyes, tries to get control of himself. "These guys, Slippers! They'll do anything . . . they're fucking *ruthless!*"

Dave moans again, and spins away, so that his back is against the wall of the dark hallway. He tilts his head back, as if trying to keep the tears in his eyes.

"I don't suppose they told you that it was the other driver's fault? Or that he turned in front of me? That the girl was in *his* car?"

"No," I admit. "None of that."

"I'd had a few glasses of wine, blew a point-oh-one—and if there are two drunk drivers in a fatal accident, they charge both with vehicular homicide. The prosecutor was supposed to plead it down to a DUI . . . but I'll bet it was your fucking drug task force friends who convinced him to withdraw the deal." Dave moans, shakes his head. "I knew. I knew it—"

"Dave, I didn't—"

"And Dave is my middle name!" he yells, and bursts into tears again. "It's not an alias! It's my *middle fucking name!* That's not the same as an alias! I haven't gone by Eddie since I was thirteen!" He wipes at his eyes. "People used to call me Special Eddie. How would you like that?" He looks around himself. "I should've let Monte board this place up, but Jamie comes up with the idea of selling this place and I just thought . . . yeah, if I could make a little money before I got disbarred . . . I could go back to school." He sighs. "I was gonna be a counselor."

Then he shakes his head. "A federal fucking task force? Do you know what that means?"

"No," I say. Honestly . . . I don't know what anything means.

"It means *federal* prison. Means they can hide us in some hole in Nebraska for fifteen years. Confiscate everything we own." He points at me. "I knew they were sniffing around, too. I could just tell. People said I was paranoid, but I knew. That's why I got that shit-bucket Nissan. I gave my mom the Benz just in case, 'cause I didn't want those fuckers taking my good car."

He's right. The Maxima *is* a shit-bucket car. I wonder if they confiscate mine, if I'll still be responsible for the payments.

"What else did they say?"

"Dave, I don't—"

He wipes his nose on his sleeve. "Come on, Slippers, just tell me."

"They said you committed an assault and . . . uh . . . intimidation?"

He nods, ashamed. "That was a long time ago. I had some anger stuff then. My ex-girlfriend . . . this older guy she was seeing." Dave wipes his pocked cheeks again. And a little snot bubble forms, just like Franklin gets. "The funny thing is . . . I felt like I had my shit together . . . you know, before the accident? You make one mistake and then—" He shakes his head. "Did they tell you I gave her CPR after the accident? The girl?"

"No."

"No," he says, "of course not," and he sighs. He stares down the hallway again. Shrugs. "Jesus, Slippers. How does everything get so fucked up?" And it's all too much for him again. Dave's head falls into his hands and he shudders with sobs. And I find myself stepping into the dark hallway, my feet crunching on the dirt floor, my hand rubbing his twitching shoulder.

"It's okay," I whisper. "It's okay, Dave."

Then Edmund AKA Dave Waller, manslaughtering, weeping drug dealer, turns back to me, his cheeks glistening, and says, through snot and tears, "Shit, Slippers. I'm never gonna practice law again, am I?"

CHAPTER 29

Lincoln Log Dreams

I HAD A ROUND TIN of those little toy logs when I was a kid. All you could really build was cabins; still . . . I loved them, the feel, the smell, the way they fit together. In my dream, they're just as small as I remember them being, but there are tens of thousands of tiny logs, and the cabin I build is massive, big enough for my family and me. It has room after room after room, opening one into the other, three floors of Lincoln Log sunken living room, bedrooms with Lincoln Log Murphy beds, home gym, log theater and game rooms and a Lincoln Log burglar alarm that beeps and beeps and—

—I wake alone, curled up on my side on the floor, staring at my glowing watch, which sits on the floor in front of me, beeping. Did I set the alarm? Did I know the watch had an alarm? The dregs of sleep blow away and I look around at the paneled walls and remember—I am in the basement of Weedland. I agreed to wait down here for an hour before I called Randy and Lt. Reese and told them I was quitting, to give my old dealers a head start—and so I sat down here on the floor, listening to them move around up there, their footfalls on the floor above me as they rushed around packing bags . . . and I must have—

I sit up, dizzy. Reach for the watch. Turn off the alarm. It's seven-thirty. I glance outside: daylight. I remember. Dave took my watch. He must've figured out how to set the alarm, brought it down here, seen me sleeping and—

Funny. I've finally gotten a good night's sleep, and it's in the basement of Weedland. Sure. The door to the grow rooms is closed, paneling replaced. I don't hear anything upstairs.

I groan and ache as I get to my feet. Make my way to the stairs. "Dave? Jamie?"

Nothing. They're gone. You can tell when you're in an empty house. I remember when I found Dad in Oregon. I packed up and set him carefully in my car—took one more run through his cold house. There was nothing there either—an emptiness that felt unnatural. I think about all of those foreclosures out there: an empty house is an abomination.

I find my phone and keys on the little Formica table. There is, of course, no sign of my money. I suppose that was asking a lot—getting a $9,000 refund from the dealers you've betrayed. I pick up my phone and check the missed calls. Two from my house: one at 6 a.m., and one at 6:30, both from Lisa. One at 6:40 from a number I don't recognize. And one from Jamie about ten minutes ago. There are no messages.

My car sits outside alone, in front of the house where I pulled up last night. Even the red Camaro is gone. I hesitate before leaving, wondering if I should lock the door behind me. I look up and down the street, at the houses in Weedland. There's a line of old diseased trees lining the road, their trunks flaking bark, the sidewalk rising and cracking from their roots. I lock the door and go.

I get in my car. I consider calling Lisa—but I'm not sure what to say, where to start. So I just drive. The highway winds and straightens, flat farmland gives way to clusters of trees and I ease into the squat downtown of my city, a low fog hanging over it like a basement ceiling.

When I pull up to my house, there is a Stehne Lumber flatbed truck parked in front.

What kind of man was I?

I ease past the flatbed, pull into the driveway.

Chuck Stehne is standing at the end of my driveway, in a big brown work coat and brown gloves, thick arms crossed like rope. He looks uneasy, confused. Probably because he sees the same thing I see.

I climb out of my car. "What are you doing, Dad?"

It's a stupid question; I can see what my father is doing. He's doing what I should be doing: building his son a treeless tree fort. He's got the plans open on the sidewalk, a brick holding the pages down; he's just started to saw wood. An extension cord snakes out from the open front door.

I glance over at Chuck, but he won't meet my eyes.

"When I pulled up he was already working," Chuck says. "I told him you wanted me to take all of this back . . . but he told me to go to hell."

Before I can remark on Chuck's going to hell, Dad says, "Hold this," and I take the end of one of the eight-foot posts and hold it over a corner of the woodpile while Dad scratches a straight line with one of Franklin's Spiderman pencils. Dad's hands are raw and red in the cold. He's still wearing his pajama bottoms and his Go Army sweatshirt. He's in socks. There's no sign of his remote control. "Brace it with your leg," he says. I do and Dad picks up a circular saw that I don't own and makes a clean cut, straight down his straight line, the wood grain protesting at the end before it breaks and Dad's end falls softly into the saw-dusted lawn.

When the saw is done humming, I say, as gently as I can, "Dad, where'd you get that?"

He looks up, confused. Then he looks at the saw in his hand. "Isn't it mine?"

There's also a framing hammer, and a heavy-duty electric drill. I pick up the drill, turn it over and see my neighbor's name stenciled on the back.

Chuck Stehne shifts his weight in his work boots. So here we are.

Dad has just started work on the base of the fort, cutting the first eight-foot four-by-four in half. I breathe in sawdust and cool morning air. He hasn't done enough to keep me from returning the wood, of course; I can always pay for a single cut four-by.

I take another whiff of sawdust. It's a nice smell, like something cooking. I have a vague memory of the smell, but there's nothing visual to go with it. "I'm sorry to make you come all the way out here," I tell Chuck. "But it looks like we're keeping the wood."

Chuck nods and his cool, blue eyes drift up to the second story of our house, then back to the woodpile and the senile old man wielding a circular saw. He starts to move away, and then seems to stop; he hasn't taken a step—it's more of a flinch. "You know," he says. "I could help . . . if you want." He quickly adds, "Or not."

Then Chuck Stehne sighs, looks once more at the house and says, quietly, "Look. For what it's worth? I didn't tell her about . . . you know . . . the whole pot thing?"

I have no idea what to say. *Thanks* seems a little much.

Dad goes back to reading the plans.

Chuck goes on: "I think you should know . . ." He sighs. "I mean . . . I guess I'd want to know . . . if I was you . . . first of all, we didn't . . . and it wasn't something anyone . . . you know . . . what I mean is . . ." He screws up his face. "And whatever *did* . . .

you know . . . happen . . . it was my fault . . . Lisa, she didn't . . .
what I mean is . . ."

"It's okay," I finally say—putting myself out of my misery by
holding my hands up. Christ, I'd rather he showed me pictures
than leave all those unfinished sentences.

Then Chuck Stehne, Prince of Lumberland, nods, sighs again,
and starts for his truck, although he still seems desperate to say . . .
something. He pauses, then seems to think better of it, then gives a
what-the-hell shrug, and finally says it: "I really do love her."

There it is. My head falls to my chest.

"It wasn't something . . . I mean, we weren't . . . Anyway . . ."
And then, when he has done all the damage one person could
possibly do with nothing more than sighs, nods and stammering,
unfinished thoughts, he starts for his truck again.

Then Chuck Stehne climbs into the cab of his flatbed truck,
pulls the door shut, sits for a minute before starting it and—
finally—pulls away. And I look up at our bedroom window, but
all I get is a flat reflection of the gray sky.

"You gonna help or you just gonna stand there holding your
dick?"

And so my father and I continue to build the base of Frontier
Fort II. I get him some shoes and gloves. We saw some more posts,
then lay two of them on the ground, four feet apart, and then we
put two more on top of those, perpendicular to them, and two
more on top of those.

I look up every few minutes, and once I catch Lisa in the
window, staring down on us. I hold my hands up . . . in a double
wave, or a sign of surrender. But she just backs away from the
window. A few minutes later, the boys come out, in coats and hats
and gloves. The door closes before I can catch Lisa's eye.

"I thought you said this wood was a mistake," Teddy says.

"Sometimes you just make the best of your mistakes," I say, accidentally parenting.

"So . . . we can keep it?"

"Sure."

"No *way!*" says Franklin, and he picks up one of the spikes and swings it like a sword.

The fort comes together pretty quickly. I'm surprised how often Dad refers to the plans as we work. At first I think it's the dementia—that he's forgetting what he reads, but then I flash on a long-ago Christmas, Dad returning every few seconds to the little folded Japanese instructions as he built me a slot-car racetrack. I guess it's one of those things I'm supposed to learn, maybe the only thing—*pay attention to the goddamned instructions. Follow the* rules, *dipshit.* I watch Dad drill 3/16-inch pilot holes, watch the way he eyes it and lines it up so the drill goes straight down through the base beams. He has Teddy hold a framing square on the base to make sure we're at 90 degrees and then he has Franklin go get one of the six-inch spikes.

"How big is—" Franklin starts to ask.

"Big as your foot," Dad says.

Steam escapes from the mouths of the Prior men.

Dad drives the first spike through the base of our fort and then the next one. It's a simple base—sixteen posts, eight going in each direction, spiked crosswise to form a nice, solid foundation. The spikes echo like gunfire as Dad pounds them.

"Floor next," Dad says, reading the plans. We lay out eight of the longer posts, the eight-footers. Dad shows the boys how to use spikes to make sure the floorboards are uniformly spaced.

We've been out about two hours and are about two-thirds done when I look up and see a newer four-by-four Ford pickup truck coming down our street slowly, as if looking for an address. The truck parks in front of my house. A very unhappy Lt. Reese climbs out, wearing a heavy coat, a watchman's cap and a scowl.

I set the framing hammer down. "You might have to finish without me," I tell Dad.

"Well, look here," Lt. Reese says as he walks up the sidewalk. "If it isn't the guy who managed, in twenty-four hours, to fuck up a six-month investigation."

"I'm sorry."

He laughs bitterly. "Don't apologize. I told you what would happen if you fucked up." Then he looks past me. "Hey, I know that pile of shit. Is that Frontier Fort number two?"

"Yeah."

"I built the same thing for my kids. Ten years ago. Wife didn't want them falling out of a tree. They played in it for twenty minutes and haven't been in it since. But the stupid thing will be there fifty years after my house falls down. Why are you making it in your front yard? Who builds a goddamn fort in his front yard?"

"That's just where my dad started it."

"And who builds a goddamn tree fort in November?"

"My dad . . . he's kind of senile."

Lt. Reese looks past me. "All that wood." Shakes his head. "It's easy to build, but it's twice as expensive because of all those four-bys. Thing's a waste of trees."

Then the lieutenant calls past me. "Hey. Grandpa! You gotta use the twelve-inch spikes for the last row!"

I turn. Dad is, indeed, holding a six-inch spike.

Lt. Reese walks over and picks up the plans. "I know it says to use shorter spikes, but you need this one to go through the floor-boards, too. See?" He grabs the drill, puts in the longer bit and deepens the hole, then takes a longer spike and sinks it while Dad swings the hammer and drives the spike through. It makes a sharp report that echoes down the street. I flinch each time he hits it. Lt. Reese steps away. "See?" he says again.

Lt. Reese sits on the porch and watches us cut the doors. "I can wait," he says.

And so, with the sun burning off the morning fog, supervised by the surly lieutenant from the regional drug task force—who occasionally calls out instructions ("Reverse the drill!") my father, my sons and I successfully build Frontier Fort Number Two in my front yard.

We're leveling the sidewalls when Lt. Reese says, "Hey. You got any coffee in there?"

I go inside to make it, but in the kitchen I see that Lisa has already made a pot. I get a cup for Dad, one for Lt. Reese and one for me. We sit on the front porch, holding the warm cups in our cold hands, watching the boys play in their finished fort. It's bulky, but not at all roomy; like everything in life, Frontier Fort II is both bigger and smaller than I thought it would be. There are no secret rooms. No Murphy beds or home gyms. Not even a roof. It's just some square walls sitting on a smaller square a few feet above the ground. Even the boys aren't quite sure exactly how to "play" in it, or how to play anything without a controller in their hands. It strikes me that I am at least two years late in building my boys their treeless tree fort.

We sit on the cold porch, steam from our coffee in our faces, watching the boys jump from the walls.

"So did you get him?" I ask. "Dave?"

"Get him?" Lt. Reese laughs. "We could've arrested him any time we wanted. God, you really are stupid." Then: a sigh. "Idiots turned themselves in, just like we were afraid they would. Lawyers called this morning. They all want deals. We're fucked." He sips at his coffee. In his disappointment, I remember what Randy told me and I think I finally understand: the last thing they wanted was to arrest Dave and Monte, to shut down the operation. With their grant running out at the end of the year, and their emergency budget presentation coming up, what they really needed was some reason to keep the operation going so the task force could get two more years funding. They needed tape of me pretending to buy Monte's business, so they could string the thing out for a while. But I panicked and blabbed and ruined the whole thing.

Lt. Reese finishes his coffee. "We should get going. There's a lot of paperwork."

I pull the watch from my pocket and hold it out to him. "And this. Is it—"

"Yeah." He shrugs. "Just a watch. With a backlight. It was Randy's idea . . . he figured you'd get suspicious if you didn't think you were wired up. I wanted to put a fake body wire on you but Randy thought you'd piss your pants so he came up with this James Bond bullshit." He takes the watch, puts it in his pocket. "I guess this is what happens when you're pushed for time. You make mistakes."

"What's going to happen to those kids," I say. "To Jamie?"

"Oh, I wouldn't worry about him," Lt. Reese says cryptically. I think this confirms what I figured out last night. That if I was OH-2 . . . there had to be a -1. "So Jamie was—"

He just smiles. "Don't ask me that."

"None of those guys seemed like criminal masterminds," I say. "Even Dave wasn't as bad as you made him out to be. I think he was just caught up in it, like I was, over our heads."

"Caught up? Over your head?" This is apparently the wrong thing to say to Lt. Reese, who spins on me, his old shitty self. "You were dealing drugs, fuck-nuts! You know the definition of a fuck-ing drug dealer, *Slippers*? Someone who deals drugs!"

My boys have looked up from the tree fort. I hold up my hand to quiet Lt. Reese.

He continues more quietly: "The only difference between you and Dave? Is that you *sucked* at it. You think you're different 'cause . . . what? You got kids? 'Cause you used to have a job?"

Lt. Reese hands me his coffee cup, sighs. "You know the worst part of what I do: nobody ever deserves it. Nobody ever thinks they're wrong. You're all a bunch of assholes walking around crying, 'It ain't fair . . . I didn't mean it . . . I got a bad deal.' "

"Amen," says Dad.

Lt. Reese and I both look over at Dad, who rocks back and forth, staring off into space.

Lt. Reese reaches over and pats my father on the back. Then he stands. "You ready?"

"Can I go in and tell my wife?"

Lt. Reese looks at his empty cup. Sighs. "Get your dad and me some more coffee first."

I get them each a cup. "Five minutes," Lt. Reese says.

I nod. I don't see the boys in the fort, so I walk over. They're sitting on the floor, cross-legged in opposite corners, like boxers between rounds. They're playing their Gameboys. Fifteen minutes in their new eleven-hundred-dollar fort and they're back to playing video games.

"I love you guys."

They look up, confused. "Okay," Teddy says. I step into the fort. It really is solidly built. I feel strangely . . . proud. I bend down and hug them. Even Teddy hugs me back, awkwardly, but I'll take it. They don't ask where I'm going.

"Bye Dad," I say. "I'm going to jail."

He toasts me with his steaming coffee.

Then I start back toward the house. The stairs creak under my feet. The door to our bedroom is closed. I start to knock—then I grab the knob and open the door. Lisa looks startled. She's staring out the window, chewing her thumbnail, her phone at her ear.

Wearing her heavy coat. She looks back and sees me. Her eyes are red and bleary. "I have to call you back," she says into the phone. She closes it and turns to face me.

Our big suitcase is open on the bed. Nothing in it. I don't know what this means. Has she not packed yet? Or changed her mind? Or is she expecting me to go?

She looks up and I catch her eyes—green, frightened.

I look down at the bed underneath that suitcase. "Lisa . . . I . . ." What do you say? Where do you start? "I am so sorry."

CHAPTER 30

After 7/11

Bankruptcy turns out to be like an outdoor concert Lisa and I went to once. The gates were thrown open suddenly and we sprinted down this hill, way too fast, the crowd out of control, and I squeezed Lisa's hand and we ran, but we could've slipped so easily, fallen, gotten trampled. "Don't look back," I just kept saying, "just keep moving forward."

It turns out they have a Chapter 7 *and* a Chapter 11 bankruptcy. I try not to dwell on the significance of the numbers. After disaster shopping for a while, Lisa and I decide to go with Chapter 13 (all of these prime, odd numbers . . . alone out there . . . disconnected from the pack), which is bankruptcy for people who are making *some* money, but not nearly enough to meet their debts. It's not a great deal, but it's certainly a better deal for us than for our creditors. The court takes everything we have, which is not much, and divvies it among the sharks. Anything we were making payments on goes back to the lenders—even our living room furniture, which we were close to paying off, even our dryer. Then we get to start from scratch, only with less stuff and with shitty credit.

A few years ago, shitty credit wouldn't have mattered; we could've bought Graceland. Now . . . the conservator assigned to our case feigns trying to help us keep our house, but there's no way. When the packet from Providential Equity finally arrives, it turns out we can't even get into their mortgage modification program. The numbers aren't even close to penciling out and now that I have a conviction, for possession of narcotics with intent to deliver (I'm out on probation), we are no longer eligible. So, just months after giving me a reprieve, my friends in Benicia—Gilbert and Joy— end up with my house. It doesn't help my case with Lisa, either, that I withheld not only being a drug dealer, but also the letter about our house being foreclosed. I wish she were angry, but all I get from her now is fatigue . . . cold, indifferent resignation.

The day before we are officially served with eviction papers by a sympathetic Sheriff's deputy, we have a big garage sale, and watch people haul away the shit we should've gotten rid of years ago. It's almost cathartic. I think Lisa does pretty well with her compulsive shopping boxes, maybe even turns a profit on the plush toys. I'm happy for her. The boys sell a bunch of their old games and toys, too, and make enough to buy a Wii. I'm happy for them, too.

And then . . . we move. Or at least I move, with the boys, to a two-bedroom apartment in a shrub-covered 1970s triplex on a busy street twenty blocks from downtown.

Lisa needs some space. Some time. The old me would've pointed out that they're really the same—space and time, on a four-dimensional smooth continuum that theoretically allows for even more dimensions and explains such phenomena as time-dilation (although this relativity doesn't explain the munchies) and I'd have been halfway to string theory as she was loading up her car. But the new me—quiet, humbled—just says, "Okay." And, "Take as long as you need."

She moves in with Dani, although I imagine she spends her

nights at Chuck's. We agree that I'll keep the boys in the apartment with me for the time being, until she gets settled. Since my apartment is near her optometrist's office, Lisa will come by after school every day and stay with them until I get home from work—which is often quite late. When I get home she goes to Dani's—or to Chuck's. I don't ask. This way, we hope, our split will disrupt the boys as little as possible. Sometimes when she's there I'll walk to Dad's nursing home—which is less than a mile away—and watch TV with him. The boys aren't happy about any of this; we tell them that sometimes Moms and Dads just need a little time apart, but they know. They take turns with self-pity and surliness, like video game controllers they hand back and forth.

I've yet to go back to our old house since we lost it . . . but Lisa confesses that she sometimes drives through our old neighborhood. I wish she wouldn't torture herself that way. One night, when we're having pizza in the apartment with the boys—we decide to keep having dinner together once a week, for their sake—Lisa tells me with disdain that our house sold at auction for three-fifty, two thirds of what we owed. "Doesn't that make you furious?" she asks.

It might make me angry if I drove by the house and saw for myself, but since my car went back to the bank I travel by bus now and it would take at least one transfer and . . . I don't know . . . I guess the truth is that I don't want to see it. I don't want to be reminded of all that I lost, all that I gave away. I slowly replace the furniture that we lost or sold at our garage sale with second-hand stuff; I hook the boys' Wii up to an old 19-inch TV. After our second dinner with the boys—fish sticks and fries—Lisa teases me about my latest purchase: an orange couch with cigarette marks on the arms. I explain they were out of moss green, cigarette-burned couches. The apartment's best feature is a balcony, which is built at tree-level, and when we're done with dinner we move our chairs out there and sit. I tell Lisa that I can't wait for spring, to sit out there and watch the boys ride their bikes. She smiles politely.

On the grass in front of our triplex is the big wooden Frontier Fort, which I had moved over from the house. The boys hardly ever play in it but there are two rotten neighbor boys who are younger (and who swear like teenagers) and they seem to like it. And *I* like having it there.

Teddy hates sharing a room, but I think Franklin likes it. He sleeps better with someone else in the room. Every morning I walk them to school, and then take the bus to Earl Ruscom's real estate office building, where he's opened the little headquarters of *Biz-Daily Online* (I was able to talk him out of the awful name *Can-Do Times*) in a little twelve-by-twenty room, consisting of—for now—two desks and a white board. When I accepted the job I had to admit to Earl that I'd been arrested and charged with possessing and intending to deliver marijuana. Earl's eyes narrowed and I steeled myself for trouble. "No shit? You were dealing weed?" Then he leaned in close. "Can you still get some?" I told him that I couldn't. He hired me anyway.

My old dying newspaper just keeps laying people off—half the staff is now gone, including Ike, who has gone back to school to be a teacher—so there's no shortage of writers for me to hire to do upbeat freelance stories for almost no money. In spite of Earl's mandate that we write "positive business stories," we find ourselves doing a lot of stories about businesses going under. I think we might last a couple of years ourselves before Earl gets tired of losing money and I have to write a cheerful story about our own demise.

Every time I take the bus to work, I recall how our old house was around the corner from a bus stop, how I used to watch that big bifurcated bus roll past every day without giving it much thought; I certainly never thought I'd be on it. I do remember seeing people at the stop and sometimes I'd catch their eyes, think vague thoughts about their lives, and get a surge of my old atrophying empathy. What were their lives like? Was it awful to be so poor? I'd see kids sitting with their parents, waiting for the bus, and I'd feel worst about my own pity for them, my passing-by-at-forty-miles-an-hour-in-heated-leather-seat pity.

The first time I waited for the bus I felt self-conscious, as if I were watching myself with that same pitiful detachment. A car went by my stop and I saw myself in a woman's eyes as she passed: *Look at that poor guy in the nice wool coat. What do you suppose happened to him? Could it ever happen to* my *husband?* On the bus that day, I sat next to a large woman reading a pulpy novel. I started to read over her shoulder—I couldn't help it; it was a sex scene—but she moved the book. It felt as if everyone on the bus saw through me.

At the next stop a woman, maybe nineteen, got on, followed by a little boy no more than four, and a rail-thin man with the gapped smile of a meth-user. The boy had one glove on his right hand and was holding up his left hand—red, bare and cold—while his mother finished a lecture that must have started long before they got on.

"Because I told you not to lose it, that's why! Gloves ain't free, TJ. That's your last pair for the whole winter. You just gonna have to wear that one."

"I don't know what happened to it," the boy said with great wonder. "It was on my hand."

"Well it ain't now," his mother said. They moved down the aisle toward the back of the bus, mother in front, boy in the middle, father behind, and as they passed me, the little boy turned back to his father. They were in this together. "It's okay, Dad," said TJ. "Look." He smiled at his own cleverness. "I got pockets." And he shoved his bare hand in his pants pocket.

The father put his hand on his son's head and made eye contact with me, smiled proudly, and I swear to God I have never felt such shame—such deep, cleansing shame. I put my judgmental face in my spoiled hands and I wept quietly. The woman with the sexy book got up and moved to another seat.

Christ. It is the only unforgivable thing, really . . . to feel sorry for yourself.

The next day I took a pair of Franklin's old gloves and put them in my messenger bag. I carry those gloves in my bag every day now, but of course I've yet to see TJ or his dad. In the meantime, whenever I feel like a failure—not an uncommon feeling—I take those gloves out of my bag, imagine that father touching his boy's head and hope I'm half as good a man.

After being assessed by the nursing home, my own good father has been moved to the memory unit. It's paid for by Medicare and his VA benefits. I'm not going to pretend that he's happy—but he has his remote and one of the cable networks has begun showing *The Rockford Files* every day at 11 a.m. Dad has built his day around that. His clear memories come in fainter now . . . I wonder if he might be better off when they don't come in at all. One day Lisa offers to pick Dad up and bring him over for dinner. I gladly accept. On Dad's second visit, she even cooks, makes him chipped beef; but he asks her not to make it anymore. Says he doesn't like it.

What he does like is the treeless tree fort. He and I sit on the balcony and watch the cursing neighbor boys climb around on it, Dad laughing every time they swear: *Fuck you, Travis! Fuck you, Alvin.* Dad loves this show; he doubles over like Travis and Alvin are Martin and Lewis, funniest thing he's ever heard.

Teddy and Franklin go to a little public school four blocks away but I made sure the new apartment was in a better district than the little Sing-Sing school in our old neighborhood. The boys seem okay with their new school. They miss their friends but they love not wearing uniforms. There's even a Math-Quest team at the public school.

Biz-Daily exists only online for the first month, but when we finally finish our first print issue, the thing is gorgeous. We sell out of it. I can even imagine the thing making money someday—if companies can ever afford to advertise again. In the back of our first printed edition are two features that I pushed hard for, both of which turn out to be popular, the Stoned Stock Analyst, in which I make random picks under the pseudonym Jay Wollie (he's already up four percent by pushing fast food stocks), and The Poetfolio, which I write under my own name:

Recovery

We're like bored ghosts—over our horror
as we wait for dispensation
on the hard wooden pews
of bankruptcy court
and next to me
this old ruddy trader
who's been reading the paper
whistles at something in the stock pages.

"If only," he says, "I had about twenty G's"
and I complete: "you wouldn't be here?"
but he slaps at the paper, "No, look
don't you see, it's already
here—the next thing . . ." and I'll be
damned if I can help myself:
"What do you mean?"
Then one by one he lists them
the drugs I already know

"We had tech and pharms
war, biotech and of course housing."
And now? I say, leading, but he won't
give it away, he just shrugs
and says it again: "The next thing."

An hour later we are broke but free
and as we part in the hallway
it's all I can do to not beg the man
for that last tip, that final stake
like some idiot junkie who
kicks smack by going on crack
kicks crack by going on meth
kicks meth by going on smack—
jonesing for the next thing, because
relapse is what we mean
when we say recovery.

And maybe there's a sort of bankruptcy for marriages, too. At least, that's what I tell Lisa one night after we've had dinner with the boys, and they've gone on to bed, and we're sitting on that balcony having a glass of wine. "Marital bankruptcy," she says, and almost smiles.

Sure—I say, unable to look her in the eyes—a new start. No debts, no blame, no punishment: marital bankruptcy. Like we're new people. (She: hot woman awaiting her divorce papers; me: middle-aged drug dealer on probation.)

Marital bankruptcy isn't quite the carefree little joke that our old mulligan was; and when I glance up, Lisa looks away sadly. "I'm here," I say. "Take your time. I'm not going anywhere."

She says, quietly, "Don't, Matthew." But we have another glass of wine, and that night, she nestles in behind me in our king-sized bed; the beds are the only big pieces of furniture I saved, and ours takes up most of the tiny bedroom in this apartment. I know better than to ask what this means—having her next to me like this. I know better than to say anything. I just sleep . . . my wife's knees pressed into the backs of mine.

In the morning she's gone, and for days, she doesn't say anything about it. But a week later, she stays again, and a week after that, we make love. It's awkward at first, bumping, apologizing; we turn out to be exactly like new people, tentative, trying to find our way back. But afterward, we sleep.

I usually have some time to think on the bus, and in the drizzling morning after I make love to my wife, I bounce on the curb and light-step my way through sighing split doors, my mood untouchable, even by an especially potent burst of bus-funk (let's see, I'm getting sweat, diesel fuel and off-brand tobacco, perfectly balanced, with a slight finish of unwashed ass) and I drop into a plastic seat like some grinning fool, and that's when I happen to catch, out the bus window, a for-sale sign, a little wooden post planted on a weedy strip of sidewalk in front of a shocked bungalow (*Price Reduced!*), the plywood door of a forced repo where some other poor shit was run over, and my mind starts to race again (*how long must you spend in exile*) as I begin to calculate the down and monthly on a place like that (can't be much . . . doable, no?) and like a kid irrationally looking for a specific song on an old car radio, I spin station to station—maybe get an advance . . . make a couple of smart investments . . . qualify for a loan . . . flip that house—I land on a breathless commercial I heard just the other day featuring my old Aussie real estate agent (*Interest rites my neevah be this low ageen. NEEVAH!*) and I suppose the devil needs only the tiniest hoofhold because two stops later I'm actually ginning the numbers, (*ponziing myself!*) and I'm up to my ears in that peculiar bastard of American calculus, that ol' bad math, macro-optimistic flawed formula of Keynesian interventionist Mall-of-the-Americas bliss, endless exponential derivation—*the Theory of "UP"*—big sloppy bang of perpetual growth, long-view, as the winking brokers used to say, their BMW sedans and Lexus SUVs parked with the wheels car-ad cocked, their view of *your future* always a step on an endless climb, steeper, steeper, faster and faster in the widening gyre, interim between collapses shrinking—fall . . . recovery . . . boom; fall, recovery, boom; fallrecoveryboom; fa-boom—a kids' carrousel ride gone out-of-control (*Get on kid, gotta get on, don't miss the ride!*) and I know better, I swear to God I know better (*It's unsustainable*—a kind of mania, a sickness, and yet)—*you deserve this, you are a fucking American*—because all you want is one more chance—all you want is for your boys to have it better than you did—all you want is what's there—all you want is—

Untenable. I know. It is untenable. And I feel myself blush. Reach into my bag and find TJ's warm gloves. When I get off the bus downtown there's an old man standing there, with a milky eye and a piece of fresh cardboard. He asks if I have a felt pen. I offer him a ballpoint, but he says people won't be able to see the writing. I give him a dollar.

That night, Lisa says it was a mistake, sleeping together.

I don't say a word.

But a week later, she stays again. After we make love that night, Lisa suddenly sits up in bed, gasping. She's had a nightmare and she's disoriented, unsure where we are. "It's okay, Lisa," I whisper. I touch her face lightly. "It's okay. It's okay."

She looks around the tiny bedroom of my crap-ass apartment. There's a long crack in the wall where the stucco on the outside has settled. She stares at that crack, and begins to cry. "I really am trying, Matt."

"I know you are," I say. "It's okay. It's okay." And all that night it feels like I'm holding my breath; for the first time I let myself think about her and Chuck. Imagine him holding her. For the first time in a long time, I don't sleep.

In the morning, I get the boys off to school and take the bus. Write my happy business news ("M-Tronic Laying Off Fewer Than Feared") and keep my eyes down on the bus. I go home to find Lisa already with the boys, making dinner. That night we sit out on the balcony. Lisa takes a deep breath and says that she feels like I should know "exactly what happened" between her and Chuck.

The past tense thrills me a little. But I say, "It's okay, Lisa . . ."

She shakes her head and says, "Maybe it's not even as bad as you're thinking."

I take a deep breath. Choose my words carefully. I tell her that of course she can tell me what happened. She can tell me anything she wants. But she doesn't have to say a word. With bankruptcy, I tell her, you're supposed to come out lean and smart and humble, free of the old obligations, the bad habits and weighty contracts that were holding you down. You get a clean break. Start from scratch. There's a reason they call it *forgiving* debts, I say. (And the trumpets blare . . . celebrating the glorious freedom of freedom!) Whatever happened with Chuck, I tell Lisa, it was as much my fault as theirs . . . more maybe. And whatever happened, it's okay. It's okay. I plan to just keep saying this until it feels true: It's okay, it's okay, it's okay, it's . . .

She nods slightly, and stares out the window. For a long time, we're quiet.

And then I lean in gently, whisper: "It was the bald spot, wasn't it?"

Then one day, I get my biweekly check and see that Earl has padded it a little, so I hit the bank on the way home and I arrive at the apartment to find Lisa playing Yahtzee with the boys. I ask if she wants to take the boys to a movie. I can still only afford two tickets, so Lisa and I sit in the mall and share an ice cream cone while the boys are in the theater. We can hear muffled explosions coming from one of the theaters.

I reach over for the cone.

"No. You don't get anymore." Lisa holds it away from me. "You don't eat it right."

"How are you supposed to eat it?"

"You're supposed to lick it. You gum it like an old man."

"I'm using my lips. You can't get enough with just your tongue. You just move the ice cream all around."

"So I'm just supposed to settle for a dainty little lick while you get a big gummy mouthful? That's not fair. I should get ten licks for every one of your old Abe Vigoda gums."

"How about five licks for every Abe Vigoda?"

"Eight."

I grab the ice cream from her, and hold it away, and she's wrestling me for it and that's when I look up to see my old pothead friends, Jamie and Skeet, coming out of the theater.

Skeet's got my loafers on.

I ended up spending two nights in jail, booked on charges of possession with intent to deliver. I was arraigned, posted bond, and went home. As quickly as I could, I pled guilty; because of my cooperation, the prosecutor agreed to overlook the fact that I tried to buy two pounds and it's only the three ounces I get credit for trying to sell. Because of my clean record, the fact that I have a job and am supporting two boys, and have a recommendation from Randy and Lt. Reese, I got into a deferral program; if I complete my drug classes and keep pissing clean urine, the charge could eventually disappear entirely from my record.

Monte has also pled guilty, to more serious charges; Lt. Reese tells me he'll probably get a break in sentencing, too, since he is cooperating fully. Like Monte, I may be called to testify against Dave if his case goes to trial. I'm not looking forward to that, but all I can do is tell the truth. Lt. Reese tells me not to worry. He thinks Dave will eventually plead out, too, and that he and Monte will end up doing no more than a couple of years each. In the end, I ended up liking Lt. Reese a lot. He's . . . I don't know . . . genuine. He laughed mercilessly at my story of selling pot to my old editor, speaking into my phony glowing watch. I suppose I originally thought his bad-cop thing was an act, but the guy really is a prick. Just like Randy really is a nice guy. Unfortunately, their task force did lose its funding and they're back at their old jobs, Randy with the city, Lt. Reese doing school drug presentations for the state patrol (I like to imagine it: "Okay, listen up you little fucksticks."). One day Randy called out of the blue to see if I wanted to go to his church. I thanked him but said no. He told me that Dave was close to accepting Jesus Christ as his personal savior. "That's great, Randy!" I said. And I really was glad for him; I imagine that saving someone is an incredible feeling. But it was Dave I felt best for. I pictured his many failings going into that salvation garbage can and I was so happy for him I could barely stand it.

As for Jamie, as far as I know, he was never charged with anything. I recall what Randy said about professional CI's and I wonder if maybe he isn't doing that. He would be great; certainly the best I ever saw: smart, calm, quick on his feet. Funny how you fail to see people for what they really are—

In the mall now, Skeet doesn't see me at all, but Jamie does, sees right into me, and knows. He gives a little smile, and then hesitates . . . I feel the same thing . . . but what would we say? Finally, Jamie gives me a short nod, looks down, and he and Skeet move on.

"Who was that?" Lisa grabs the ice cream back from me.

"My old weed dealer," I say.

"Oh."

And here we are.

Sitting in a mall where I am gently trying to win back my beautiful wife, while our boys see a movie on the twenty bucks it has taken me three months to save, and Lisa and I fight over a single ice cream cone. I think we are supposed to somehow be better off now, out from under all of those middle-class weights and obligations and debts, all the lies that we stacked above our heads like teetering lumber. As Lisa said, we're trying.

But it's not easy, realizing how we fucked it all up. And that turns out to be the hardest thing to live with, not the regret or the fear, but the realization that the edge is so close to where we live. We're like children after a thunderstorm. It's okay, I whisper to Lisa on those nights that I convince her to stay with me. It's okay. Just keep moving forward. Don't look back. It's okay.

Maybe we will be happy again—maybe we'll even come out of this happier. But I can't help wondering if we couldn't be happy in our big old house, with our old nice furniture, with our old second car, with enough money for *four* movie tickets.

For two ice cream cones.

No, we miss our things.

But we have pockets.

And Lisa and me—we're okay.

ACKNOWLEDGMENTS

Thank you to Sam Ligon, Jim Lynch, Dan Butterworth, Sherman Alexie, Dan Spalding and Eric Albrecht for various insights, inspirations and encouragements; to Cal Morgan and Warren Frazier; and most of all to Ralph Walter, Danny Westneat, Som Jordan and all of my dismayed and displaced newspaper friends, whose talent and commitment deserve a better world.